Secrets on River Road

Leanne Tyler

Coverdesign by Mallory Kane

ISBN: 1515349330
ISBN-13: 978-1515349334

Other Titles By Leanne Tyler

Audiobook
Ava: Love Letters

Anthologies
Through the Garden Gate
A Christmas Kiss is on Her List

Novellas
Ava: Love Letters
It's Always Been You
Victory's Gate

Short Stories
A Country Kitchen Christmas

Novels
Season of Love
Because of Rebecca
The Good Luck Charm
The Good Luck Spell
The Good Luck Potion

Acknowledgments

This book is very dear to my heart. It was inspired by a photograph of a young girl I discovered while working in a photo lab. A woman brought in several old pictures found in chest in the attic. I asked if I could have a copy of the girl's photo and the woman agreed. I used the photo as inspiration and soon discovered the story of Madison Franklin and her time at Wyndam House. I hope you enjoy the story too.

Chapter One

Charleston, South Carolina
May 1920

The sun sank low in the horizon, casting shadows on the large, Georgian house up on the hill as I stepped off the small bus with my suitcase on River Road in South Carolina that early spring day. Butterflies played havoc in my stomach and my heart fluttered as I took the first few steps up the winding drive toward what lay ahead.

It felt strange to be at Wyndam House, but the letter I'd received a few days before beckoned me to come with haste. I could recall being in this house only once before. I had been six years old and my parents had brought me for my grandmother Millicent's funeral. As soon as we'd arrived, I'd been tucked away in the upstairs nursery despite my mother's protests, but she'd given in to the two older ladies that I later learned were my great-aunts.

I remember being escorted by a well-dressed woman in a black dress and stark white scalloped apron. She wore these funny looking wedge shoes that squeaked when she walked. I fixed my eyes on the tidy little hat that sat firmly on her mass of auburn hair as I made my way up the long, winding, marble staircase. My leather slippers made clicking sounds on the glistening floor as she showed me into the large room at the top of the stairs. One wall was lined with bookshelves that held leather bound editions of the Classics. A few wooden toys lay neatly arranged on a small table—as if they were there just for me. However, I didn't play with them. Instead, I found a pretty picture book and curled up on the cushioned window seat so I could watch all the people arrive who had come to say goodbye to my grandmother.

I had wanted to be part of the procession that followed her coffin from the house to the private graveyard on the large estate, but I wasn't allowed. I didn't cry, not even once during that horrible weekend. Looking back, I find it odd since grandmother and I had been very close. She spoiled me with shopping trips, picnics at White Point Garden and carriage rides along the harbor every time I went to visit her on the Battery in Charleston, which wasn't as often as we would have liked. That is where she had lived until a few months before her death. For some unknown reason, she had left the grand house by the Charleston Harbor–where the Ashley and the Cooper Rivers meet–and moved to Wyndam House where neither my mother nor I could visit her.

Wyndam House. It had been off-limits to my family for a reason I did not know and my mother would not say. Yet, as if I had always been part of this family and this house, I had been invited to come stay–for an undisclosed period–with two women that my only memory of involved them calling me Maddy and pinching my cheeks affectionately when I felt like my world had come to an end.

These two women–Mossie and Maude–were my grandmother's sisters and since their father, my great-grandfather's passingwere very well off. When he died last year he left them his entire estate, which included the large Georgian house up on the hill. From what my mother told me, the house was built after the Civil War to replace the original plantation house that had been burnt to the ground when Sherman marched northward after burning Atlanta. It had taken many years after the war to replace the house, because of the long Reconstruction period that left Charleston in such economic devastation, but my great-grandfather succeeded in building a house that replicated the former splendor of the original.

It isn't pleasant to think a family can be divided by wealth, but I believe this is the case with mine. I grew up on a small farm with more love than many receive. I suppose it was easy being an only child and an only grandchild as well as great-grandchild, but that did not mean I knew my great-grandfather Wyndam. He was a mystery to me and now that he is dead, I can only wonder what kind of a man he was and why he never wanted to be part of my life. My mother said it was better for me not to ask questions, but how can one *not* question the estrangement of relatives?

My eyes were opened to the problem within my family at my grandmother's funeral. A problem that a six-year-old doesn't fully understand but is aware of nonetheless because of the strain and distance between family members. I'm sure people outside of the family knew about it because I recall how the mourners at the wake looked at me strangely and murmured to one another when I shyly passed by, tightly holding my mother's hand.

I was never happier to be out of that house and on my way home again to Camden and the beautiful farmland my father worked with his brothers and cousins. My father's family had always been close, and I believe that is why my mother's family puzzled me so much. They were distant and a mystery to me.

My parents occasionally referred to the day of the funeral as the mark of a new chapter in all of our lives, but I never understood what they meant. I had worried that it meant that they'd one day suddenly leave me too and I would be summoned to live in that house on River Road.

We lived happily together until I was seventeen. Then our lives changed drastically because my father was shot and killed while in town on business. A few drunken men had been letting off steam about the war in Europe that the United States had yet to join. My mother had been devastated because her father, Ronald Madison, had been killed when she was only four after attending a political meeting at Society Hall in Charleston. Losing both men she loved at the hand of a gun was more than she could take. It was a full year before my mother fully recovered from the shock of my father's death. But we survived, even after the United States entered the war and times became hard for everyone.

"Wyndam women always make do," my mother said time and time again when things seemed to be at their worst. Though I knew things could have been better if my great-grandfather hadn't done what he did after my grandmother's death.

We had to sell most of the farmland to relatives so we could keep our house. My mother took a job in town at the local grocery as a clerk, while I went to school during the day and tutored younger children at night. We managed. We didn't have much to spare–no one did–but we never went hungry.

The funny thing was, whenever we thought we were on our last leg a letter would always arrive from these two aunts and my mother would begin crying and then everything would get better again. Those letters were like Christmas for us. They didn't come often, but when they did they always made my mother smile again.

That is why I couldn't ignore the request for a visit from my two great-aunts. And so, after so many years, here I am back at Wyndam House for a long, overdue visit to repay them for their wonderful letters that cheered my mother during her lowest times. And to thank them for whatever they said that made our lives a little easier.

Standing on the porch of Wyndam House, I felt a sense of longing that lay within the estate. The feeling was so overwhelming it drew me closer to the door before my knock was even answered. I assumed the maid would appear, but it was my great-aunts who came to the door together. They looked the same as I remembered, as if time had spared them from aging a day in the past fourteen years.

"Maddy," one of the women said affectionately, pulling me into the house. The other grabbed my small suitcase and closed the door behind me.

"It's such a blessing to have you here," the other murmured leading me through the foyer, past a marble-topped table and crystal-cut vase with fresh roses, to the parlor where tea was already set out.

I took a seat on the moss green sofa amidst piles of rose and cream throw cushions and studied the two women, trying to recall which was Maude and which was Mossie. The silence was tense as I stared at them and them at me.

"Well Moss, I suppose we could offer Madison a cup of tea." Maude finally broke the awkward silence that permeated the room.

"Yes, of course, forgive us dear." Mossie reached for the tea service and poured three cups of the hot liquid. "Do you like cream, sugar, or lemon?"

"Sugar, thank you." I studied them even more closely now that I knew which was which. Maude was the younger, even though they were both in their sixties. Her hair fell short of her shoulders and it was salt 'n pepper where the gray was taking over the dark brown. Her face was oval, as was Mossie's, but she had high cheekbones that made her look regal with her shining blue eyes and wire-rimmed glasses. Mossie, on the other hand, had short white hair and was a little plump for her height. Her eyes were a warm brown, hidden behind wire-rimmed glasses.

I could see my grandmother's mannerisms in them, and I wondered how they felt about the years she was not with them during her life. I knew that if I had had a sister, or even a brother, I would have wanted us to be as close as possible during our lives. I would not have wanted anything or anyone to come between us.

"How is your mother, Madison?" Maude asked, causing me to quickly recall how I had left her that morning. She was not thrilled by my sudden decision to visit the aunts, even though she was grateful they asked. She would have preferred I had waited until she could accompany me on this visit, but the letter seemed so urgent I felt I could not delay my arrival.

"She's well, isn't she?" Mossie asked when I didn't immediately reply.

"Oh yes. She's fine. She was surprised by your letter, as was I."

Maude and Mossie looked at one another and then smiled.

"I would have expected that," Maude said. "Hope must wonder why we did not ask her to come as well."

"Yes, I do say we might have offended the dear girl." Mossie set her cup of tea and saucer back on the silver tray.

"Never mind that now, Mossie, we did this for a reason and I think Maddy is wondering why." Maude sounded a little impatient.

"Yes, I suppose you are right, Maude." She folded her linen napkin in her lap and looked at her sister hesitantly. "But shouldn't we show Madison to her room first?"

Maude frowned and set her cup on the silver tray in front of me. She did it so daintily it didn't even make a sound. Then she looked up at me with a warm smile. "Are you tired, Madison? Forgive us for not thinking of your comfort. It is getting late and dinner will be served soon. I am sure you are famished after your long trip and would like to freshen up a bit. Come, and we'll show you to your room."

Without another word, my great-aunts stood and escorted me from the parlor, up the marble staircase, to the second floor. A lovely floral runner extended from the top of the stairs to the bottom, cushioning the sound of our steps, though in my mind, I could still hear the clicking my shoes had once made on the marble. I had found my aunts amusing with their endless chatter as if I had not even been in the room. I could see how they lived alone in this large house without being dreadfully lonely now. They were a lively pair.

"Madison, this room once belonged to your grandmother." Mossie opened the door to the large room.

The sight overwhelmed me. The room was larger than mine at home; in fact, it could hold three full beds with room left over. The ceiling was vaulted as it was all through the house. A bay window with a cushioned widow seat was at one of end of the room and another large window was at the other. The furnishings were Chippendale, and included a bed, dressing table and chair, a settee and a high backed wing chair. An oriental rug covered a small section of the polished hardwood floor.

"Father made sure each of us girls had our own room when he rebuilt the house after the war," Mossie continued.

"Mother would have loved it, I know," Maude said.

"Yes, yes. Father always said it was her little piece of paradise that he created here, even if she didn't get to share it with him." Mossie walked over to the large bay window and opened the curtains, allowing the fading sunlight to drift into the room.

Maude fingered a delicate lace covering that lay on top of the dresser. "Mother died during the war while father was off fighting for the Confederacy. She became ill shortly after the war broke out."

"Mother never got over giving birth to Millicent. She was sickly from that time on, Maude," Mossie corrected her sister. "Father knew she was ill and worried about her dreadfully while he was in the war. He told me so many times over the years."

Maude frowned at her sister for an instant and then smiled again. "Well, enough of that," she said, looking embarrassed that they had slipped into reminiscing. She came over to where I stood, taking in the room and their chattering. "Madison will just have enough time to change before dinner as it is. We must leave her now."

"Yes, Yes. Do forgive us, dear, for rattling on about the past." Mossie touched my cheek affectionately before the two disappeared from the room.

When they were gone, I walked over to the bay window and sat on the window seat. I didn't really know how to take my two great-aunts. They were nothing like I expected, nor were they like my father's aunts whom I had grown up around. They acted as if I had always been a close part of their lives, yet I felt as if we were meeting for the first time. I knew so little about them, really. The fact that I still didn't know why I had been asked to come to Wyndam House bothered me. Maude had been ready to tell I was sure of it, but Mossie had been hesitant. Why? Was there a great mystery these two were about to reveal to me? Only time would tell.

Maude had been right. I only had enough time to change into a fresh dress and splash cool water on my face before the maid announced dinner was served. Maude and Mossie had also changed from their floral print day dresses to soft pastel, taffeta dinner gowns, making me feel out of place in my cotton sack dress as I entered the spacious dining room.

I was overwhelmed by the heady perfume of tangy nectar that reminded me of being in a peach orchard as I took my place at the grand, oval cherry table, which extended across the length of the peach, accented room. A sparkling, crystal chandelier hung over the table and the crystals glistened like dewdrops catching the last rays of sunlight, giving the room an added touch of grandeur.

Without realizing what I was doing, I took in

several deep breaths, almost tasting the juicy ripeness of a peach. This behavior caused Maude and Mossie to look up from their plates.

"Is something wrong?" Maude motioned for the maid to come forward.

"Yes, dear, aren't you feeling well?" Mossie chimed in, sitting on the edge of her plush seat.

"No. Nothing is wrong." I felt my face flush at the realization of what I had been doing.

"Are you sure?" Mossie watched me closely.

"I'm not accustomed to eating in a room like this."

They nodded as if my explanation made logical sense as we all began to eat our dinner.

"I'm sure Hope has made a lovely home for you in Camden," Maude said.

I wasn't sure how to take her comment. Was she implying I grew up in squalor because I had not been fortune enough to grow up in the shadows of Wyndam House? Camden was not a poverty-stricken town. It happened to be the oldest inland town in South Carolina with just as many prestigious families as Charleston. Several confederate officers came from there so it was not a backward town. Though I suppose the prejudice of the low country still prevails. Charlestonians have always looked down their noses at individuals who come from the up-country. My father always referred to the fact whenever snide remarks were made about where we lived.

I put down my fork, wiped my mouth with my

napkin unable to finish my dinner. "Yes, our home is lovely. Nothing like Wyndam House, but you would have seen how nice it is if you had ever bothered to come for a visit."

My tone was curt, but I felt I needed to defend my home. The stunned expressions on their faces told me my response took them by surprise. I could not sit here and be criticized by them when they knew nothing about my upbringing or me. I began to have doubts about coming to Charleston after all. Perhaps my mother had been right to try and persuade me to stay in Camden.

Mossie blanched and sputtered a reply. "Yes, I am sure. But dear, you must realize Maude and I have not been away from the house in many, many years. We took care of father until last year when he passed away."

"Mossie, I think Madison is speaking of more than just our visiting Camden." Maude winked at me with a friendly smile. That gesture put me at ease and I felt foolish for getting my feathers ruffled.

Mossie reached for her crystal goblet of water stopping midway and looked at her sister as if she were unsure about something. "Do you really think so?"

Maude nodded and gave Mossie an impertinent look before the older woman conceded. She smiled and turned toward the maid. "Bring dessert and coffee to the parlor."

"Yes ma'am," the auburn-haired maid said before disappearing through the swinging doors into the kitchen.

"Shall we retire to the parlor?" Maude asked, standing up and leading the way.

Walking to the parlor, I noticed a change in Mossie. She was hesitant as if mentally wrestling with a decision she was not happy with. I wondered if she didn't share Maude's opinion about why I was visiting them. Or was it something else that made her not want to discuss this?

A fire burned low in the fireplace and soft classical music played on the phonograph as we entered the parlor.

"Don't you just love Mozart?" Mossie took a seat in one of the cream upholstered, high-backed Queen Anne chairs adjacent to the sofa.

"It is nice," I said, taking a seat on the grand-piano stool in front of the large picture window. I had never seen a piano like this one before. It was not upright like the one at the small church my mother and I attended in Camden. It extended outward and the keys were genuine ivories.

"Do you play, Madison?" Maude asked, taking a seat on the sofa.

"No." I ran my hand over the polished ivory keys letting my fingers touch them lightly. I had always wanted to learn to play, but that wasn't possible. We couldn't afford the extra expense.

The conversation ended and awkwardness filled the room until the maid carried in the tray with coffee and dessert, which brought Mossie to life again.

"Come, Madison, and try this. It's my favorite," she cooed, taking the small plate the maid served.

I was amused by the woman's enthusiasm over food. The pie was delicious, and I could see why Mossie helped herself to a second piece, even though Maude chastised her for it. But, I could not forget why we had come into the parlor. I had been patient enough and it was time I learned why I was invited to Wyndam House after twenty years of my life. Why hadn't my great-grandfather wanted me to visit him when I was a child?

All of these questions tormented me as we went through the motions of eating dessert like a family enjoying the stillness of the night. But, we weren't a true family. We were practically strangers.

Maude must have sensed my anxiety as we listened to the music play because she kept watching me closely, but she did not make a move to put me at ease. Were they simply teasing me? Perhaps my mother was right when she said I should not rush to do as they asked. I hadn't given the implications of my coming here on their first request much thought, but now I wondered if I had not set myself up to be a pawn that they could toy with for their own amusement.

The strain of traveling across the state began to take its toll on me and I scooted deeper into the sofa, laying my head back against the cushion as the music played on. I could feel my eyelids grow heavy as the music filled the room and it became difficult to focus on the soft chatter between the aunts. I believe I had drifted off to sleep for a few moments when I suddenly heard Maude say something about an inheritance that was in question. Her voice was soft and lulling as she talked with Mossie, as if they were alone in the room, even though I was only a cushion away on the sofa.

"Father never mentioned it before his death," Mossie said in a low voice.

"Yes, but it is written in his will nonetheless." Maude sounded exasperated.

They obviously believed I was sleeping or they wouldn't have talked so freely. I knew I shouldn't eavesdrop on them, but I so wanted to find out answers to my questions so I remained silent.

"I still don't think it should be brought up just yet." A cup and saucer rattled as Mossie spoke. "It took us this long to have the courage to bring her here. Madison doesn't need to know. We agreed we'd tell her when she arrived, but I don't know, Maude. I believe she will be satisfied in knowing we want to get to know her. We don't have to drop such a burden on her at once. You saw how she reacted at dinner when you innocently made that comment on how she lived in Camden. This visit is a first step for us. We must be cautious if we want to bridge the gap in the family. We shouldn't move too quickly and risk losing her."

"I'm afraid if we stay silent we may lose her anyway." Maude was silent for some time before she spoke again, moving restlessly on her end of the sofa. "But the stipulation to the inheritance stands, Mossie. We cannot forget that," she paused. "I suppose I am too anxious. I want to make up for all those years father kept us from Millicent, Hope and Madison. We should have been there for them when Edward was killed, but instead, we stayed away."

"I know, Maude. I know. But father had such a hold on us. He made us feel we would be betraying him if we contacted Hope," Mossie said.

There was another brief silence and then I felt Maude move back into the sofa. She reached her hand over to pat my arm.

"Madison, wake up, dear." Her voice was soft and soothing and sounded so much like my grandmother that for a moment a thrill ran through my slumbering senses as I recalled the nights I spent with her on the battery so long ago.

Chapter Two

The next morning I lay in bed thinking about the conversation I'd overheard between my great-aunts the night before. They'd mentioned an inheritance with a stipulation that was left in their father's will, but he'd never spoken to them about it before his death. And whatever the provision was, it had taken them time after his death to feel up to dealing with it.

Pushing the covers back I sat up, recalling something Mossie had said about not 'dropping a burden on me all at once'. What burden? The only burden I was feeling was the uncertainty of why I was here at Wyndam House.

I was beginning to feel I had been tricked into coming because my great-aunts were lonely. Why else would two elderly ladies want a houseguest when they are finally free from nursing their ailing father?

"Madison, dear," Mossie called from the other side of my closed bedroom door before slowly opening it. "Oh good, you are up."

"Good morning." I quickly looked through my everyday cotton sack dresses hanging in the closet to see which one would be appropriate to wear today. I never cared much about the style of my clothes because in Camden I wore what every other young woman did. But here, I felt a division between my great-aunts and me because my clothes felt ordinary compared to the polished fabrics of their dresses.

"Did you sleep well? You were so tired last night. Maude and I were afraid we bored you with music and dessert in the parlor. It has been many years since we were your age and so many things have changed. Mercy, how long ago that was…"

I smiled at her as I began brushing my short, cropped brown hair. "Surely it wasn't that long ago. Mother said you and Maude entertained regularly when she was growing up."

A gleam came to her brown eyes and they sparkled behind her wire-rimmed glasses. "Yes we did. Your grandmother was the belle of the ball when we were younger. That's why she caught the eye of Ronald Madison when she was only fifteen! Do you know much about your grandfather whom you were named for?"

I shook my head. My mother told me some tales when I was younger, but I had a feeling hearing them from Mossie would be a treat. "I know he married grandmother when she was young and he died when my mother was four."

"Yes. Yes. Such a tragedy, but Ronald Madison was a fine man shot down in his prime. He was considered part of the Charleston gentry. He marched with the Confederacy when he was only eleven. Did you know that? He played the drums. That is where he met father." Mossie went to the settee and made herself comfortable while I dressed.

"Father approved highly of Ronald. I do believe that is why he allowed Millicent to marry at fifteen when neither Maude nor I had been spoken for yet. It was highly irregular. Ronald took Millicent away to live in the city on the Charleston Harbor. Father hadn't expected that, but he understood because Ronald was very active in the government and he needed to be close to this office and other officials. Some said he could have easily gone on to be governor of South Carolina if he hadn't been fatally shot at such an early age."

Mossie shook her head, took off her glasses, and wiped her eyes with her lace handkerchief, pausing for a few moments before continuing. "Millicent was so brave. She dressed herself and Hope in black and they marched right down King Street behind the horse drawn glass carriage bearing his coffin to the cemetery. Father took the news badly, and insisted Millicent move back to Wyndam with Hope for fear the shooting was not random and they might be in danger. But no, your grandmother wouldn't hear of leaving her home. She said it was the nearest thing to being with Ronald and she was not separating herself from him."

As I listened to Mossie, I wondered why my mother hadn't told me this story. It showed how much her parents meant to one another.

"You must come with Maude and me for a drive down River Road, Madison. It's because of you that we are going out. We haven't stepped foot off of the estate in years." Mossie scrambled to her feet. "Afterwards we'll take you for a walk around the grounds and show you just what your great-grandfather salvaged after the war."

"I'd love to come, Aunt Mossie, but shouldn't we discuss why I'm here? Your letter sounded as if something was dreadfully urgent. That is why I'm here."

Mossie looked horrified. She began to fidget and look around the room quickly as if searching for the answer. After a moment she placed both hands on her cheeks as if she was beside herself. Then she threw her hands up in the air in exasperation. "Really, Madison, that can wait. Come along, dear, Maude is waiting on us in the car with our driver, Godfrey."

"So much for that," I murmured under my breath, grabbing my small purse on the way out of the room.

The drive down River Road was fascinating

not only for the scenery but because I had never road in a closed in automobile before. Aunt Maude and Mossie's car was a 1914 Case Limousine and their driver sat up front separated from us by a privacy glass. It shouldn't have surprised me that great-grandfather would own such an expensive automobile fit for the king of England, but it did.

I had traveled down part of River Road the day before while on the bus, but I hadn't really paid attention to the view. I'd been too preoccupied thinking about getting to Wyndam House and seeing my great-aunts. I also couldn't help thinking about my mother being alone in Camden. We'd never been apart for very long before.

"How old do you suppose these trees are, Maude?" Mossie asked, shaking her head as she looked up at the tall, moss-draped oaks that lined the road as far as the eye could see.

"Older than you and me, that's for sure." Maude strained her neck out the car window to look up at the trees.

"Father said he climbed these trees when he was a boy," Mossie rattled on looking at me with a smile. Her eyes brightened, and then she gave me a serious look. "Have you ever climbed a tree, Madison?"

I grinned at her for being so serious when asking such a question. "Yes. I have climbed a tree or two with my male cousins in Camden. There was an apple orchard next to our farm the boys loved to sneak over to."

"Did you feel you could reach the sky from the top of it?" Maude half-turned in her seat as she spoke, surprising me by the question.

I really didn't know how to answer her. I had never thought about it when I was playing with my cousins all those years ago, but I could see the question was important to her. "I suppose one could feel that way," I replied, noticing how some of the trees closer to the Ashley River were knotted with bulging roots stretching above the ground along the river's bank.

"I always thought so," Maude said, sounding remorseful.

Had she wanted to climb trees when she was younger, but her gender and circumstances at the time prevented her from doing so? I, on the other hand had been free to play as I wished. Looking at the way Maude had replied made me see just how free I had truly been growing up.

There had been a confinement when my great-aunts were growing up. It had more to do with society's views than just the Civil War and Reconstruction periods of the South. Family appearances and acceptability had still been a strong virtue people clung to. It separated the social classes as well as how much money one had. But during the economic hardships of Reconstruction, it played a major factor in who remained gentry and who sank to the lower class. Therefore, proper young ladies didn't climb trees, nor did they run about playing with rambunctious boys.

"Climbing trees isn't all that fun," I said, hoping to cheer her a little and make her see she hadn't missed anything. "I remember scraping my knees and tearing my dresses, which didn't make my mother happy."

"I'm sure Hope didn't scold you," Maude said matter of fact as if she knew my mother very well. Perhaps Maude had known her when she was growing up in Charleston, but I felt my mother was not the same young woman they remembered. She didn't cling to the memories of growing up on the Battery in Charleston or living in the shadows of Wyndam House.

As for scolding me for climbing trees, no, she hadn't. She really had never scolded me during my life other than to sit me down and talk the matter over so I would know the appropriate way to conduct myself while other children my age boasted about trips to the woodshed, especially my male cousins. I don't think I was a perfect child. I had my faults just like everyone else, but my mother viewed life a little differently. I never questioned why. I only hoped it had to do with her background as a child. My grandmother claimed my mother was just like her and that I would be the same when I grew up because I carried the dreaded 'Wyndam Trait' as she called it.

I didn't know what trait my grandmother was referring to but the statement stuck with me and over the years I watched my mother closely. How she interacted with my father, his brothers and their wives, and especially the few friends she made in Camden. And, in the privacy of my bedroom, I would stand in front of the full-length mirror and study myself. The way I smiled, the way I wore my hair, the way I would sit down or pick up my glass at the dinner table. Sadly enough, through all of this careful study I could not find what my grandmother was talking about until after my father died. And there, as if it had been a freckle on my face that I had forgotten about, I saw it. It was my mother's independent nature. It had been overshadowed by my father's presence so I never really saw it.

I'm certain my father saw it for he said that he never had to worry about Hope being alone if something ever happened to him.

"She'd take care of the farm just like I would," he said with all the confidence that made me believe my future was secure. However, after his death, it had taken some time for us to get over the loss. Afterwards my mom had blossomed into her own person. Even when the war broke out in Europe and so many families faced hardships having to send their sons and husbands off to fight, my mom faced the toughest decision for our welfare. She sold our farm land to my father's brothers to prevent losing it all together. She did what she had to do just like my father would have.

"Is something wrong, Madison?" Maude asked as

the driver turned off the main road onto a long, winding drive.

"Yes, dear, where did that pretty smile of yours disappear to?" Mossie asked, adjusting her wire-rimmed glasses on her nose as if to see me better.

"I was thinking about my father and Camden." I stared out the window at the house we were approaching. It was unlike any of the other houses we'd passed along River Road. This house looked like it was a century old and far more the plantation style than Wyndam House. "Where are we?"

Maude and Mossie smiled brightly as if delighted by my question and apparent interest.

"I knew she'd like it." Mossie clapped her hands together.

"This is Drayton Hall. It's the only plantation house that wasn't destroyed when Union troops marched through during the war," Maude spoke with pride.

"How's that?" I asked, knowing the Union Army wasn't likely to pick and choose which property to burn or to spare when they were rampantly burning the land.

Mossie laughed and clapped her hands again. "No one can say Charlestonians do not know how to salvage what is most precious to them."

I arched a brow, wondering what she meant.

"It is rumored that Drayton's slaves told Union soldiers the house was infested with smallpox. Of course, smallpox did run its course through the area during the Civil War and Charles Drayton was a doctor," Maude said as if swearing on the man's honor that this was the truth. "Those blue coats turned tail and ran."

"Oh Maude, you really shouldn't say that, but it's the truth." Mossie shook her head and laughed. "Father always said so."

If there was one thing I was learning about my great-aunts, it was that they worshipped their father's words. Anything he did or said was gospel to them. It's no wonder that they never went against his wishes to see my mother or me during all those years. I still have to wonder how my grandmother was permitted to return to Wyndam House before she died. Did my great-grandfather have a change of heart? Or did these two plead for their sister to spend her last days with them?

I wanted very much to find out the answers to these questions and more. However, another thing I was learning about my great-aunts was they didn't like answering my questions about that time in their lives. They were brilliant at finding a diversion to change the subject.

"Both of you have excellent memories," I commented as Godfrey turned the car around and we returned to River Road.

"Thank you, Madison," Maude said while Mossie nodded.

"I suppose you would not remember how my grandmother faired after my grandfather was killed, would you?"

Mossie sat up straighter in the seat. "Yes, why yes, I do. She faired exceptionally well in Charleston. Father kept a close watch over her, though he did so from a distance without her being the wiser."

"Millicent was extremely independent," Maude pointed out. "Father always said that was why he couldn't convince her to come back to Wyndam House."

"Father blamed Millicent for being too independent and for teaching Hope to be the same way. That's why…"Mossie stopped in mid-sentence when Maude shifted her feet, nudging Mossie's leg. The two exchanged private looks and I knew another opportunity to find out about my family's dreaded history was over. But I wouldn't give up. I'd keep asking questions.

"Why what?" I asked with all innocence.

"Why she stayed in Charleston," Mossie said, but I knew that wasn't the real answer.

"Madison, before we head back home, there is one other place we would like for you to see," Maude announced trying to draw my attention to a new subject.

"Oh yes, Maddy, I know you will love it even more than Drayton Hall. Father did. That is why we have such a beautiful landscape in the back of

Wyndam House," Mossie said, piquing my curiosity.

What Maude and Mossie were referring to was a breathtaking fifty-acre flower garden that extended over a five-hundred acre estate. The foliage was lush and inviting to the senses with an array of vivid colors. We took a brief walk along the foot of the garden so Maude and Mossie could speak with the gardener who once worked for them when they were much younger. While they talked, I spotted swans down by a pool of water.

The garden was like paradise. I couldn't imagine anyone wanted to leave once they came, but sadly we did. Maude and Mossie wanted to get back to Wyndam House before lunch was served. They had a surprise for me. I couldn't help but get my hopes up that they were finally going to tell me why they had asked me to come for a visit. The more they talked about the past and the more I learned about my mysterious family, the more I desperately wanted to know everything.

Lunch was served in the backyard at noon. Maude and Mossie were so giddy I felt they were up to no good as they led me around to the back of Wyndam House. I was a little surprised they hadn't blindfolded me so I would have a grand unveiling of their precious yard.

"Well?" Maude asked when we finally made our way down the twenty or so stone steps that led to a lovely valley shaded on one side by moss-draped oak and cypress trees making a boundary for the large man-made pond where swans swam.

I had a feeling I was looking at a miniature of the fifty-acre garden we had visited earlier. There was a gorgeous, white Victorian-style gazebo and a white bridge that arched over the water to the trees on the other side. It was a quaint paradise I knew I could lose myself in during my stay with the aunts.

"It's lovely." I left them at the stone steps and walked on to the gazebo where lunch had been set up for us.

Maude and Mossie followed at a slower pace as if they were seeing the garden for the first time and wanted to absorb its splendor.

"Father had it landscaped after the Magnolia gardens," Mossie said, taking a seat at the table.

"The Draytons were truly honored," Maude assured me as she took her napkin from the side of her plate and placed it in her lap.

I didn't doubt that, but no one could replicate the gardens at Magnolia Plantation to perfection. One could plant the same flowers and lay them out similarly, but the Magnolia gardens had a character all their own which, from what Maude and Mossie told me, stemmed back to the late 1600s.

"How did you get the swans to come here?" I asked as we ate our lunch of watercress sandwiches and carrot soup.

"Why, they have always lived here," Mossie said, getting a look in her eye again as she remembered the past. "Father loved them so. He made sure they were not killed during the war. He created a mirage around the pond to prevent anyone from knowing it was here. That is an outsider. But we knew. It saved our lives."

"A mirage?" I tried to picture in my mind what Mossie was talking about and how it could possibly have saved their lives.

"Father transplanted plants around the pond. Large bushes were dug up by the slaves from different parts of the estate and carried down to the pond area to make it look like an overgrown, impassable thicket. They spent several weeks working on it before father went to join his comrades in the war."

"I'm surprised the Union soldiers didn't burn their way through it when they destroyed the house." I glanced over at the swans gliding on the water.

"Yes. Yes. We all feared it would happen when they came that dreadful night. Mother had been very ill and all the slaves had run off by that point or they might have been killed when their quarters were burned." Mossie shook her head. She had stopped eating her lunch all together.

"All except Delci. She was like our mother's sister. They had grown up together and she came to Wyndam House when mother married father. She took care of us when we were born and she stayed on with us even though she had the chance at freedom. Delci was the only person we had to care for us after mother passed on until father could come home to us when the war finally ended. She even stayed after father told her she could leave because she didn't want to see her Miriam's babes getting on poorly. Not that Delci doubted father could care for us, but because she knew he had too much to do on the estate preparing us a place to live." Maude patted her sister's hand because the dear woman was softly sobbing.

"It was Delci who took us into the mirage when the soldiers came. Mother had been dead only a few weeks. Father hadn't even been able to come home for her funeral." Mossie wiped her eyes with her handkerchief. "Millicent was only four and Maude was six. I was the oldest at nine, but still a babe myself. We couldn't understand why the soldiers would want to burn our house down nor why our mother was dead and our father didn't come home to us when we needed him so."

There was a brief silence that overcame the gazebo as Mossie sobbed for a time long gone. Again today I was feeling a difference in our worlds. It reached much farther than climbing trees and proper etiquette. It touched on who we were and what we made of our lives. My aunts had been greatly affected by the Civil War and the time surrounding it. They lived for a short time when slaves cared for their needs. It was a time I couldn't have imagined being a part of because I didn't feel that anyone was better than another human being.

God had created us all and placed us here on the earth. We should all live in peace together, but that had never been possible. Countries had been fighting one another for centuries, and even the United States struggled within, forcing brother to fight against brother for what they believed.

With the World War, we all feared the world would come to an end. Who couldn't imagine powerful countries fighting one another without total destruction being the end result? I knew my life had been affected by the war. It came when my mother and I were still struggling to overcome my father's death. We hadn't fought in the war or sent a brother or a husband to fight, but we lost because of it. We felt the pain others felt when the news of death arrived. We experienced the anguish and fear of our country's participation in the war itself.

I can only imagine how terrifying it was for three little girls and one woman to seek shelter from the enemy in a mirage that could have easily been destroyed by fire along with the rest of the plantation. If that had happened it would have been the end of the Wyndams as we know them. My mother would never have been born because Millicent Wyndam would not have met Ronald Madison. My father's life would have been altered greatly. He may have never met his first and only love.

I remember him taking me on his lap in the evenings while mother cleared the supper dishes. He'd bounce me on his knee until I giggled and then hug me tight before beginning his tales. After my grandmother's death, I wanted to know how we came to live in Camden instead of Charleston. Why my grandmother hadn't come to live with us when she was so sick instead of going to a place where we couldn't visit her.

My father had looked me squarely in the eye and asked if I really wanted to know all of this. The house suddenly became quiet, and my mother came from the kitchen to join us by the fireplace. I was delighted that my quest for a tale had brought her to join us, but she didn't look so happy. There had been sadness in her brown eyes as she reached for my father's hand.

"Of course, daddy." I squirmed on his lap. "Tell me, ple-e-a-se."

My father glanced at my mother and they exchanged a little nod before my father began his story. "We live in Camden because this was my home when I was a little boy. I grew up on this farm with my brothers and cousins just like you are growing up with their children. You like living here, don't you?"

"Yes, daddy," I replied recalling how Jeb and Deter would tie me up to a tree and dance around like Indians before Toby would come galloping in on his stick horse and rescue me. Each day they'd take turns being Indians and the lone cowboy, but I always had to play the 'damsel in distress' as they called it.

"Well, in Charleston there isn't any of our family,"

he said. "My family has always lived in Camden and that is why we live here instead of Charleston where your grandmother lived."

I remember wrinkling my nose and thought on that for a moment or two. I frowned because this hadn't been the type of story he usually told before sending me off to bed. There wasn't excitement and adventure, and I wondered if I hadn't asked the right question tonight.

"But Grandma is family and she lived in Charleston," I said, crossing my arms over my chest.

"Yes. She did and so did I, but after I met your father while attending the College of Charleston, we decided to come here to live," my mother explained in her gentle, warm voice.

"I bet you made Grandma cry," I said, getting down off of my father's lap. "I know I would have cried if you moved so far away from me. And now she's dead."

I ran from the room to my bedroom with them both calling after me.

"Madison…"

"Madison, dear are you all right?" Maude reached across the table and touching my arm.

"Yes, dear, you look like you were a thousand miles away." Mossie gently pulled my cloth napkin from between my clenched hands.

For a moment I felt lost. I was no longer a child who could sit on her father's lap and listen to him tell stories about life. I was a young woman who had questions to be answered. And I wanted answers.

I took a deep breath and looked my aunts squarely in the eye. "Why did you ask me to come to visit you? Why did you write asking me to come with such urgency in your words? I have a right to know. I have a right to know why I couldn't visit my grandmother when she was so ill before she died. I have a right to know why my great-grandfather didn't want me in his life. I have a right to know."

Maude looked pained by my outburst and I was certain she was going to answer me, but Mossie shook her head.

"Madison, dear, there is nothing to be so upset about." She gently squeezed my hand. "It's all in the past, and we are so glad you are here with us now."

"You are glad?" The sound of my voice rose until I was almost shouting. "Why wasn't Richard Wyndam glad to have me in his life? Why wasn't he overjoyed that he had a great-granddaughter to share this beautiful estate with? I don't want it, if that is what you are looking so scared about. I would just like to have gotten to know him. To have been allowed to visit while my grandmother was here, not after she was dead."

"Madison, it is such a difficult thing to speak of," Maude said in a calming voice. "But, you should know that Mossie and I have always wanted you in our lives. Father did too, but there was principle."

"Principle? Like when he had grandmother's will declared invalid?" I pulled my hand from Mossie's grasp. "Well, I have principle too. I came here thinking you were in desperate need of my help. I thought there was possibly something wrong. I left my mother alone in Camden because I thought you needed me more, but that doesn't seem to be the case. I'll be leaving in the morning."

I left them in the gazebo staring after me. I marched up the stone steps without looking back. I shook with disbelief that I had become so outraged with them. I never raised my voice. I never shouted at anyone. It hadn't helped my situation. I didn't feel better. Instead, I felt like I was giving up before the fight really got started.

I spent the rest of the day in my room with a headache. I couldn't lie down without the back of my head hurting. I couldn't sit up without feeling so tired and dizzy-headed that I wanted to lie down again. So I compromised. I took the bed pillows over to the bay window and sat back against the wall with my head resting between the cool windowpane and the pillows.

It was while I rested this way that I noticed the pond was clearly visible from this room. I'd sat at the window the evening before, but I hadn't noticed it. I had been marveling at the surprise of my great-aunts' behavior and not really looking out the window. Now, as I watched the sun sink low in the horizon, dipping behind the tree line, the pond became less visible to the eye, but when the moonlight reflected on the water, it looked almost magical.

I wondered if my grandmother had spent evenings sitting on this very window seat staring down at the water. Had she dreamily thought about her Ronald after the ball when they first met? Did she fantasize about a life with the man she loved? I would never know the answers to these questions because they were hidden well within the walls of Wyndam House. If my great-aunts knew, I was sure they would never tell freely because it would bring up such a distressing time for them. But, deep inside of me there was this need to know. It was stronger now than it had ever been before in my life and I could not push it out of my mind. I had to find out about my family's past. I had to know why my mother and I were not allowed to come to Wyndam House all these years. And I had to know why my great-aunts suddenly invited me to come for a visit. Why hadn't they asked my mother to come? Why were they keeping these answers from me?

As these questions ran through my head, it hurt more and more and I couldn't find comfort. I squirmed on the window seat, shifting my weight from side to side until I finally found a comfortable position that didn't cause my head to ache.

I finally drifted off to sleep, not opening my eyes again until the sun was casting shadows into the garden down below, and I could see the swans gathered on the small landmass in the center of the pond. They were bathing and sunning themselves in the morning sunlight. I couldn't help but smile at the sight. It was so relaxing and peaceful to watch them.

I stretched my legs down the window seat and straightened my back before standing up. My head felt better but my stomach felt empty. I took the pillows back to the bed and noticed a tray of buttered-toast, jam and juice had been set out for me over by the settee. I took a piece of toast and walked over to the closet to begin my packing, except my clothes were gone. Startled, I went over to the bed and felt underneath for my suitcase, but it wasn't there either.

Tiredly, I sank down on the bed and finished the piece of toast while trying to convince myself there wasn't anything to panic about. My aunts were trying to keep me from leaving. Perhaps sometime during the night Maude and Mossie had finally come to an agreement that they should tell me what I wanted to know. I would speak to them about it as soon as I finished my breakfast. But, I would make it perfectly clear to them that I would only stay on if they told me what I wanted to know. Surely they couldn't deny me that much.

A half-hour later I found Maude and Mossie in the kitchen going through the cabinets giving instructions to the maid on what groceries to purchase. Neither acknowledged my presence right away, and I assumed they were showing me their displeasure over my outburst the afternoon before.

"Did you sleep well, Madison?" Maude finally asked, pouring herself a fresh cup of coffee before walking over to the small kitchen table that looked too modern to belong in a house of such antiquity.

"Somewhat." I got myself a cup of coffee as well. "My clothes are missing. You wouldn't happen to know where they are, would you?"

There was silence, and I looked up. Mossie looked shocked. Maude smiled mischievously and the maid turned away quickly.

"That would cause you a problem in leaving, wouldn't it?" Maude asked, picking up the morning newspaper as if we were discussing nothing more than the weather.

"I'm afraid not." I walked to the kitchen window where I began sipping my coffee, waiting for them to take the bait. "I have more clothes in Camden. It will be less of a burden to travel empty handed." And empty handed is exactly how I felt. If I left now, I would have accomplished nothing by coming here.

"Excuse me, miss," the maid spoke up. "I heard the misses talking last night and took the liberty of packing for you last night. You will find your bag in the foyer when you are ready to leave."

"Oh, Bea, how thoughtful of you." Mossie clapped

her hands together as if this was the most exciting news.

"Bea, do we still have the number three bus schedule?" Maude turned the page in the newspaper that she was pretending to be engrossed in reading.

"Yes, ma'am." She went to the small secretary on the opposite side of the kitchen and opened up a drawer, retrieving a yellow paper about the size of a postcard and handed it to me.

"Thank you." I looked at the schedule and wondered how I was going to maneuver a conversation with my aunts that would allow me to get the answers to my questions in time to catch the bus that morning.

"I really wish you weren't so set on leaving." Mossie sighed as she arranged the fresh cut flowers into a vase.

Maude put the newspaper down and looked at her sister. "Moss, you know Madison made up her mind yesterday to leave. She is free to do as she pleases even if it is cutting our first visit together so short."

"Yes. Yes, I know." Mossie cut the stem on one of the flowers with a pair of floral sheers so it would fit uniformly in the vase with the others. "But I had so hoped she would stay long enough for us to have a dinner party so we could introduce her to our friends."

I listened as my great-aunts conversed as if I were not even in the room. It shouldn't have surprised me since they had been doing it ever since I arrived. The mention of the dinner party was a perfect out for me to stay and I believe Mossie knew it.

"A dinner party?" I crossed my arms over my chest as I contemplated the idea.

"Yes, dear, wouldn't that be lovely?" Mossie asked, glancing expectantly at me over the top of the flower arrangement.

"Now Moss, don't go trying to change Madison's mind about leaving. As she said yesterday at the gazebo, our letter brought her here thinking there was a family emergency. If she doesn't want to stay to get to know us better, then that is her decision."

My pulse quickened and my blood pressure rose at the insinuation Maude was making about me. How dare she turn this on me? I was about to protest when I realized she was cleverly manipulating me with her words the way she had at the dinner table on my first evening here.

"I would like more than anything to stay and get to know each of you better, and if that is the real reason you brought me to Wyndam House, then why didn't you say so when I asked?"

"Well, Madison." Mossie carried the vase over to the kitchen table. "I thought you would have realized this on your own."

I rolled my eyes upward and pursed my lips together.

Maude winked at me and gave a little nod as if she knew I was smarter than Mossie was giving me credit for. "Why don't you stay and find out?"

"Humph," I grunted. "Maybe I will." I left the kitchen, but not before laying the bus schedule on the secretary.

I went to the foyer to retrieve my suitcase, but it was not there. I placed my hands on my hips and shook my head as I looked around the beauty of the finely built home. Was I crazy for staying?

Chapter Three

Later that day I found my way down to the gazebo with my writing tablet, pencil box, and journal. Since I was going to be staying on, I had to write my mother to let her know I had arrived safely and what my plans were. I really didn't know how long I would be staying, but I knew that if I didn't press too hard I could enjoy the time at Wyndam House. And maybe with time I would find the answers I was looking for.

My mind kept going back to the thought of my grandmother living here when she was a young girl. She never spoke of that time when I was with her in Charleston. I suppose that is why when she suddenly moved back to Wyndam House before her death I didn't understand. I hadn't known this part of her life.

My mother seldom talked of the Madison family,

since they had died long before I was born. Her father had been an only child and his father had originally come from Europe when he was a young boy. That is all she ever told me about her father's family; perhaps she didn't know any more than those details.

Thinking about my mother made me long to be with her again in Camden. I took out my writing table and began a letter.

May 11, 1920

Dear Mother,

I hope you are doing well while I am away. I know you must be lonely because there is loneliness in my heart for you that I cannot deny. I promise to return home soon. I don't know when that will be just yet, because I want to learn more about the Wyndam side of our family.

Wyndam House is a glorious place. It's far more likeable than I remember from my first visit. I have been made to feel at home while staying here. Aunt Maude and Aunt Mossie have shown me the beauty of River Road. They also took me on a sightseeing trip to Drayton Hall and Magnolia Plantation before finally showing me their own luxury garden at the back of the estate. That is where I am now, sitting in the gazebo by the water, watching the swans glide across the pond and breathing in the heady fragrance of the lush flowers in bloom.

Aunt Maude and Aunt Mossie are a joy, but I have to admit they are quite different from father's aunts. They send their best and hope they didn't offend you by only asking me to come for a visit. It wasn't their intention.

This visit is still a mystery to me. I feel they're keeping why they asked me to come a secret even though I have asked repeatedly. They have a habit of speaking of me as if I'm not even in the room, which is frustrating at times, but I'm learning not to mind because I find out what they are really thinking through their endless conversations.

They are planning a dinner party in my honor. It's exciting that they'd want to honor me in this way. I just hope the guest list isn't too long and that it will be an informal affair. I'll write more about it when I have details.

I am staying in grandmother's old room. It's a warm and comfortable room. I like the bay window very much because it looks down on the pond and I can watch the swans frolicking on the water. I'll try to send you a sketch in my next letter.

I miss you terribly.

Love,

Madison

I laid my pen aside and looked out over the water, trying to imagine it as it had been during the Civil War when my great-aunts and grandmother were hiding while Union soldiers burned their house down. It was an awful and eerie thought, and it made me shiver as I tore the page from my tablet.

As I addressed the envelope, I caught a glimpse of something moving near the water. I looked up to see if someone was there, but I didn't see anyone. Still, I had the feeling I was not alone. I looked around again to see if I could spot someone near the water, but everything appeared as peaceful as before. All except for the shadows made by the trees.

There was serenity about this place, yet, I had the feeling that someone or something was out there watching me. I tried to push the thought aside, but it wouldn't go away. I told myself I was over reacting because I had been thinking about my aunts and grandmother hiding from Union soldiers as they burned everything in sight. Still, this did not ease my mind.

I left the gazebo and went down to the arched bridge for a better look. The swans squawked and fluttered from their horde and began to swim again. It was the queerest thing. I turned and looked up at the house wondering if Maude or Mossie might be looking out of one of the windows down to the gazebo. But, I did not see them. The fact that I was obviously alone did not calm me as I went back up to my writing spot. My heart beat faster and I found my hand running nervously up and down the back of my neck.

"Excuse me, miss." The maid, Bea, appeared out of nowhere. I jumped and let out a little scream. She carried a tray with a glass pitcher of lemonade and a single glass of ice. "I was asked to bring you this. Are you all right, miss?"

"You startled me, that's all." I took several deep, calming breaths before I took the tray from the maid. My hands were still shaky and the contents rattled as I placed them on the table in the gazebo. "Thank you, Bea."

"I'm sorry, miss. Can I bring you anything else?"

"This will be fine." I poured myself a glass of the lemonade and sipped it, chastising myself for thinking someone or something was out there watching. I quickly dismissed the episode.

For the next few days Maude and Mossie talked nonstop about the dinner party they were giving. It consumed their every waking moment, giving me little time to pursue my questions with them. They met with their banker to check on their financial affairs before doing anything else, which made me wonder if the Wyndam estate might be in need of funds. This brought back to mind the conversation I had overheard them having in the parlor on my first night here. They spoke of placing a burden on me. I could only wonder if they needed me to help them raise money for the estate, but I couldn't think how to do so if they asked. I didn't have any wealth. The Franklin family had little but their land, and it seemed their land would soon consume them financially.

I decided not to bring up the matter with them until I had more proof that the estate was in a financial bind. It would be quite embarrassing for us all if I tried to salvage something that didn't need saving. Yet, I didn't want my great-aunts going to great lengths to throw a formal dinner party on my account if it would drain them of what little savings they had.

"Madison, dear, are you all right?" Mossie smiled at me as she stepped out of the house from the back door. "You have that look on your face again, child. Is something bothering you? You know you can tell me if there is."

I smiled. She had her pruning shears and flower basket ready for her morning ritual of providing fresh cut flowers for the foyer table.

"I hope you and Maude aren't going to much trouble with this dinner party. A small gathering would be more than enough if you insist on having the dinner. I really wouldn't feel disappointed if you decided to forget the idea."

"Nonsense." Mossie wrapped her arm around my shoulders and gave a little squeeze as we walked further down into the garden. "You shouldn't worry about the dinner party. Maude and I have everything under control. We've hired a caterer who will oversee everything. All we have to do is provide the guest list, decide on a menu and wear our prettiest dresses."

I tried to smile at her, but my mind went back to my wardrobe. I didn't have the type of dress Mossie was referring to. One of my cotton sack dresses with all its fashion wouldn't be appropriate attire for a formal gathering.

"Now don't you fret." Mossie patted my shoulder. "Maude and I are planning on taking you into Charleston to buy you some new dresses because we are certain once we present you at the dinner party, you will be receiving numerous invitations for engagements later on in the summer."

I tensed thinking about this. I rarely attended large gatherings. The largest had been when I graduated from high school in Camden. There had been twenty in my class—mostly girls. Many of the boys had dropped out to join the army to fight for the United States over in Europe.

I knew I didn't have the grace or sophistication of my great-aunts who were accustomed to sharing intellectual conversation over dinner with individuals like themselves. How could I ever fit in among these people? After all, I was from the up-country and they were from the low. Surely this stigmatization was still present in the back of their minds.

"Thank you, Aunt Mossie." I kissed her check. "But you don't have to go to the trouble of doing that."

Mossie frowned, looking displeased. It was the first time I had seen her do that. There was also sadness behind her eyes as well. She walked over to one of the flower bushes and began snipping stems to put in her basket, moving from bush to bush until she had enough flowers before she spoke again.

"We want to do it, Madison. It will make us both very happy to see you looking like the beautiful young woman you are. You favor your grandmother when she was your age and to see you wearing a beautiful dress and catching the young men's eyes will make us feel Millicent is still with us."

"You miss her, don't you?"

"More every day." With a sigh, she sat down at the table in the gazebo and I joined her. "I regret all those years we were apart. I regret turning her away when she tried to speak with father. It was wrong of me, Madison, but I knew father wasn't ready to speak with her. Loyalty sometimes keeps people apart just as much as pride."

"You obviously did what you thought was right at the time."

"Did I?" She sounded unsure and stood up with her basket and headed back up to the stone steps. I followed her.

"Was it right of me to turn my youngest sister away when I could see she was lonely? She missed her family and it was all fathers' fault. Her daughter had left Charleston because of him and she couldn't be with her sisters either. How right was it of me to keep Maude from going to her for a visit?"

I could see Mossie was plagued by her actions all those years ago. She wanted to make amends and she obviously hoped to accomplish this through me.

"You did what you thought was right at the time, didn't you? You obviously didn't want more strife to come to your family. Maybe you had no right to keep Maude from seeing Millicent, but you acted out of what you thought was her best interest to keep the peace with your father."

Mossie looked at me as if seeing me for the first time. She shook her head. "You sound like Millicent, Madison, did you know that? She said the same thing when she was dying. I begged her to forgive me, and she said she already had because she knew I acted out of love when I turned her away."

"Then you should be satisfied knowing that." However, I wasn't satisfied with the little information she had revealed. It only gave me more unanswered questions.

After Mossie left the garden, I returned to the gazebo, curled up in one of the chairs, and opened up my journal. I had promised my mother a sketch of the garden and I was having difficulty drawing it the way I wanted her to see it. I was certain she had once come to the garden when she was younger before whatever made Richard Wyndam so upset that he refused to allow his youngest daughter and her child to return to Wyndam House.

That's why my drawing had to be perfect. I wanted her to recall the beauty of it as if she were here at Wyndam House again. I don't consider myself an artist by any means, but I like to draw. My father always loved my pictures. He even framed a sketch I did of the farm when I was thirteen. He hung it over his easy chair in the living room so all could see. I had been uncertain about my ability until that day, but knowing he cherished my hobby that much gave me the encouragement to do more.

I leaned back in the chair and looked out over the water. I watched the swans pick at one another, flutter their wings and glide away only to return after a short swim to start the process all over again. Such a simple life.

Across the water a bird sat in the top of a large oak tree. Its breast was stuck out and its beak was lifted heavenward as it sang a joyful tune. A plop came from the water's edge, drawing my attention back to the pond. Ripples spread outward, leaving telltale signs that a frog had joined the swans in their wet haven. I watched as the ripples vanished and then reappear as the frog bobbed up and down, catching the moths and bugs that skimmed the top of the water.

I sketched this scene in my drawing and put the bird in the top of one of the trees. As I worked, I lost track of the time, and when I looked up again the sun was moving over the trees, almost dipping below the other side of them. I laid my journal on the table and stood up to stretch before walking to the edge of the gazebo for one final look at the pond before going back to the house.

The tranquility of the spot was still visible to my eye even if I had been frightened by the thought of someone watching me the other day. Because of that, I was hesitant as I inspected my surroundings. I compared the view and my artwork until I was satisfied with the drawing. But, as I laid the journal back down, I noticed something odd in the brush around the water's edge. It was as if two eyes were looking out of the picture at me, eyes that drew me into their own world.

A short gasp escaped my throat. I looked out at the pond again and searched the water's edge. The eerie feeling engulfed me again and a chill ran up my spine. It wasn't Bea bringing refreshments this time. Someone was near, out there in the brush on the other side of the pond watching me. They had been there for quite some time or I wouldn't have mysteriously drawn them into my picture. I had obviously been too engrossed, concentrating on my sketch to realize it.

I closed my journal and left it lying on the table in

the gazebo before walking down to the water's edge, hesitating only a few moments before crossing the wooden bridge to the grove of trees on the other side. Whoever was out there needed to stop lurking and make their presence known.

The swans seemed mesmerized by my movements as they clustered close to the small mound of earth in the center of the pond. I imagined I had their support as I walked on the wooden bridge watching for a sign of movement in the direction of the trees. I tried not to appear timid as I walked because I didn't want to seem an easy target if the person meant me harm.

At the edge of the grove of trees, I stopped and looked around as if I was searching for something. I didn't want whoever was out there suspecting my true motive for crossing the bridge. There was no movement of any kind around the trees, and I felt disappointed and relieved at the same time that the person might have left. So I began picking cattails along the water's edge as I aimlessly walked back toward the bridge. And then, out of nowhere, there he was.

I sucked in a deep breath and stepped back as my eyes slowly traveled from a pair of shining, brown leather shoes to wheat-colored linen trousers that narrowed at a trim waistline blending into a crisp cream colored shirt and leather suspenders. His hands were tucked into his pockets and he rocked back and forth on his heels with a grin on his face so perilously white it made me almost miss his dazzling cobalt blue eyes on first glance. His skin was tanned and it made his sandy blond hair look almost white.

"Did the cat eat your tongue?" he asked pointedly when I didn't say a word, but kept staring at him in disbelief. I don't know if I was shocked more by his sudden appearance or by the fact that he was so devilishly handsome. Chill bumps ran up and down my spine, this time from adrenaline instead of fear.

"W-wh-at?" I blinked and tried to regain my composure.

"I said, did the cat eat your tongue?" he repeated in a thick southern drawl.

My face warmed and I looked away, dropping the cattails. I was at a loss for words and I really didn't know why I had been staring at him. He wasn't the first handsome male I had ever seen.

"You aren't from around these parts, are you?" He continued to rock back and forth on his heels, grinning like a Cheshire cat, his pearly white teeth gleaming.

"No. I'm from Camden." I ran a hand up the back of my neck and glanced out over the pond to keep from staring at him. I suddenly felt awkward, which puzzled me because my playmates growing up were all male cousins so this stranger's presence shouldn't unnerve me.

"Camden." He nodded his head. "Don't reckon' I been there before."

"Oh. Do you travel?"

"Been to Europe and the Pacific Islands." His reply was matter of fact.

"In the war?" Was that why his skin was so tanned?

"Yes and no." He lost his grin as he looked out over the pond at the gazebo. "I love it here. You like coming here?"

I found that question strange, but I suppose it was a way to make conversation and get away from something one didn't want to talk about. "Yes. It's so peaceful and quiet except, of course, when the swans get rambunctious."

He gave me a long sideways look as if he were studying me. Not that he needed to, since he had obviously been watching me for quite some time now from his hiding place in the bushes.

"You know this is private property you are on?" He casually leaned back against the bridge railing and crossed one leg over the other at the ankles.

"Oh?" I wondered what he was getting at. His tone sounded like he was giving me a warning.

He took a deep breath and nodded. "I know the place looks almost deserted, but there are two elderly spinster ladies that live in the house upon the hill. You really shouldn't be sneaking on their land."

His chastisement surprised me and my mouth dropped open as I sucked in my breath and almost laughed at him. Here he was trespassing on Wyndam land and he had the gall to warn me of doing so.

"I know Maude and Mossie Wyndam wouldn't mind if you asked permission to visit their garden," he continued dryly, obviously ignoring my reaction.

"Why should I do that? I'm already here."

He chuckled and shook his head. "I can see that, but the elderly are a queer bunch, especially those with money. You could easily be arrested and thrown in jail."

"Is that so? Then we'd both be locked up, wouldn't we?"

"No." He uncrossed his ankles, bushed away from the bridge railing and stood tall again. "I'm not the one trespassing."

That statement made me laugh, and he looked utterly dismayed as if I were mad.

"What do you find so amusing?" His brows arched and he cocked his head to one side.

"Do you have permission to be here?"

He didn't answer.

I rolled my eyes heavenward and planted my hands on my hips. "You've got some nerve lecturing me when you're the one trespassing on Wyndam land. Just who are you, anyway?"

"I know who I am. The question is who are you?" His words were thick with southern cockiness.

I shook my head. I had wasted enough time with this silly chatter. I stooped down and picked up my cattails and headed back across the bridge.

"Where do you think you are going?" He caught

my arm as I passed him.

"Home. Now take your hand off me. I'll be late for supper and Aunt Maude and Mossie will be worried."

His dumbfounded expression was priceless as he let my arm go. "Your aunts?"

"Yes, those two elderly spinster ladies you referred to are my grandmother's sisters." I smiled sweetly. "Will you come by for a visit again soon?"

He didn't answer and I didn't wait for him to. I giggled to myself as I walked back to the gazebo to collect my journal, writing table, and drawing pencils before heading up the stone steps to the house. I didn't give him the satisfaction of looking back because I knew he was watching my every move. I could feel those penetrating cobalt blue eyes on me.

Chapter Four

That night as I lay in bed I couldn't fall asleep for thinking about the handsome stranger I'd met at the pond. I wanted to know why he had been watching me from the brush, but I had been too stunned to ask. I should have given him a piece of my mind on his behavior, but all I could do was stare at him.

I turned onto my side and punched my pillow vowing that I would not act this way again if he did return to the garden when I was there. He had better, that was all I could say. He had better.

The next morning I dressed carefully and worked with my hair longer than usual. Maude and Mossie were taking me into town to look at dresses for the dinner party. I was a little nervous as we drove into town, but Maude and Mossie didn't seem to notice. They were too engrossed in remembering their shopping trip for the ball when my grandmother had met my grandfather.

"Do you suppose Millicent would have caught Ronald's eye if she had worn that red gown father wouldn't let her purchase?"

Maude shook her head. "That red dress made her look wanton. I believe Ronald would have not been impressed with it. But clothing does not make a person, Moss. I don't believe Ronald chose Milli for what she was wearing."

Mossie sighed. "No, but first impressions are very important."

First impressions. The thought lingered in my mind as I thought of my encounter down in the garden with the mysterious young man who had been watching me. Had I made a good impression on him? He had definitely made a lasting one on me. I'd spent hours the night before writing in my journal about those cobalt blue eyes of his. It was more than their color that captivated me. It was the way they drew me into him, almost making me see the world through his eyes. I wanted to know more about him. Who was he and where did he live?

"Come along, Madison," Maude urged when I was slow getting out of the car at the dress store.

A jazzy tune played on the wooden radio as we entered the store. I was immediately in awe at the finery that was presented for sale in the store. There were dresses made from the finest water color silk to be had as well as tailored suits for men. Other fabrics were available as well like taffeta and organza, satin and velvet, sequins and pearl beaded, linen and polished cotton but each were in their own section of the store. The shoes were of the latest style and color made from hand sewn leather.

Maude and Mossie were right at home browsing the selections, but I felt out of place as I carefully walked between the aisles of garments. I hesitated before touching the fabric of one dress I liked in particular. It was a majestic blue and I couldn't help smiling because it made me think of his eyes–those fascinating cobalt eyes.

"Oh, Madison," Mossie cooed coming over to where I stood. "I like that. Don't you?"

"Yes." I wasn't thinking about the dress, but him. He'd been to Europe and the Pacific Islands. Had he served during the war? Was that the reason he'd lost his grin when I asked him about it?

His southern drawl was not like the people from South Carolina. It had a distinct difference about it, but I could not decipher where he was from.

"Is something the matter?" Maude asked, stopping her browsing.

I quickly put away my thoughts about him and concentrated on the matter at hand. "Would this be suitable for the dinner party?"

"Most certainly." Mossie took the dress off the rack and held it up for Maude to get a better look.

"You'll look lovely in it, Madison. The blue will compliment your brown eyes." Maude immediately motioned for the sales lady to come over to help us further with our selections. After picking out a few more outfits, she led me to a dressing room in the back of the store.

The blue dress was long, and the majestic blue silk and sequined fabric cascaded down my frame, collecting in folds around my feet. It was made in the S-curve which became popular during the turn of the century. I found the style emphasized certain features of my body, giving them a more voluptuous appearance than my small, slender frame possessed. And when I moved, the dress shimmered, reminding me of a dress my mother had worn once. It had been for her tenth wedding anniversary. My father had splurged and taken her to the finest restaurant in Camden and to a play at the theater. My mother had talked about that night so many times after he died. She said it wasn't so much that he'd spent money on her, but that he had thought to do something she hadn't done since she was a young girl living with her mother in Charleston.

The sales lady picked out several more dresses suitable for a season in Charleston as Maude and Mossie referred to it. One of the dresses was a sleeveless, white crepe belted at the waist and the sales lady said I'd get plenty of use out of it. I tried protesting because I didn't really plan on being with them at Wyndam House long enough to need so many new clothes. A season could last up to twelve weeks or so and there was no way I was going to be away from my mother and beautiful Camden that long.

Among the garments that Maude and Mossie insisted on purchasing were a few day dresses that would be suitable for making and receiving calls. They rattled on about etiquette and social grace until I had second thoughts about staying on and agreeing to the dinner party. I wasn't thrilled at the prospect of spending my days confined to a parlor having tea and small talk with people I didn't even know just because they were the right sort of people. When I told Maude and Mossie that on the way back to River Road they were aghast.

"B-b-but, Madison," Mossie sputtered. "It will be expected of you dear."

"Why?"

"Because it is the way we do it here," Mossie explained.

"Well I won't." I crossed my arms and leaned back in the car seat.

"Madison," Maude said in a stern tone. "We will not insist you carry on every day this way, however, the courteous thing will be to accept calls when they are made and to return calls respectfully so no one will feel snubbed by the Wyndams."

"Yes. Yes, my dear, that is all we ask." Mossie nodded.

The thought of wearing the new clothes and having to put on airs just so I would not be accused of effrontery was absurd. But as my father always said, "The low-country is far different from the up-country. You may not see that now, but one day you will just like I did."

It was too late in the day to go down to the gazebo after the shopping trip with Maude and Mossie. I was exhausted and I practically fell asleep as soon as my head hit the pillow after a late dinner. However, I woke early the next morning with a crushing thought that *he* might have spent time lurking in the garden waiting for me to show up and I never did. A guilty feeling washed over me because I had off-handedly given him an invitation to drop by.

How rude of me not to have remembered. But maybe my forgetting would work in my favor. He might see my failure to appear as playing coy. Though, I wasn't one to play games.

I prepared my bath and soaked thinking about when I might see him again. What I'd say. What I'd wear. Not one of my new dresses. No. A simple sack dress would do just fine for a chance encounter with him. If I put too much effort in our next meeting he might leap to the wrong conclusion and that would never do.

After dressing, I ran down the stairs and grabbed a muffin from the breakfast platter that Bea left on the kitchen table. I had my journal tucked under my arm and was almost out the back door when Maude came into the kitchen still wearing her wrapper.

"I thought that was you I heard running down the stairs." She smiled. "Are you off somewhere so early this morning?"

"M-m-m-h," I murmured chewing the bite of the muffin I'd taken.

"Anywhere I might find interesting?" She poured herself a cup of coffee.

"Just down to the garden to work on a sketch for my mother." I wiped crumbs away from my mouth with a napkin. "The sunlight is just at the right angle this time of the day."

Maude nodded. "Hope loved to draw when she was a girl, but Millicent was the true artist. She had discipline that Hope never seemed to grasp. Father always said Millicent could have been famous if she had not given up when she married Ronald. Of course, she saw it differently. She said there was too much time consumed running a household and taking care of a baby to draw. I suppose she was right." Maude took a sip of her coffee. "You won't let marriage stop you from drawing, will you? You won't let others stand in your way because of silly pride either, will you?"

I shook my head. "I will always find the time to draw."

"Of course you won't." Maude smiled. "You're too bright a young woman to let that happen. Run along now or your sunlight will be all wrong."

I grabbed an apple from the breakfast tray and slipped out the back door. I had had no idea that my mother drew, nor my grandmother. I thought sketching was only something I did. Why hadn't my mother ever said anything?

I was almost down to the gazebo when I noticed a shadow at the entrance. I stopped walking to get a better look and then *he* stepped forward so I could see him better.

"Good morning," I called taking the remainder of the stone steps at a faster pace without thinking. I shouldn't have been the first to speak, nor should I have hurried my pace, he might think I was eager to see him–which I was, but he didn't need to know that.

He nodded curtly, leaning his lanky frame against one of the posts at the entrance of the gazebo. His ankles were crossed and his pant legs looked wrinkled. His arms were crossed over his chest and I noticed his shirt looked rumpled. Had he slept here last night waiting on me to show up?

"Where have you been?" His voice sounded dry as I slowly moved past him to the table where I laid my journal and small box of drawing pencils.

I arched a brow. So he had been waiting for me. I swallowed the smile that threatened to form at my mouth. "Confined in Charleston."

"Shopping no doubt." He pivoted so he was now facing me. His tone was still dry with a note of irritation.

"Afraid so. What about you?"

"So you really are the infamous great granddaughter of Richard Wyndam." He looked me up and down as if I didn't measure up.

I was beginning to prefer his Cheshire cat grin to the look he was wearing. "What do you mean, infamous? What do you know about me?"

He shrugged before pushing himself away from the post and coming over to the table. He placed his hands in the center and leaned forward, coming almost nose to nose with me. "You don't know, do you?"

I pursed my lips together tightly, wondering if I was ever going to get a straight answer to my questions. Why wouldn't anyone give me an answer? I started to ask him to tell me what he knew, but he was being so arrogant I didn't dare.

"Of course I do." I lied and made the mistake of looking into his deep, penetrating, blue eyes.

"No you don't." He finally broke into a grin. He straightened his frame and gave me another look over before he turned and walked out of the gazebo.

I watched dumfounded for a moment before I realized he was leaving. "Wait!" I called going to the entrance of the gazebo.

He stopped and looked back over his shoulder.

"Where are you going?"

"To bed. I'll see you this evening, Madison." He disappeared quickly over the arched bridge and into the bushes before I had time to recover from the fact he knew my name. I sank against the post where he had been only a few minutes ago. The spot was warm and I felt flustered. He knew about me. He knew who I was and that there was a definite problem with the Wyndam family. And worst of all, he knew I had no idea why.

I clenched my fist and looked up into the sky and screamed. Aunt Maude and Aunt Mossie were running out of time. If they did not tell me what I wanted to know soon, then I'd be forced to find the answers second hand. Tick-tock.

Chapter Five

After dinner that evening, I excused myself, pretending to be exhausted. Instead of going up the stairs to bed, I headed to the kitchen, making sure Bea was not still cleaning up, before I slipped out the back door. The sun was setting low in the trees sending shadows of crimson and orange around the pond while the moonlight was just beginning to shine giving a clear view of the stone steps as I made my way down to the gazebo. It was empty when I reached the garden, but I did not expect him to be waiting there, I only hoped he came soon.

I sat in the entrance of the gazebo on the step and watched as the swans glided lazily on the water. There was a cool breeze blowing and I felt extremely relaxed as I waited listening to the crickets chirping and the plopping sounds as the frogs bobbed up and down, catching their dinner.

I was keeping an eye on the bushes on the other side of the pond for any sign of him to appear, but he didn't come that way. Instead, he came from the opposite side of the gazebo with his hands behind his back and whistling "Dixie."

I turned slightly and watched as he made his way to where I sat. He was wearing that Cheshire-cat grin again and I couldn't help but smile back.

"Ah the fair maiden returns." He stopped in front of me and dramatically dropped down to one knee. "Please accept this token of friendship."

I didn't know what to expect as he brought his arm from behind his back and presented me with a bouquet of Tiger lilies.

"A pure and natural flower to compliment the fair maiden."

I took the bouquet and smelled the flowers before looking up at him. "Thank you."

There was an awkward silence as he sat down beside me in the entrance of the gazebo. I really didn't know what to say to him even though I desperately wanted to know his name, but I couldn't very well blurt that out. I also wanted to know how he knew who I was and why he had been lurking in the garden the other evening.

"Is something wrong?" he asked when I didn't speak right away.

I shook my head and looked up at him as the

moonlight cast shadows over his face. "How did you know who I was?"

"I asked my grandfather."

"And who is your grandfather?"

"A neighbor of your aunts."

I don't know why I had expected him to give me a name in response, but if he was going to keep his identity a secret then I was just going to have to excuse myself. "Well, if that is all he is then he should keep his nose out of other's business."

I left my flowers lying in the gazebo and marched down to the bridge. To my dismay, I heard him chuckling behind me.

"That's a haughty reply for someone who doesn't even know what business she is referring to."

My spine tensed at the truth in his words and it stung that he knew so much about my situation. "I know more than you think."

"Not enough."

No, not enough. I didn't want to admit he was right so instead I said, "This is my first visit with my grandmother's sisters."

"Yes." He came up behind me and I could feel the warmth radiating off his body he stood so close behind me.

"My grandmother died when I was very young, that is all." I tried to make him believe that was the reason.

"Yes. My grandfather speaks highly of Ronald and

Millicent Madison."

I turned around facing him. "Did he know them?" I immediately regretted how desperate I sounded.

He nodded and reached for my hand. "You want to know, don't you? But they won't tell you?"

I found his perception of the situation unnerving, not to mention his touching my hand. There was no point in denying he was right. "No. They won't tell me. I've tried since I arrived to find out answers to my questions. Every time I think they are about to tell me they shy away from it. I don't know why it's so difficult to tell me why I was never allowed to come here except for my grandmother's funeral."

He nodded and let my hand go. "My grandfather said I shouldn't get involved, but there is too much you want to know for me not to try and help you."

A glimmer of hope was suddenly sparkling. Excitement began to bubble to life within me and it was all I could do to keep from bursting. "Then you know why I never knew my great-grandfather?"

"My grandfather does. I think you should meet him. I'll come for you tomorrow after lunch. Will you be here?"

"Yes. I'll be here. I'll make sure of it."

"Good. Until then." He turned to leave.

"Wait."

He turned back. "What is it?"

"I don't even know your name."

He chuckled and extended his hand to me. "I'm

Conner Montgomery."

Conner. Conner. I repeated to myself. The name fit him. "I'm Madison Franklin."

"I'll see you around two tomorrow, Madison." He left me standing by the arched bridge in the moonlight.

Two tomorrow. I'd have to make sure that Maude and Mossie did not have plans for me tomorrow afternoon. Surely they had too much to do with the dinner party approaching to keep them busy at home.

I spent most of the next morning with my great-aunts to ensure they would not be in need of my presence during the afternoon. After lunch, I went to my room and put on one of my new dresses for making calls, fixed my hair, and applied a little blush and lipstick. I wanted to make a good impression on Conner's grandfather. *Conner.* I liked his name.

At a quarter till two I picked up my journal and box of drawing pencils and headed down the stairs. I was quiet as I walked from the stairs to the kitchen so not to disturb Maude and Mossie who were in the dining room with the maid, giving instructions for cleaning the house in preparation for the dinner party that was soon approaching.

I was careful as I walked down the stone steps to stay clear out of sight of the dining room window. I didn't want them to see me and wonder why I was going to the garden dressed in one of my new dresses. Once at the gazebo, I sat down in the entrance way and waited for him to arrive. I opened up my journal and began randomly sketching lines. I was surprised when a perfect caricature of Conner became visible on the page.

"Let me see," he said, appearing from nowhere to stand over me.

I snapped the journal closed and held it tightly against my chest, shaking my head. I didn't want him to think I was romanticizing over him. I hardly knew him after all. "It isn't finished yet."

He sighed heavily and extended his hand out to me. "When it is then?"

"Maybe." I took his hand and stood up, noticing he was only a few inches taller than me.

"I hope you are not disappointed if you don't find out everything you want to know with today's visit." He took a step away from me as if we had been standing too close together.

I shrugged. I really hadn't expected to find out everything at once. Any clues to the puzzle I was trying to unravel would be a help at this point. "I don't think I will." I picked up my pencil box. "If I find out one new thing today then I'll be satisfied."

Conner smiled and offered me his hand. I took it and we headed for the arched bridge. "I should also warn you that my grandfather doesn't know I'm bringing you for an inquisition. He thinks you are coming for his famous homemade ice cream."

His Cheshire grin returned to his face and it made me feel he was up to no good this time. An amusing trait for someone his age. "Well, if I have to eat ice cream I can make the sacrifice. And I won't ask too many questions either."

He led me through the brush to a well-worn path that I wondered if my great-aunts knew about. It was obvious that he was not the first person to come sneaking into their garden this way, but I wasn't upset that he had. My visit was turning into a more pleasant one now that I met him.

We walked for quite a while, cutting through the yards of two estates before finally coming to the Montgomery House. It was different from the other houses along the way, yet it still held the distinctive character of the south. The house was built in the Georgian style just like Wyndam House, yet the portico was not square, but rounded with four columns evenly spaced on the façade. There was also a small balcony over the front door and another over a sun room on the west side of the house. A short distance from the house was a small grove of apple trees with wooden lawn chairs set around a small wooden table. Two older men were sitting there talking as we approached.

As we came closer, the two men stopped talking and looked up. I immediately felt awkward as I could tell they were looking me over by the way their eyes moved.

"You must be Miss Franklin." One of the men got up from his chair and extended his well-tanned hand to me. "I'm Duncan Claiborne."

I nodded and smiled taking his hand. "It's nice to meet you, Mr. Claiborne."

"Call me Duncan, dear, everyone does."

"Yes, do call him Duncan. I'm Conrad Montgomery." The other man didn't stand because he was busy cranking the handle on the ice cream maker. "You'll have to forgive my grandson for not making proper introductions. He seems to forget his manners at times."

"It's nice to meet you, Mr. Montgomery." He spoke the truth. I don't think I'd ever have found out Conner's name if I had not come out and asked. However, Conner didn't seem fazed by his grandfather's remark.

"Have a seat," Conrad said. I thought it odd that he had dark hair that was graying white and Conner had blond hair, but not everyone carried the same features in the family. Conrad had broad shoulders and was tall with a mid-waist bulge. He looked to be in his sixties; around the same age as Maude. So did Duncan. He was a tall man and looked to be fit for his age. He had dark hair that was neatly trimmed and he was well-tanned for early spring.

Conner waited for me to take my seat before he sat in the chair beside mine. He fidgeted, rubbing his fingers together as an awkward silence fell over us.

Duncan glanced over at Conrad and then back at me. "You look familiar, Madison. Almost as if I have met you before."

"Have you been to Camden?"

He shook his head. "I don't think you understand, dear." He grinned and his forehead wrinkled and crow's feet became visible around his eyes. "You remind me of your grandmother when she was young."

I found his way of approaching the subject of my grandmother odd, but people in the low country had their quirks.

"You've left her speechless, Duncan." Conrad chuckled causing his stomach to jiggle. "You had better explain yourself."

Duncan leaned forward in his chair resting his elbows on his knees. "What's to explain? We have Millicent's look-a-like sitting here with us."

"Did you know my grandmother well?"

"As well as anyone knows the Wyndams."

"And that isn't much." Conrad slowed the cranking motion before stopping. "Your family tends to keep to themselves. Yet they are always eager to help if there is a crisis."

"I see."

"You were just a child when she died, weren't you?" Duncan asked.

I nodded wondering if he had come to the funeral.

There had been so many strangers there that day that I could not recall if I had seen his face or not. "I was six. Her funeral was the first time I came to Wyndam House."

Conrad looked at Duncan and they exchanged a look.

Conner, who had been quiet up until now, cleared his throat. "I don't think Madison came to discuss her grandmother. She came to have some of the famous Montgomery ice cream."

I glanced at him and smiled, thankful that he was not going to allow the conversation to get too grave. I really wanted to know more than what these two were providing.

"And so she shall, Conner," Conrad said. "But first, I want to know how long Miss Franklin will be gracing us with her presence? Will you be staying on for the summer?"

I shook my head. "That really depends on my great aunts."

"Don't you wish to stay all summer?" Duncan asked.

"I'd love to, but I need to return to Camden and my mother as soon as I discover the answer to what has kept my family separated all these years."

The countenance on both of the gentleman's faced dropped and Conner shifted in his chair placing his hand at his mouth, but he did a poor job hiding the smile that appeared because of what I said.

Well, sometimes a Wyndam has to do what she has to do. Doesn't she?

Conrad and Duncan were quiet for a few minutes as they began dishing out the ice cream. Conner reached for my hand and gave it a squeeze for reassurance. It wasn't until after we each had a dish that Conrad spoke. "I see you brought a notepad and box of pencils. Does that mean you draw?"

I nodded. "I recently learned that my grandmother did as well."

"She was quite the artist." Duncan said. "Of course that was before she married. I recall the way the young men would gather around her at parties hoping she'd sketch them. It was more of a prize for Millicent to pay them that attention than to win the first dance with her."

"Did she ever sketch you?" I asked.

"No. My Ramona would have never permitted that." He shook his head. "I'm not saying she was a jealous woman because there was not a jealous bone in her body, but it would not have been proper for a married man to be sketched like the dandies."

"Now that you mention that, Duncan, I recall Richard being quite displeased with her for attracting so much attention away from her older sisters." Conrad held his spoon in mid-air. "It was unheard of for a thirteen-year-old to gather so much attention from the young bucks.

"Millicent was so different from her sisters. She was independent and she didn't care for all the lace and frills that other girls like to have on their gowns. The plainer the better. I remember Ramona talking about how that girl could take the simplest dress and make it stylish by putting it on."

I smiled, listening to Duncan and Conrad sink into reminiscing about parties and barbeques until Conner leaned over and asked me if I wanted to go for a walk. I hesitated that they might say something important that I needed to hear if we left, but their conversation soon turned to the war and all the blood-shed they had seen.

We quietly slipped away and Conner led me around the estate showing me the flower garden. Once we reached the hedge maze, we found a stone bench and sat down.

"Did you learn anything?"

"A little. I'm sure I could have learned more if I'd known what questions to ask."

"The more you come and talk to them the more you'll learn." He touched my check with a bent finger and ran it down it softly. "You'll just have to be patient."

I nodded still feeling the velvety touch of his finger long after he moved his hand away. He cared. I could see it in his eyes, his voice and his touch. I liked that, because it made me not feel so alone here.

"I should get back before Maude and Mossie begin to miss me. I don't want to alarm them if they find I'm gone."

"Of course. I'll walk you home." Conner led me out of the hedge maze back through the flower garden over to the apple grove.

Conrad and Duncan were still discussing the war. They stopped long enough to look up at us when we stopped by the picnic table to get my journal and box of pencils.

"We're going fishing tomorrow, Madison. You're welcome to come along with us," Duncan said.

Fishing. "I'll have to see what my aunts have planned for tomorrow."

"Conner can stop by and see if you can go," Conrad said. "We enjoyed you coming today."

"I enjoyed it too." I waved at them as Conner and I headed back toward Wyndam House.

About ten yards away Conner slowed his pace. "If you don't fish you could still come along and draw."

"I'd like to."

"But?"

I looked down at the ground for a quick second and then back at him. "Maude and Mossie are throwing a dinner party soon. There is so much to be done. They may have the day already planned for me."

"Then you'll come if you can and if you can't we'll see you another time." He shrugged, walking again.

"I'll come by around nine and if you aren't at the gazebo then I'll know you can't. We'll be down at the Ashley if you decide later you can sneak away."

He made everything seem so simple.

"I'll try."

We continued on in silence the rest of the way back to the garden, stopping only when we reached the small path at the edge of the brush. Conner looked at me and I looked at him. Neither one of us said anything for a few moments. I couldn't read what he was thinking, but I felt he did not really want to say goodbye any more than I did. I enjoyed his company.

"Till tomorrow, Madison," he blurted and was gone before I could stop him.

Yes tomorrow. I watched until he disappeared out of sight among the trees before I went back up to the gazebo to finish the sketch of him I'd started earlier.

After dinner that evening Maude tactfully brought up my disappearance that afternoon while Mossie was preoccupied reading a letter she had received that day.

"I was hoping we could have discussed the menu for the dinner party this afternoon, but we didn't get the chance." She set her coffee cup in the matching china saucer on her lap. "Perhaps tomorrow afternoon you will not have plans."

I nodded, watching her carefully. I half expected her to ask me not to leave the estate without permission, but she didn't and I was glad. I was not a child who should have to check in with them during the day.

"Tomorrow afternoon would be nice." I thought about going fishing. "Aunt Maude, where is a good place to go fishing?"

She almost knocked her cup and saucer off her knee when I asked this. "I wouldn't know dear. Do you like fishing?"

I looked away to hide my smile. "I haven't been since I was ten, but I might like to watch others so I can sketch them. Do you know a good place? What about the right time of day?"

"Well…I…ugh…I would suppose the Ashley would be a good place." She placed the cup and saucer a safe distance away on the coffee table. "As for the right time of day, father would go in the early morning hours, but it wouldn't be proper for a young lady to go alone.

"I wouldn't want to go that early. I'm not looking to catch a big one. I'm more interested in the flavor of the fishing trip. I've been enjoying the scenery while here. My sketches are making a beautiful memory book that I can share with my mother when I return to Camden."

Maude nodded, looking less disturbed now that I was talking about sketching instead of fishing. She glanced over at Mossie who had fallen asleep still holding her letter in her hand.

"The poor dear. She's running herself ragged getting ready for this dinner party. She wants it to be perfect as when we entertained years ago. But we're not as young as we once were."

"Please don't go to too much trouble on my account."

"Nonsense. We're doing this as much for you as for us. It's been years since we entertained. Well, since father got so ill we couldn't have company over for fear it would agitate him."

"Perhaps we should help her upstairs," I suggested.

Maude nodded.

It wasn't difficult to get Mossie to her room. She woke as we were assisting her out of the chair and she pushed us away.

"I'm not an invalid. I can walk on my own."

"No one said you were." Maude followed her to the stairs. "You fell asleep and we didn't want to leave you in the armchair all night."

"Well I don't need your help." Mossie missed the first step and lurched forward, but Maude caught her.

"Are you sure you can make it on your own?"

"Yes." Mossie slapped her hands away.

I held back not wanting to get into the sisterly squabble with them. I went to my room and closed my door, putting on my nightgown for bed. A few moments later there was a knock and Maude came in.

"Is Mossie okay?"

"Yes. She wasn't fully awake and she gets agitated sometimes. But that isn't why I came. I wanted to thank you."

"I really didn't do much."

"No, not just helping get Mossie out of the chair, but for coming when we wrote. We weren't sure you would because of the way things have been for so long."

I sucked in my breath almost afraid to say anything for fear she wouldn't continue. "Aunt Maude, whatever was wrong in the family can be resolved. Can't it?"

Maude didn't respond right away. She clutched her hands together in front of her, rubbing one thumb over the other. "Come with me."

I padded along behind her in my bare feet down the long hallway, past the other bedrooms to a large room that looked vaguely familiar. It was the nursery where I had spent the afternoon of my grandmother's funeral. I suddenly felt chills run up and down my spine at the memory.

"I know you want to know the answers, but before you do, I think you should understand your great-grandfather." Maude went over to the book shelves that lined one side of the wall and pulled out an old book with the binding tattered from age. "Once you know who Richard Wyndam was, then I believe you will see why what happened all those years ago changed our family as well as why it happened."

I looked down at the book she handed me and then back up at her. I was speechless and she left me standing in the dimly lit nursery holding the old book.

Hesitantly I went back to my room and curled under the covers. I opened the book and found an old photograph of a man, a woman, and three small girls. The youngest was just a small baby in the mother's arms. I carefully turned it over and read the names written: Richard, Miriam, Mossie, Maude, and Millicent Wyndam, October 1860.

I let out the breath I hadn't realized I held. This was my grandmother's family. Had Maude truly realized what she was doing when she gave me this book? Why now? Had Mossie made her upset tonight so she decided to go behind Mossie's back? Whatever the reason I wasn't going to question.

I studied the photo for a long time and looked at the date again. My grandmother was only two and a half months old when it was taken. It was hard to imagine. I looked closely at my great-grandmother and saw she looked much like Maude and Mossie did now. This was the first time I'd seen a photo of her. Richard Wyndam must have carried this photo with him during the war. That was the only reason it had survived the fire.

Maude and Mossie didn't talk about their mother much. I assumed it had much to do with her dying when they were so young and they didn't remember much about her. But Richard Wyndam had to have remembered her; he rebuilt the house in memory of her. Hadn't Mossie said the house was her mother's piece of paradise?

I placed the photo in the front of book to keep it safe and turned the page carefully. To my surprise it was a journal. A journal that had belonged to my great-grandfather. I closed the book immediately not wanting to read his private thoughts. I placed the book on the bedside table and turned out the light. Did I dare pry? But was it really prying to read someone's journal, especially if that person was dead? And hadn't Maude given it to me for that very purpose? She'd wanted me to get to know my great-grandfather in a way that only he could provide. He'd never made an attempt to reach out to me when he was living, not even when he had the perfect chance at my grandmother's funeral. The least he could have done was pull me into his arms and give me a hug. A hug. Would that have been too much of a gesture for him to have made?

Big drops of water began falling as I sank into the bed, and I swiped at the tears that flowed as the pent up dam of pain exploded within my chest. I shut my eyes trying to block it all out. I told myself that he wasn't important to me, but he was. He was the center of all that confused me. I had to find out why he hadn't wanted me in his life. Why had he shut me and my parents out of his life? Why had my grandmother only come home to Wyndam House before she died? Why not before? These were questions that plagued my mind and I had to find the answers to them.

Chapter Six

I woke early the next morning, my eyes swollen from all the crying I did last night. The sun was barely coming up as I made my way into the bathroom to splash water on my face and to get dressed. I wanted to crawl back in bed, but I needed to be ready when Conner arrived to go fishing. So I donned the only pair of britches I had brought with me and a button up shirt that I tied at my waist. On my way out to the gazebo to wait for him, I stopped in the kitchen to make myself a bowl of oatmeal. While it cooked, I put together some bread and cheese for sandwiches and selected some fruit to take along. After I ate, I rummaged in the pantry and found a basket to put the food in as well as a few bottles of pop.

Satisfied, I headed down to the gazebo to wait for Conner. He appeared with another bunch of tiger lilies.

My cheeks warmed. "Thank you, but you don't have to keep bringing me flowers."

He shrugged. "They make me think of you."

"That's sweet."

He picked up my basket and looked inside. "Lunch?"

I nodded, getting to my feet. "I wasn't sure how long we'd be gone or if you'd bring anything."

"Thoughtful of you." He reached for an apple and I smacked his hand away, taking the basket and putting it behind my back. "Don't be such a tomato."

The next thing I knew, he had me around the waist pulling me to him as he tried to get at the basket and the apple, but I wasn't going to let him have it even after we bumped heads.

"You don't play fair."

"Fair? Is it fair that you want to eat our picnic before we even get to where we're going?" I was standing nose to nose with him by that point, feeling his warm breath on my face.

"Fine." I thought he was giving up, but he did the one thing I hadn't anticipated. He began to tickle me.

"No!" I shrieked turning away to escape him and dropped the basket as I tried to protect myself from his onslaught. The soda pop bottles clinked together.

"Say uncle," he breathed heavily against my ear.

"Never." I pushed against him trying to make him lose his balance as I wrapped one leg around his shin. But he was as stout as a tree with roots secured deep into the ground.

"You'll never win."

"That's what you think. I grew up with male cousins. I can hold my own."

He laughed, but that was his mistake. He lost his balance and we both went tumbling to the ground, landing with a thud. For a second, I thought the fall had knocked the breath out of him. His eyes were closed and his body went limp as I scrambled to get off him and regain my lady-like composure. Concerned, I knelt down beside him to check to see if he was all right. In one swift move, he snaked his arms around me and within a second he had me trapped beneath him.

"I win." He was proudly grinning from ear to ear, his hair fell down in front of his cobalt blue eyes. He was dashingly charming in this state, and I was very aware that he had indeed outwitted me.

"You win what?" I asked pushing against his chest until there was a clear pathway so I could get up. I scrambled to my feet, dusting myself off and straightened my clothes, thankful that neither Maude nor Mossie had witnessed that shamble of decorum. They would have been mortified by the display of unruly behavior.

Conner leaned back on his left side and began picking at the blades of grass. I watched him as I gathered the picnic basket and made sure the soda bottles weren't broken. When I turned back, he hadn't made an effort to get up. There was smudge of grass stain on his soft flannel shirt at the elbow and his old blue jeans were wrinkled from wear. There was something appealing about him in this state, and I grabbed my journal and began to sketch him.

Suddenly he sat up as if he had just thought of something important. "I win the privilege of taking you to a picture show in town."

"I can't."

"Why not?" A sheepish grin spread across his face.

I ignored his question and added that to the sketch.

"Madison, stop drawing me."

I looked up at him and saw that he looked annoyed.

"Why can't you go into Charleston with me?" he asked getting to his knees and leaning back on his haunches.

"My aunts wouldn't understand how I met you. They might not approve of us meeting here in the garden without them knowing."

He stood up and walked down to the arched bridge not saying a word. Once there, he turned back toward me. "You think they would feel I wasn't suitable to call on a Wyndam, is that it?"

"No. That isn't what I meant at all." I closed my journal and stuck it and my pencil box in the basket before going down to the bridge to join him. "My aunts are going to a big deal to throw a dinner party where they plan to introduce me into Charleston society. They've been spending hours each day for the last week getting ready for the occasion. How would it look if I was seen in Charleston with you before then?"

"Do you really care about social etiquette?"

"I care about my aunts."

"Really?" he arched a brow.

"Yes. This means a lot to them."

"But does it mean that much to you?"

I shook my head. "But I'll do it for them. And I'll behave properly–though I'm not doing a good job of it so far. What little I know about society rules tells me our meetings are not proper behavior."

"Neither is wrestling."

"No. It isn't for a Wyndam, but I'm a Franklin."

He chuckled. "A Franklin from Camden." He took the picnic basket from me. "We'd better get going or Grandpa and Duncan will have already caught the fish that got away."

"There's one of those in every stream."

He caught my wrist and pulled me to him, then he gently ran his finger down my cheek. "Not every stream."

I was thankful Conner didn't wait for me to respond to what he said. Instead, he slipped his hand from my wrist to my palm and led me across the arched bridge to the path in the brush. I followed at a pace that kept up with his long stride wondering if I was being foolish with him. I should have never scuffled with him earlier. We knew too little about one another to horse around like that. Anything could have happened.

"Did those cattails back there get your tongue again?" He glanced back over his shoulder at me.

I shook my head and watched the path.

"I think they did." He shifted the basket and plucked a foxtail when we passed a patch of them, slowing his pace. I almost bumped into him when he turned. He let my hand go and ran the foxtail under my nose until I laughed, swiping the thing away from my face. "Now that's better."

"You're incorrigible."

"Only children usually are." Finished with the foxtail, he dropped it alongside the path, as he walked backwards.

"So that explains it."

He arched a brow and frowned. "What's that supposed to mean?"

I rolled my eyes and gave him an impish grin, walking past him. "The way we get along."

Conner followed for a short distance without saying a word. I figured he was thinking about what I had said. He was probably scrunching his forehead like all deep thinkers do. I glanced back at him and almost laughed because he was doing just that.

"You think you're funny, don't you?" He sounded

a little rebuffed that I had laughed at him.

"Just as funny as you."

He shook his head before he pulled me to him in one swift move, dropping the picnic basket on the ground. I started to protest, but I saw in his blue eyes that he wasn't joking around this time. He looked serious and his hold on me was firm, but not constraining. What surprised me most was that I wasn't scared. My pulse didn't race, my throat didn't constrict with dryness. I was totally relaxed in his embrace as if that is where I belonged–though I didn't care for his rough way of going about it.

His touch was soft against my back as his hand slowly glided up to my neck where he gently cradled it in his hand before lowering his mouth to mine. The kiss was brief and it took a moment before it registered what he'd done. I blinked and pushed him away.

"Conner, don't." I ran back down the path toward the garden putting as much distance as possible between me and him. Why had he done that? Did he have those kinds of feelings for me already? How? We hardly knew one another. Or was he the type of guy who liked to go around kissing girls?

"Madison. Madison, wait."

I heard the pounding of his feet as he ran after me, but I didn't slow down until I finally crossed the arched bridge and ran to the gazebo where I felt safe. I held onto the post at the back of the gazebo while I caught my breath, trying to figure out why I had run from him. If I wasn't scared of him, then what had me trembling?

"Madison." He came quietly up behind me, but he didn't attempt to touch me. I didn't turn around either. "I'm sorry; I didn't mean to scare you."

"I don't think you did." I tried to turn around but my legs wouldn't move. I could feel the warmth of his body behind me and it sent chills up and down my spine. My trembling turned to shivers and when he touched my arm, he was gentle as he turned me toward him before he wrapped his arms around my waist. I returned the hug and allowed him to hold me close until I felt in control again.

"Why'd you kiss me?"

"I like you."

"But how do you know? We only met a few days ago."

He shrugged, leaning back a little to look down at me. "I can usually judge whether I like a person soon after we meet."

"Oh, so you go around kissing everyone you like?"

He grinned. "No. That's not what I meant and you know it. Who's being incorrigible now?"

I leaned my head back against his chest. "How can you like me when I don't even know who I am anymore? I have so many unanswered questions that I can't think or do much of anything except try to unravel this web of deceit. And once I do, I have to wonder who I will become."

"I believe you know exactly who you are, Madison Franklin. You're the same person who came here from Camden. Finding the answers you seek will not change you. It will only give you more confidence in the girl you already are."

"Maybe."

"I think you are afraid of finding out that you'll never be the Wyndam your grandmother or mother were so long ago, but that doesn't matter. I like you just the way you are."

"But it does matter because who I am somehow prevented my great-grandfather from wanting me in his life. Maude gave me his journal last night to read. She thinks this might help me understand who he was and why the problem in the family occurred."

"Did you read it?"

I shook my head. "I couldn't bring myself to read his journal. Those are his personal thoughts and feelings. I can't pry."

Conner sat down at the table. "I don't think you have any other choice. It's the only way you are going to learn answers to your questions. It isn't like you can talk to the dead. Reading his journal is the closest you'll get to talking to him."

When I remained silent he stood up again. "You keep a journal, right?"

"Yes. I draw more than I write."

"And I bet your sketches tell more about what you

feel and who you are than you think. If your aunt felt comfortable giving you the journal then you should read it. You may not find out what you are looking for, but at least you might begin to understand who Richard Wyndam was." He placed a finger under my chin, tilted my head upward. "Now do you feel up to fishing or would you rather get started reading?"

I stubbornly crossed my arms over my chest. "Fine. I'll read his journal, but you'll have to bring my things back later. And no peeking inside my journal either."

He made the sign of an x over his heart. "I promise. I'll give Grandpa and Duncan your best. And thanks for the lunch. See you later." He quickly kissed me on the forehead before running down the path to the bridge and disappearing into the bushes on the other side of the pond.

I sighed, trudging back up to the house. I had much reading ahead of me. Maude and Mossie were sitting in the kitchen drinking coffee, but I didn't stop to talk. I could tell they were surprised by my attire. It was the first time I'd not worn a dress since arriving.

"How was fishing?" Maude asked.

"Change of plans. I'll be upstairs reading if you need me."

I settled on the settee to read the journal. I stared at the faded writing on the outside of the cover and then at the frayed edges. I slowly opened the book and took out the picture, staring at Miriam's features. My mother looked a little like her now, but more like my grandmother did at that age.

I placed the photo on the cushion next to me and took a deep breath for courage before I turned the page. The handwriting was crisp and legible even though it was almost sixty years old and had been written with a pencil.

July 1861

Never in my life would I have thought of keeping a journal. But that was before the war, long before I had reason to leave my Miriam and three baby girls. I was never one to put much faith in the written word other than the Holy word, but being in a place so desolate as a war where each day less men are still living, and if they are they are not always whole, one had to document the hours in hopes of it giving comfort to those left behind.

I pray that I am fortunate enough to return home to my family because my Miriam is not well. Birthing Millicent was a strain on her and the doctor warned she would be our last chance at having a son to carry on the Wyndam name. I reckon having three girls is not so bad as long as they make sound marriages when the time is right.

I try writing letters home, but there is not much to say other than I am alive and the war will surely be over soon. I have only been here less than a month even though the fighting started shortly after Sumter, but a man has obligations closer to home to see to sometimes. I could not leave my family without seeing to their protection while I was away. I just pray that they will stay safe.

August 1861

I have not had the opportunity to write in days or has it been weeks. I lose count of time anymore. Up early. To bed later. My duties have been increased because I am from the upper class in Charleston. I have now been placed in the rank of an officer in the Confederate Army. I do not feel I deserve the honor because there are others here that are more capable than me. I am not a leader and my men know it. But they are good men, loyal men, even those from the up-country. Here we are all the same. No one cares what part of South Carolina you hale from as long as you pull your weight in our unified mission to free the South from Lincoln's hold.

I closed the book and thought about what my

great-grandfather was saying. There had been a stigmatization between the low and up-country during the war. I was glad because I knew my father would have been pleased. That stigmatization seemed to rule his life for some reason. Yet, I could not help but feel remorse that my great-grandfather had thought so little of President Lincoln during the war–though many southerners felt that way when Lincoln was elected into office. South Carolina had been the first to secede from the Union. And then other states followed suit until the Confederate States of America were formed and Jefferson Davis had been elected as their president.

I tried imagining the political upheaval that my great-grandfather and the other citizens of the United States went through during those trying four years of the war. I slowly opened the book again and started reading.

Page after page I read on, overwhelmed by the hardship my great-grandfather felt being away from his family. His having to put his duty to the Confederacy before those he loved. It slowly changed him.

February 1862

The winter is brutal on us. My men are not doing as well as they should. I have tried to find them an abandoned barn to sleep in during the night or a shack that would at least keep the chilling wind off of them. I am feeling a new pressure from my comrades who boast about how well they are doing. They have cruelly implied one of my men would be better suited as a commander of this troop. He would be one if this man was from the low-country, but he isn't. He's from the up-country and they rub that fact in my face every time we meet for a drink.

I wish this war was over. How much more bloodshed can we take before the Union backs off?

April 1862

I have not written in weeks. I have been ill. The whole troop has suffered from the cold and loss of soldiers. I was shot in the leg. It was not a serious wound. The shrapnel only grazed my leg causing a scar, but there was loss of blood that left me weak. I am thankful that the musket ball did not lodge within my flesh because I would have surely lost my leg. These army doctors do not have time or patience. They amputate limbs for the littlest wounds because it is easier than facing gangrene setting up. Medicine is precious and in short supply.

I wrote my family about my illness, but there has not been a response. I do not even know if they received it. I will be going home for a brief visit when my troop passes back through South Carolina as we move farther south as summer approaches.

Easter Sunday 1862

The war has stopped for the day. The men have been given a day to rest and we are all thankful. It gives us the opportunity to wash and mend our clothing, but no one feels like celebrating, not even to attend the small service a few of the men put together. We have buried more men than I care to remember. Young and old alike. With each letter I have to send to families I am thankful that my Miriam has not received one about me.

June 1862

I just returned from visiting my family. My Miriam does not look well and most of the slaves have run off. They have taken to the notion that they are free because Mister Lincoln says so. Well I say otherwise. He was not the one who paid for them, has kept them fed and well all these years, I have. But alas, only Delci has stayed loyal to my Miriam. Miriam…

I closed the book and laid it aside, using the photograph as my marker. I walked over to the bay window and looked down into the garden. The vivid color of the flora was breathtaking and I had a feeling each plant had some significant meaning between my great-grandparents.

The door to the room opened and Bea brought in a tray for my dinner. "Miss Maude asked me to bring this up to you and said if you needed anything just ring."

"Thank you." My stomach growled as the delicious aroma of the food reached my nostrils, reminding me I'd skipped lunch. I dug into the food, but as I chewed I found it got stuck in my throat because I knew not everyone had always been able to eat a hot meal. My great-grandfather had gone into great detail in his writing about the days when his men had gone without more than a chunk of stale bread and molding cheese to satisfy their hunger.

I went back to the settee and picked up the book, turning the page and reading on. The next few passages were more detailed descriptions of major battles he'd participated in and then I saw a name I recognized.

April 1863

My troop and I have been honored by the presence of Stonewall Jackson. He travels with a fine group of men. Far better than my small troop. I find with each day that passes I despise those that come from the up-country more and more. They are far more capable than those from the low and yet we are economically better off. I do not understand it. It should be the other way around and yet it is not. Why, oh why, have

I been placed with the burden to lead these fools, these gentry' dandies who are far better off in a ballroom than a battlefield?

I have met a very interesting young man this evening. He is a drummer in Stonewall Jackson's troop. His name is Ronald Madison. His family is from Charleston, but we were not acquainted before tonight. He has been with Stonewall since he was eleven and the war began. Master Madison is a fine young man who I'm sure makes his parents very proud. If only I had been blessed with a son…

I smiled. Maude and Mossie had said their father had liked my grandfather very well. I just wondered if he had any aspirations for him to marry one of his daughters from their first meeting. Interested in what else he might have to say about Ronald Madison I read the next few pages, but there was little mention of him other than an occasional meeting during battles. It was a shame because Stonewall Jackson died a few weeks after that first meeting.

March 1864

Today is a black day. I have just received word through command that my Miriam has passed away. She had been ill for some time and I know she held on as long as she could for our daughters' sake and mine. If only she could have lasted until I could come home again. I would have sought out the finest doctor. But it was not God's will.

I have been informed that a leave from my post is not possible at this time. Word is being sent to my darling girls and arrangements are being made to take care of them until the war ends.

When, oh, when will it end? How much more bloodshed is needed? How many families will be divided?

I felt tears stream down my cheeks as I read this. I knew he had not been able to come home, but hearing the pain in his words tore at me.

I reached for a handkerchief and dried my eyes before sticking my nose back in the journal.

Chapter Seven

Two days later I closed the journal for good and emerged from my room for more than my meals and a little party preparation with my aunts. During those times, I hadn't mentioned the journal because I did not know if Mossie knew Maude had given it to me to read. The journal only contained my grandfather's time in the war and ended after Wyndam House was rebuilt. It contained his view on the Civil War and his dealings with men from both the low and the up-country. And to my dismay, there wasn't any indication that there might be another volume of his writings in the house. If there were Maude didn't know where it might be. I came away with just as many unanswered questions–if not more.

I still didn't know the awful truth that divided the Wyndam family all those years ago. I know it wasn't my grandmother marrying my grandfather. And I don't believe it was his untimely death either. Something happened during my mother's lifetime before I was born, but what?

My level of frustration at keeping secrets had escalated. I wanted to run down the hallway and wake Maude and Mossie, demand they answer my questions. But I couldn't do that. Not today. Today was their day. It was the day of the dinner party. I had to put aside my feelings and pretend it was the happiest day of my life for their sake.

Getting out of bed, I slipped on my wrapper and house slippers before going into the bathroom and running a comb through my short cropped hair. My hair. What a travesty. It had little body, which was the reason I cut it short when the style became popular at the end of the World War. Maude promised to have a hair dresser stop by today to fix it before the party. I just hoped the poor woman did not leave here screaming for mercy.

A short time later, after I dressed, I went downstairs and found Maude and Mossie sitting at the dining room table enjoying their morning coffee.

"Well, Madison, what did you learn?" Mossie asked, smiling at me.

I pulled out a chair and sat down, surprised that she knew what I had been doing all along. "My great-grandfather hated the war. He despised the men he led into battle. He despised being put in that leadership role. He stopped writing as soon as he rebuilt Wyndam

House. There was not one word about the family problem recorded in that journal."

"I think you learned more than you know." Maude set her coffee cup down on the table. "I gave you that journal to find out who Richard Wyndam was. Not the family problem."

"He was unhappy during the war because he felt inadequate at his job and knew a number of other men, especially those from the up-country, who could do his job better. Yet he respected those men."

Maude nodded. "Is that all?"

"He was a man who cared about his family deeply; some might say more than he did his country or fellow man. Yet he lived his life to see that his country survived the turmoil of the Civil War and Reconstruction. He never got over the death of his beloved Miriam. He dedicated the rebuilding of their home to her, fashioning every room with something to remind him of her."

A smile spread across Maude's face. "He loved us all the same. He didn't make a difference between Mossie, Millicent, or me. I believe that is why he allowed Millicent to go ahead and marry before Mossie and me."

"Father was loving." Mossie spread butter and then some jam on a muffin. "We all loved him."

I didn't doubt that for a minute, but I wanted to know more. I wanted to know what caused the rift between such a loving family. "Did my grandmother love him?"

Mossie dropped her butter knife and looked at me as if I'd asked whether Millicent had killed him. "Yes."

Maude cleared her throat. "Millicent certainly loved father. He was the only parent that she ever knew besides Delci. Mother passed when she was just a toddler. She always said she could not even remember the sound of mother's voice, but father she knew."

"If they were so close, then how did they drift so far apart?" I received a sharp look from both of them.

"Father had his reasons." Mossie picked up her napkin and wiped the corner of her mouth. "Millicent wasn't always the easiest woman to get along with."

"Now Mossie, you know she wasn't that bad. She was just different from us. She had her own convictions that father didn't always agree with."

"That may be true, but Millicent never knew when she went too far. If she'd been more mindful of her place then she wouldn't have allowed Hope..."

Maude shook her head furiously at Mossie who immediately stopped talking.

"What? What did my mother do?"

"Nothing, dear. Really there was nothing. Mossie is chasing rabbits, remembering things incorrectly. Isn't that right, Moss?"

She nodded and gave me a weak smile. "I've never been a parent so what I might have found outlandish behavior Millicent wouldn't."

"Besides, today isn't the day to get into any of this. We have much to do before this evening." Maude stood. "Finish your breakfast Madison and then I want you to go upstairs and take a nice long hot bath. Bea is preparing it for you now. When you finish, the hair dresser will be waiting for you and then the seamstress will do a final fitting of your dress. Today should be your day, so relax and enjoy."

Hmmm. How was I going to relax with so much to do before dinner tonight? I had to figure out a way to squeeze in time to see Conner if possible. He'd come to the garden and lingered looking for me each morning I'd been reading the journal. I'd seen him from my bedroom window. But would he be down there today?

Following Maude's orders I put all thoughts of Conner aside for the moment and went upstairs for my bath. As I lay soaking in the tub, my mind wondered to this evening and meeting guests at the front door. In my day dream the only guest this evening was Conner. I greeted him wearing the majestic blue dress and he wore a dark suit with his hair combed over to the side. He grinned, taking my hand in his before raising it to his lips for a kiss. Then, he whisked me away to the gazebo where we danced in the moonlight to the sounds of the frogs croaking, the crickets chirping, and the gentle summer breeze blowing. Aunt Maude and Mossie were devastated by my behavior and they banished me from Wyndam House.

I giggled softly running the sponge over my arms

and down my legs. A knock came at the door and I dropped the sponge.

"Pardon me, Miss," Bea opened the door far enough for me to see her face. "The hair dresser is early. Will you be much longer?"

I sighed. So much for my relaxing bath. "I'll be right out."

"Then I'll show her right up."

When the door closed, I stood up and wrapped the towel around my body before stepping out of the tub. I quickly dried off and slipped my wrapper on, tying the belt before meeting the hair dresser in my bedroom.

Madame Claire from the European Boutique in Charleston was a middle-aged woman with graying hair, but she looked fabulous. And in no time at all, she had me looking like I had been given a new head of hair. It had body and the finger curl that was normally reserved for when it felt like behaving, flattered my features.

After that I had only enough time to put on my foundation garments before the seamstress arrived. I put on the dress and she went over it to make sure every seam was properly sewn and that the hem was the right length before I met back with the hairdresser for a few pointers on my make-up.

By the time all of this was completed I had an hour to spare before the guests arrived and certainly no time to sneak down to the garden on the off chance that Conner was lurking in the shadows. I just hoped if he came today he understood why I had not waved from my window.

Downstairs Maude and Mossie were in the dining room fussing over which guest should sit where.

"I really think we should place Madison in the middle seat on the right side of the table so everyone will have an opportunity to speak with her during the meal." Mossie placed the elegant name card in front of the place setting.

"Is the right side the best, or should it be the left?" Maude asked.

"Will that really matter?"

Both Maude and Mossie looked up, surprised to see me for the first time all gussied up. Mossie dropped the cards she held and clapped her hands together, becoming misty eyed.

"Heavens above." She crossed to me in one fluid motion as if in a trance. "You are a vision, my dear."

"You do look wonderful." Maude picked up the cards one by one that had been carelessly scattered all over the grandly-set table.

"Thank you."

There were twelve place settings of china with sparkling crystal goblets and polished golden flatware. The crystal chandelier was already glistening as the sun dipped down behind the trees.

"Madison, I want you to greet our guests with me at the door when they arrive. So come to the foyer with me and I'll show you what to do."

I glanced at Maude and she nodded, giving her approval. I took a deep breath to steady the flutter of nerves that sprang up. I had no idea who was on the guest list. What if Conner wasn't on it? I really shouldn't expect him to be. Neither Maude nor Mossie even knew about him. I should have thought of that and made an effort to introduce him to them, but would that have mattered? I prayed he wouldn't think I was shunning him if he wasn't invited tonight. If he did, I'd try to make him understand I had no control over the guest list.

At precisely seven sharp, the doorbell rang. Mossie and Maude stood to the side forming the receiving line and motioned for me to join them as Bea went forward and opened the door. The couple that arrived I knew from attending Sunday services and that made me relax a little.

"Madison, this is the Reverend Holster and his wife Eliza."

"It's a pleasure to have you with us tonight," I said, shaking their hands.

"Likewise, dear," Eliza said. She was a rather plump woman. Her husband on the other hand was tall and slender reminding me of the nursery rhyme about Jack Sprat.

The next couple that arrived was the banker and his wife. I had met him the day he came to discuss Maude and Mossie's finances. He had a nice smile and his wife was very beautiful and at least ten years younger than him.

By this time Bea had left us at the door to serve drinks to our guests in the parlor while the hired pianist played one of Mossie's favorite concertos.

The next guests to arrive were the Mayor, his wife Sonya and her sister Catherine. So far all the guests had been older than me and were influential people in the community. However, if this was supposed to be my debut into Charleston society, didn't it seem logical for some of the guests tonight to be younger than forty?

Before these guests found their way into the parlor, the next couple arrived.

"Mossie, Maude," a graying women clearly in her sixties cooed coming through the door and giving my aunts a long hug. "It has been too long."

"Anna." They said in unison as they returned her hug.

I watched as they exchanged pleasantries before they finally turned to me as if I'd been momentarily forgotten.

"Madison, this is our oldest friend. Anna Whitfield and her grandson, Thomas," Maude explained.

I smiled and greeted them, noticing that at least her grandson was much younger than the other guests, but he had to be in his mid-thirties and much too old for my liking.

I followed them into the parlor sad that there was no Connor or his grandfather Conrad or Duncan

Claiborne here tonight. I just hoped that my dinner companion was not Thomas Whitfield.

The dinner party wasn't what I imagined, but then I really hadn't known what to expect. We ate the lavish catered meal. We talked about politics and religion, two subjects I'd always heard were not proper at social gatherings. We listened to music because the pianist played all through dinner. From where I sat it looked like Maude and Mossie were enjoying themselves immensely and that is what mattered most. I put forward my best effort to appear as if I were having a good time, but in reality I was counting the minutes until I could slip out the back of the house and go down to the gazebo.

The different conversations around me were lively but I missed out on the ending to an enthralling story when the mayor leaned closer to me and asked if I had tasted the divine hollandaise sauce.

"It's heavenly."

He nodded his head and leaned a bit closer as if sharing a dark secret. "I like a fine sauce of this nature with my asparagus, but Sonya doesn't like for me to have them. She believes they are too rich and bad for my disposition."

"That's too bad. I think a good sauce sets off a dish like a good painting sets off a room."

"Do you like art?" His eyes grew large with interest.

"Yes. From what I have been told I carry my grandmother's eye for drawing. Did you ever see her work?"

The mayor shook his head. "I was just a boy when she was first married. Though, I have heard others speak of her skill as an artist over the years. Unfortunately I have never seen any of her work, even though I did visit her on the Battery before your mother married and moved away."

"Oh?" This had my curiosity piqued. "Did you know my mother?"

"I was acquainted with her like most of Charleston who moved in the same circles. Hope was a lovely young woman; it was a shame we lost her the way we did."

I was about to ask him what he meant by that because she was definitely alive and well when Thomas Whitfield rose from his chair and proposed a toast in my honor. Everyone raised their glasses welcoming me to Charleston. I smiled, but his gesture did not win my favor and I wondered what his motive had been. Did his grandmother or my aunts put him up to it?

Not long after this everyone retired to the parlor for dessert and coffee. Thomas offered me his arm and I took it, allowing him to lead me into the other room because I didn't want to be rude. He began talking about himself, his family, and their money and continued all through dessert. I smiled and nodded but found him a bore. He was nothing like Conner and I began to miss his Cheshire grin and those devastating blue eyes.

As soon as I could slip away, I began to mingle with the other guests, putting as much distance as possible between me and Thomas. But every time I looked he seemed to be following my movement around the room. Finally I joined Maude and Mossie talking with Catherine and Anna, hoping I could urge them to call it a night. I had already received two invitations to visit with Eliza Holster and the mayor's wife next week.

After the last guest departed and Maude and Mossie retired upstairs, I was finally able to slip out the back and go down to the gazebo. The moonlight was shining bright on the pond and I could see a light coming from the gazebo. It looked like the glow from a lantern and my heart began to flutter with anticipation that Conner was there waiting for me. I had so much I wanted to tell him.

I lifted the hem of my dress and carefully hurried down the stone steps. I didn't even take a moment to worry about my aunts possibly spotting me out of their bedroom windows. I heard whistling coming from within the gazebo as I approached. I stopped to listen to the tune and then I puckered my lips and whistled the tune back when I saw Conner standing in the moonlight with his back toward me. He was wearing the same wheat colored linen pants he'd worn the first day we met with the brown leather suspenders and cream colored shirt. He turned slowly and the surprise written on his face when he saw me made me smile.

"Conner."

"Madison?" He picked up his lantern and shined the light toward me. "Why are you all dolled up?"

"Have you been waiting out here long?"

"Was the dinner party tonight?"

"Yes. I'm sorry you weren't invited. My aunts had their friends instead of inviting people I would have something in common with. I should have insisted they added you after we met."

He stepped toward me, hanging the lantern on the post. "I'd never be invited to a Wyndam affair. So don't worry about it."

"Why not?"

"It isn't important why." He walked around me. "Man, you clean up well, Franklin. You're the bees knees."

"Thank you, sir." I curtsied and laughed.

"Would it be too forward of me to ask for the first dance?" He sounded all proper as he held out his hand for me to take.

"No, not at all." I placed my hand in his before he brought me up close to his body and we began to waltz to the music of the night.

"You're a very pretty woman, Madison." He

stared deep into my eyes, making me feel all warm inside.

"Such flattery," I scoffed making light of his compliment.

"I'm serious." He stopped dancing and tilted my chin upward with his thumb so I was looking straight into those penetrating cobalt eyes of his.

I sucked in my breath, waiting for him to steal another kiss, but he didn't. Instead he held me closer and began to dance again, running his hand up and down my back, pressing the tiny pearl buttons against my skin.

We danced for what seemed like hours in the silence of the night until I heard Maude's troubled voice calling my name from up at the house. At first the sound of her voice was far off like in a foggy dream, but then it became more distinct and closer, breaking the trance we were in.

Conner and I looked at one another, and his lips quickly brushed over mine before he grabbed the lantern and ran off into the might, leaving me wanting him. I was staring after him when Maude reached the gazebo.

"Madison, didn't you hear me calling out to you?" Her breathing was labored and I could see enough of her features in the moonlight to detect a frown. "Who was that boy you were down here with?"

I ignored her question and asked one of my own. "The party was wonderful wasn't it?"

"Well yes it was. We hope it will be the first of many. But don't try changing the subject on me. Why didn't you answer when I called? And who was that boy?"

"Conner Montgomery." I slipped my arm through hers and we began climbing the stone steps toward the house.

"Conrad Montgomery's grandson?"

"Yes. Do you know him?"

"Not really, but I had heard he was off fighting in the war. I didn't realize he was back here. How'd you meet?"

"By chance. It's quite funny really. He thought I was a trespasser using your garden."

Chapter Eight

That night I fell asleep and slept like a log. I don't believe I moved a muscle the whole night, because I woke in the same spot I was in the night before, feeling rested and happy. I was dressed and finished making my bed when a knock came at my door.

"Madison, dear, are you awake?" Mossie opened the door and came inside, going straight to the drawn curtains and whisking them back to allow the warm sunlight to flood the room. "I hope you slept well."

"I did. You appear quite chipper this morning."

"I'm still basking in the joy of our successful dinner party last night."

I nodded.

"I realized this morning that I went to bed last night without asking if you received any invitations."

Of course, that would be the icing on her cake to

know I was being invited to teas and luncheons. "I did. Two actually. I'm having tea with Eliza this Sunday after church. And next week I've been invited by Sonya and Catherine to come pick flowers in their garden."

"Excellent. They will see to it that other young women closer to your age are included in these events and from there you will be launched. Just wait, you'll begin to receive phone calls and invitations and before long your social calendar will be full. Oh yes, last night was a success."

"Is that really important?"

"Certainly, dear. A Wyndam has always held high regard within the social circles in Charleston. It's high time you took your rightful place."

Rightful place?

"I will try to make you happy."

Mossie looked at me. "Don't do it for me, dear. It should be for you. Don't you want to fulfill your obligations as a Wyndam?"

"No. No I don't." I shook my head. "All I want is to be a part of this family."

"But the two go together. "

"I see." I didn't really, but I knew she'd never understand so I crossed my arms over my chest, giving myself a hug to keep calm. "So having tea and picking flowers with women old enough to be my mother will trickle into my being accepted into Charleston society?"

"Yes." Mossie sat down on the settee. "Right now

you are still perceived as an outsider since you didn't grown up here, but by spending time with these influential women you will be made welcome in most every home in Charleston. Eliza will be having a get together, but she will first want to get to know you better. Once she does she will select the right young men and women to introduce you to. And if I know Sonya, she is already planning the summer event that most of the young men and women in town will want to attend."

I nodded.

"Last night was just a small affair, but your real debut into Charleston society will come when Sonya Peterson gives the Fourth of July ball."

Fourth of July ball.

That was still weeks away. It sounded like my short visit was turning into a prolonged stay even though that isn't what I came for. My stomach tensed, knowing I'd have to endure several gatherings like last night, boring events that would leave me wishing I were anywhere but there. When I'd much rather be down in the garden, sketching and spending time with Conner. He really was still a stranger to me, but for some reason I felt close to him.

"That sounds lovely, Aunt Mossie, but I didn't come to Wyndam House to be turned into a social butterfly. I came to learn about our family history and what caused the division that separated us for so long. Is it really necessary to distract me with social obligations?"

"Distract you?" Mossie blew out a quick breath. "Why on earth would you think that's what I'm suggesting? Nothing could be farther from the truth. Maude and I want you to be a part of our lives, dear. We want you to feel that Wyndam House is your home. You belong here."

Deep inside I wanted to feel that way too, but I couldn't forget the unanswered questions that they refused to address. Or the fact that I had never been personally invited to visit before now. And every time we got on or near that subject I simply wanted to scream. But I knew I couldn't do that. It wasn't ladylike and it would not help my cause. So I approached it gently.

"If you really want me to feel at home here and part of your lives then let me in on this deep dark secret you are keeping."

"We aren't keeping a secret from you." Mossie shook her head.

"Then tell me why your father didn't want me in his life."

She nervously fidgeted on the settee and stood abruptly, walking to the door. "This is all too much to get into this early in the morning. Come down and have breakfast. I'll join you once I find Maude."

"You can't keep avoiding my questions. Mossie. Mossie!" I hurried after her, but she had disappeared down the hallway into one of the many rooms. I clenched my fists and closed my eyes until the urge to scream at the top of my lungs passed.

When I finally went downstairs, I didn't look for Maude or Mossie to have breakfast with them. Instead I went to the kitchen, grabbing an apple and a banana from the fruit bowl before leaving the house. I didn't stop at the gazebo but headed to the arched bridge, disturbing the swans in my haste to put as much distance from my great aunts as possible. I just hoped Conner was up for a visitor this morning.

The walk to the Montgomery House was lonely, but I enjoyed the solitude as I ate the fruit. It helped me clear my head and get my frustration in check before seeing Conner again. Only a few days ago, we'd walked this same path together and I had been happy. I wanted to be happy again, not frustrated.

When the house came in sight, I saw Duncan Claiborne walking across the lawn to a shed-like structure a small distance away. I called to him and he stopped, waving to me.

"Good morning, dear. I hear there was a big event going on over at the Wyndam estate last evening. Did you enjoy yourself?"

"For a few moments." I recalled the dance I shared with Conner in the moonlight.

"Don't you go for all that fancy smancy stuff?"

"Apparently not as much as my aunts do. But I put on a good show for them so they didn't notice."

Duncan shook his head. "Isn't it a pity that we find these things out about ourselves at the oddest times?" He began to walk again and motioned for me to follow. "Perhaps you'll like what I have to show you."

He had my curiosity piqued by that comment and I followed him without hesitation to the shed. He reached into his pant pocket and pulled out a key to unlock the door. Stepping inside, he pulled on a cord to turn on the bare light bulb hanging there.

"Wow." I walked inside amazed at the floor to ceiling shelves full of every kind of trinket to be thought of. Jars–ceramic and glass–that looked to be fifty years old or more sat on shelves and fishing poles made of bamboo and light weight metal structures hung along one wall. There were funny looking objects with hooks coming out of their ends that hung along the bottom of one shelf. And if that wasn't enough, there was a felt board displaying arrow heads and rock-like masses hanging on the back wall over a small work table.

"Does that mean you like what you see?" Duncan asked when I had finished walking around the shed, but didn't say anything more.

I looked at him and I feared my mouth was hanging open, not sure what else to say about his treasure horde. "I think it's amazing. Where did you find all of this?"

He smiled. "I started collecting after the war when I was a boy. Some of it came from North Carolina where I was born and the rest I've picked up around Charleston and other parts of South Carolina."

"There must be so much you can tell about history from these pieces." Maybe he even knew something about the Wyndam family that he could tell me since he was obviously a connoisseur of artifacts.

He walked over to a blue jar. "I picked this one up from a French man. He brought it over from France with him."

"It's incredible," I said, noticing a shell container on the top shelf. I pointed to it. "Did you get this in Charleston?"

"No. That came from the Pacific islands." He smiled, putting the jar back and reaching for the shell container. "Conner brought that to me when he returned from service."

I nodded, having almost forgotten that he had been in the war. He never mentioned his time in the service whenever we talked. For that matter he didn't discuss his family either. And when I thought about it for a moment he really didn't talk about himself much at all. I'd have to change that.

"Duncan, did you know my family very well when you were growing up?" I asked.

"As well as anyone knows the Wyndams." He put the shell container back on the shelf.

"And is that very well? Or do you know them by name only?"

He turned and looked at me. "You're very troubled by your family, aren't you, child?"

I nodded. "No one will tell me what the deep dark secret is that divided the family."

Duncan grinned. "Don't be frustrated, Madison. I don't think even your great-grandfather could have told you if you'd asked him this question."

"Why not?"

"Because the problem started more than forty years ago, Madison. That's a long time for someone to remember the root of a problem. Over the years a person's mind will contemplate the issue and see it from their point of view only. In reality, the true problem will be reshaped by the mind and it might not be the initial problem any longer because fear and doubt will set in. As time passes, if the problem isn't resolved it becomes harder for the individuals to do something about it."

I nodded, not really getting what he meant. All I knew is nothing had been resolved with my great-grandfather before he died.

"Richard Wyndam was a complex man, Madison. He clung to his standing in society. Some said he fought with all his might to keep the Wyndams from sinking to poverty after the war. He worked day and night to rebuild the house that was burned to the ground by the Union soldiers. He bartered and paid whatever the cost to get the finest materials around to make the house what it is today. Yet, his daughters were always finely dressed as any of the other gentry when they attended balls and cotillions. It was as if the Wyndams had a fortune that the other Charlestons didn't know about."

Duncan reached up and pulled the cord, turning the light bulb off as he led me back outside of the shed. "Some said that Richard Wyndam did all of this by working his former slaves for little wages, others said he had stashed away the family fortune before going off to war. No one knows for sure except those two aunts of yours. They could tell you how their father managed."

I waited for him to shut and lock the shed back before we walked over to the apple trees and sat in the lawn chairs.

"I know I haven't answered your question, Madison. There was a rumor running when Millicent married Ronald that she was with child, but that did not prove true. Your mother wasn't born until a year after their wedding date. I think many felt Richard was going a little far allowing his youngest to wed before the older girls. But Millicent had been a jewel. She was too young to remember the war so she didn't carry the battle scars her sisters did and that made her a prize for any young man to try to win her favor. But strangely enough, your grandmother didn't have many suitors, even though she attracted much attention during balls, sketching. It wasn't until she met Ronald Madison that she took real interest in anyone. The two of them instantly connected and Millicent blossomed overnight from a young girl to a budding woman, outshining her sisters."

Duncan reached into his pants pocket and brought out a knife and a piece of wood. He began shaving off thin layers of the wood. "After Millicent and Ronald married, talk about the Wyndams soon subsided. It didn't seem to matter to the town how Richard Wyndam had rebuilt his house because his daughter had made such a good match. You see, Ronald Madison had already won favor with society and with his political influence the Wyndams were respectable without scandal once more. That is until Ronald was shot and your grandmother refused to come home from the Battery. She was only nineteen with a four-year-old to raise alone at the time. I remember Ramona commenting on how brave she was for taking on that task alone, but that didn't mean she agreed with Millicent. On the contrary. Many of the women in town kept a close eye on Millicent, but she never gave them cause to speak ill of her. She never even accepted a male caller to her home unless he was accompanied with his wife or sister. And if one was not available to the gentleman then she invited a friend and her husband over to join them for the evening. It was all quite platonic."

"How did my great-grandfather feel about this?"

"Oh, everyone approved so it would have been wrong for him to object. If he had then it would have been as if he knew something that the public didn't and then your grandmother's name and reputation would have been tarnished."

I nodded, watching him whittle as I processed everything he'd told me. "Do you think this led to the division with the Wyndams?"

"I doubt it. Like I said, everything appeared fine except for Millicent not returning to Wyndam House."

I sighed, relaxing in the chair, enjoying the morning breeze.

"Madison?" Conner called running across the yard from the house to where we sat. He looked surprised when he reached us. "I didn't expect you to come by."

"I hope you don't mind. I had to get out of the house. I've had enough of my aunts for the day."

He laughed, looking at his watch. "But it is only ten."

"And she's been here for a good hour already."

"Duncan showed me his shed."

"So he's been showing off his junk?"

"Junk?" Duncan scoffed. "I'll have you know that my trinkets are valuable. And what isn't now will be one day, you mark my word."

Conner sat down on the ground and rolled his eyes. "To you maybe, but to me it's junk."

"I think Duncan has a very nice collection of antiquities."

"Antiquities!" Conner shook his head. "Don't inflate the value. There may be antiques among the pieces, but I doubt it is worth anything."

"That isn't nice to say, Conner." I frowned at his insensitivity. And here I thought seeing him again would make me happy.

"It's okay, Madison, he has a right to his opinion, but we both know better." Duncan winked at me.

I smiled. "True."

"You would agree with him." Conner jumped up to his feet.

"What is that supposed to mean?" I asked.

He didn't answer my question, but grabbed my hands and pulled me up from my chair. "We'll see you later, Duncan."

"You kids have fun," the man called not looking up from the piece he was whittling.

We were clear of the apple trees when I demanded he explain what he meant earlier.

He shrugged. "You don't know any better than to side with him."

"I know more than you think." I smacked him on the arm, feeling better just being near him.

He pulled me into his arms and kissed me. And I returned his kiss, wrapping my arms around his neck.

Holding my hand, Conner led me down into the hedge maze. Neither one of us said a word, but we didn't need to. And when he did speak again I wished he'd stayed silent.

"What have your aunts done now that sent you this way so early in the morning?"

"The usual. They refuse to answer my questions. But today was worse. Mossie went on and on about how they wanted nothing more than for me to feel a part of the family and that I belong here at Wyndam House. And then she went so far as to tell me they weren't keeping secrets."

"That is frustrating."

"I wanted to scream."

"So you left instead."

"Yes."

"I'm just glad it had nothing to do with Maude catching us in the garden last night. I felt bad leaving you to face her alone, but I feared she'd try to stop us from seeing one another if I stayed."

"She couldn't do that."

"Yes she could. I'd be trespassing on her land and she could have called the sheriff."

"But you were with me. Surely that gives you permission to be there. In fact, I give you permission to come by anytime you want."

He smiled. "It isn't yours to give, Madison."

My heart began to ache at the thought of anyone stopping me from seeing him ever again. And then my temples began to throb. I placed my hands on the sides of my face to try to stop the pain I felt. "Conner, just stop talking about this."

He led me over to a shaded area in the hedge where there was a stone bench. "Have you eaten today?"

"Some fruit. I didn't have much of an appetite after talking to Mossie."

He nodded, looking at me intently. "It's warm out. You need water. Let's get you to the house for some refreshment and a proper meal."

"No. I'm fine." My stomach growled.

"You think you are invincible, is that it Franklin?" He stood, reaching out his hand to me. "Come along and I'll fix you the best southern omelet you've ever tasted.

I stood and slowly followed him to the back of house where we went into the kitchen. It reminded me of the kitchen at Wyndam House and I wondered if the inside of the house was similar as well.

"Your grandfather has a beautiful piece of property." I sat on the stool at the counter where he pointed for me to sit.

He washed his hands before he went to the icebox and got out eggs and cheese, then he went to a hanging wire tier basket where onions, green peppers and mushrooms were kept.

"Yes, it is beautiful, but unlike you, I will inherit this land when he passes on. Not that I'm looking forward to that happening, but I prefer living in Charleston better than Dalton, Georgia with my parents." He opened up a drawer and pulled out a knife.

Dalton, Georgia. That explained his thick accent.

"So your parents are still alive?"

"You sound surprised. I know I haven't talked about them before, but I prefer not to think about them if I can. They didn't approve of me going to Europe and fighting in the war. They thought it was a cause that was best settled by Europeans even if the United States had joined the war."

"But you went. It must have felt odd to go against their wishes."

"No, not really." He chopped the onion on the wooden chop block. "I don't know why I went. I think I had an itch that couldn't get scratched any other way. War isn't as fascinating as one thinks. The blood. The rampage of death. Who can honestly say they prefer living a life like that to lazily spending their days down by the Ashley holding a bamboo fishing pole in their hand waiting for the right fish to come along?"

"Apparently you must have thought so."

He raised his knife and pointed it at me. "And I was a fool too."

I watched him jab the end of a knife into a green pepper and stick it under the water faucet, washing it. Then he dried it on a towel before chopping it into chucks.

I sighed, glancing around the kitchen at the wicker and straw baskets that lined the room near the ceiling.

"I'm glad you weren't killed."

"I am too." Conner grinned at me. The look in his blue eyes said he was thinking that for the same reason I was and I looked away quickly.

I got up off the stool to put a little distance between us and went over to a large picture window that looked out over the back lawn. Conrad and Duncan were walking along the fence row where the apple trees were.

"How long have they been friends?" I asked to change the subject.

"Who?" Conner left the counter and came over to the window to have a look. "Oh Grandpa and Duncan. Since they were twenty I believe. Duncan moved here with his bride after they married."

"I think a lasting friendship like that is marvelous." My thoughts went to Maude and Mossie. They were more than sisters, they were best friends as well.

"Yeah," Conner went back to the counter and opened up a cabinet for a bowl. He put the chopped onions and peppers in there before getting a skillet out and lighting the stove.

The room became quiet again and I looked at the few pictures that hung on the walls as Conner prepared the omelets.

"What about your family in Camden?" he asked, surprising me because I thought he had all the facts about me already.

"There's my mother and my father's family. My father died three years ago. Actually he was killed. A man shot him while he was in town on business. It was not intentional. My father was at the wrong place at the wrong time I guess."

Before I knew it, Conner had me wrapped in his arms, holding me tight. "Oh Madison, I'm sorry."

For once I did not welcome his embrace. His reaction to my grief irritated me and I pushed him away. "Don't feel sorry for me. I grieved for him a long time ago. I knew him. I had seventeen years with him. If you want to feel sorry for me about something then be sorry that Richard Wyndam didn't give…"

"Madison." He placed a finger over my mouth so I would not say it.

I pushed his finger away. "But it's true. I think your butter is burning."

He ran over to the stove, grabbed a pot holder and moved the skillet off the burner.

I sat down at the counter again and decided to stay out of his way and not distract him or he'd ruin his omelets. He'd just dished them up when the back door opened and Maude stepped inside with Conrad and Duncan. Surprised by her appearance I jumped up from the stool and Conner dropped the plates.

There was a brief silence and I noticed that Duncan was biting back a smile since this was no time to be amused.

"Aunt Maude, what are you doing here?"

"I think that should be obvious, Madison. I've come to see where you run off to during the day."

Duncan pulled her a chair from the table for her to sit down. She smiled and did just that. "When you weren't in our garden, I crossed the bridge and saw the well-worn path. I followed it and I am so thankful I met these two gentlemen when I did. I was just thankful that they knew you or I do believe I would have fainted from the walk. This spring is really getting hot."

"Hotter than usual," Duncan handed her a lace fan. "Can I get you something to drink, Miss Wyndam?"

Maude looked at him suspiciously for a moment then nodded. When he was gone she looked back at me. "Well, Maddy, what do you have to say for yourself? Mossie asked you to come down to breakfast and instead you take off. I suppose this young man here is the explanation for your disappearance this morning and the reason you were down at the gazebo last night after the party."

I really didn't like her making me feel like a child being reprimanded for doing something wrong, especially in front of Conner, Conrad and Duncan. "Can't we discuss this at home?"

"No. If we wait, then I will have to tell Mossie where I found you. I don't think her heart can take it."

I didn't like the way she put the Montgomerys down and further insinuated I was doing something wrong by being here.

"Then at least can't we step outside and discuss it?"

"No." I'd never seen her so stubborn. She took the glass of water from Duncan and took one sip before getting to her feet.

I looked at Conner, but he was busy cleaning up the ruined omelets. And Conrad looked uneasy. "Then I suppose the only thing I can do is leave. I'm sorry our breakfast was ruined."

"I'm the one who is sorry for being a klutz," Conner said dumping the broken plates and ruined food in the trash.

"Madison, let me drive you and your aunt back to Wyndam House. She's in no condition to walk back," Duncan said.

Maude snapped the fan shut and laid it on the table. "I am more than capable of getting back home on my own. I do not need you to drive us."

"We'll be fine, Duncan. Thank you for the offer. And thank you for having me. I've enjoyed my visit."

"Come along, Madison," Maude said taking my hand and leading me to the door. Again making me feel like a child being scolded.

When we were clear of the house and back on the path to Wyndam House, she stopped and gave me a stern look. "Your behavior today is outrageous, but then, you are Hope's daughter, aren't you. I shouldn't expect anything less."

I stared after her as she trotted down the path without me. Why had she said that? That was twice she'd made comments about my mother. Did the family problem have to do with my mother's behavior growing up? Maybe I should be asking her a few questions instead of expecting my great aunts to tell me all.

I hurried down the path to catch up with Maude, but she was walking at a brisk pace so it wasn't easy. I found her pace odd, especially for a woman who had nearly fainted on the way to find me because of the heat. It was clear she sure was not having any trouble returning to Wyndam house.

"What do you mean by I'm Hope's daughter?"

"Your mother never did care for her station in life, and I see that she is raising you to be just the same."

Her reply felt like a slap in the face.

"Did my mother do something that caused the rift in the family?" Even though I asked the question, I was certain it wasn't true. My mother was not a prim woman, but she didn't go around disregarding others. She had class just like Maude and Mossie. She was a true Wyndam and would have fit perfectly within their society circles if she had wanted. Maybe that was it. Had my mother shunned their way of life?

Maude didn't reply to my question. She only

walked at a faster pace making me work to keep up with her which proved she'd feigned weakness back at the Montgomery House.

When we finally reached the house Maude went to the kitchen and straight up to her room. I, however, stopped by the icebox and made myself a sandwich out of the roast beef that was left over from the night before.

I hated that Conner had worked so hard on the omelets only to have them spoiled when he dropped the plates. I can only imagine what he must have thought when Maude walked in the door.

"Madison, dear, do you know why Maude is so upset?" Mossie asked coming into the kitchen a few moments later. "Did you have words?"

I motioned for Mossie to sit down at the kitchen table with me while I ate. Maybe it was time to play my aunts against one another. It couldn't hurt. I wasn't having much luck anyway.

"Not really. Maude is a little upset at herself I think. She said something I don't think she really meant to about my mother."

Mossie's brows arched. "She did?"

I nodded and took a long drink of my iced tea. "Something about how I am Hope's daughter and she shouldn't have expected anything less from me because Hope never cared about her station in life."

Mossie turned pale and shook her head slowly. "She must have gotten too hot outside. I better go check on her."

"You do that."

She stood and started out of the kitchen, but stopped to look back at me. "Will you be writing Hope today?"

"Yes. I think I will."

"Do give her my love."

"Oh I will." I smiled to myself.

When I went up to my room, I saw Maude's bedroom door open so I peeped inside as I walked by. She was lying across her bed with a hand dramatically placed palm up on her forehead and Mossie was sitting in a chair by the bed. They talked softly and both looked distressed. Good. Maybe I was getting somewhere with them finally.

I went to my room and closed the door for privacy. At the small desk I took out a clean sheet of paper to write to my mother

June 5, 1920

Dear Mother,

I hope you are well. It has been several weeks since I wrote you last and I am sure you are wondering why I have not returned home yet. I know I was only coming for a visit, but Aunt Maude and Mossie have

plans for me to stay the full season. I don't know if I will or not because I'm not getting anywhere fast with my search for answers. I am trying to learn about the Wyndam family history and why there has been a division between generations.

No one is willing to answer me completely. I keep getting bits and pieces as if I am solving a mystery. I'm not a mystery sleuth, but if Aunt Maude and Mossie have their way, I will be one by the time I leave here.

I have some good news though. I have met a wonderful young man and we have become fast friends. His name is Conner Montgomery and he is living with his grandfather a few houses away on River Road. His parents live in Dalton, Georgia. We met by chance in the garden here at Wyndam House one evening. He thought I was trespassing when he was the one doing so when he spotted me from the path on the farther side of the pond. I believe you will like him when you meet.

My letter may be disturbing to you, mother, but Aunt Maude said something to me that did not make sense. She said I was your daughter and that you never gave a thought to your station in life and that I was following in your footsteps. I have to tell you that this alarms me, because I do not see you this way at all. But if what Aunt Maude said is true then I may be looking for answers to my questions in the wrong places.

I must ask you and I pray you will be truthful, did you do something that caused great-grandfather Wyndam to disapprove? Is that why we were not allowed to see grandmother when she was ill? If you did, I promise not to judge and I will try to understand. I just want to know why I was never given the opportunity to know this side of the family until now.

I'll be waiting to hear from you. Remember, I love you, mother.

Love,

Madison

P.S. What did you think of my sketch of the garden and pond? Did it make you remember it from when you were a young girl?

Chapter Nine

The next few days were awkward. Maude and Mossie kept their distance even when we were in the same room sharing a meal or in the parlor in the evenings before retiring for the day. I'm sure I didn't make it easier for them since I was quiet and still feeling fed up with their procrastination in answering my questions. Despite this, I carried out my social duties. I went to tea at the reverend's and then spent a whole afternoon picking flowers with the mayor's wife and her sister. True to Mossie's word, both outings had included one or two young ladies for me to get to know.

About a week later, I was in the garden with Conner feeding the swans near the bridge when the maid came running out the back of the house calling my name.

"Miss Madison, Miss Madison," Bea called.

Conner stood up and darted toward the bushes so he wouldn't be seen, but I stopped him. He had to stop disappearing every time someone came to the garden. He wasn't trespassing. He was my guest.

"She won't say anything." I held onto his arm as Bea came closer.

The maid was out of breath by the time she reached the arched bridge. "Beg your pardon for interrupting, but your mother is here."

"My mother?"

Bea nodded. "The misses are receiving her in the parlor. They sent me to get you and your friend."

Conner stiffened beside me, but I squeezed his arm to let him know it was okay.

"We'll be there in a moment." I took a deep breath and looked up at Conner. "You have just officially been invited to Wyndam House. Shall we go?"

He nodded, tossing the rest of the bread pieces into the water for the swans. "Wonder what they want?"

"My mother is here. I wrote about you in my last letter. I would say she is interested in meeting my new friend."

His mischievous Cheshire cat grin spread across his face. "What exactly did you say about me?"

"Nothing good I assure you." I started toward the stone steps with him close behind me.

"Good. Then she won't be shocked when she sees me."

I stopped mid-step and almost stumbled forward at his statement. I didn't like it when he said things of that nature. It was almost as if he knew something I didn't or that he was putting himself down. "No. She won't be surprised at all when she finds out you really do have a cat's smile."

He chuckled grabbing me around the waist and pulling me back against him. "Are you making fun of how I look, Madison?"

"Why ever would I do that?" I said trying to mimic his deep southern accent.

"Because you're a devious young woman." He turned me around until I was facing him.

"That's because I've been taking lessons from the expert."

"Is that so?

I nodded, then turned and dashed up the stone steps to the back of the house with him close on my heels. Even with him so close I was smaller and faster than him so I reached the back door before he did. I tried to catch my breath before opening the door and walking into the kitchen, but it was difficult when he caught up to me and began tickling me.

I squealed in spite of myself and Bea gave us a stern look as she finished a pitcher of lemonade. "They're still waiting in the parlor."

"Sorry." I straightened my dress and took his hand, leading him to the parlor. As we approached, I heard my mother's voice clearly. It was a glorious sound and I hadn't realized how terribly I had missed hearing it.

"I'm so glad that you decided to come," Mossie said.

"Oh, I couldn't stay away a moment more," my mom said. "Not after I received Madison's letter. She is so determined to learn about the family that I couldn't allow her to pester you further."

"She isn't pestering us. We love having her here." Maude smiled when Conner and I appeared in the doorway and motioned us to join them.

My mom stood and hugged me tight. When she let me go she turned to look at Conner. "Madison, aren't you going to introduce us to your friend?"

"Mom, this is Conner Montgomery. Conner, this is my mother Hope Franklin."

"It's a pleasure to meet you, ma'am."

"The pleasure is mine." Mom smiled.

"Will you be staying on for the summer?"

"I might." She winked at me. "I hear you have been keeping my daughter company in the garden and that she has been by your family's home a few times as well."

"Yes ma'am," Conner said.

"Then you won't mind if I steal her away from you this afternoon? I would like to catch up with her since we have been apart for so long. I promise I won't keep her a moment longer than is necessary."

Conner must have sensed her sincerity because I

noticed him relax and the tightness that had formed in my stomach eased as well.

"No problem at all. I'm late for a fishing trip as it is. So if you'll excuse me I'll take my leave." Conner turned to Maude and Mossie. "It was a pleasure seeing you both today."

"Yes. Do come again," Mossie called as he left the parlor. I left with him and showed him to the front door.

"I wish you didn't have to go," I said.

"But I do. And you should to spend all the time you need with your mom." He squeezed my hand affectionately at the door. "I'll see you soon."

I nodded, knowing he wouldn't stay away long. I waited until he disappeared around the corner of the house before I shut the door and returned to the parlor.

My mom had smoothly maneuvered Conner out of the house so that it was just family now. I could only imagine what she had to say to me and our aunts.

"Oh, what a charming young man. Madison. What did you say his name was?" Mossie asked when I returned.

"Conner Montgomery. His grandfather is Conrad Montgomery. They live a few houses away."

"Oh yes. I believe I know who you mean."

"Well," Maude said. "This is a treat to have three generations of Wyndam women under one roof."

"Yes, it certainly is." Mossie handed me a glass of lemonade that Bea had brought in while I was seeing

Conner to the door.

I took it and sat down beside my mom on the sofa. There was a short silence in the room as we all sipped our beverages. I watched as Maude and Mossie exchanged looks and I felt skittish as I waited for someone to say something, but neither one seemed anxious to get into a conversation.

On the other hand, my mom didn't wait. She set her glass on the coaster on the coffee table. "I was quite surprised when I received Madison's last letter. She said you were telling her how I had disgraced the family."

I hadn't said that. Had I?

The temperature dropped several degrees in the room. However, Maude and Mossie appeared unaffected by it.

"I don't believe I put it that way at all," Maude spoke in her defense.

"It doesn't matter how you put it," my mother said. "It's what you were implying that disturbs me."

"Now, Hope dear, don't get all flustered over a little misunderstanding," Mossie said tactfully.

"Misunderstanding." Mom gave a little laugh. "Yes, that's what it has always been, isn't it?"

"Father had every right to feel the way he did." Mossie sounded defensive.

"And it didn't matter how he hurt my mother, did it?"

"Hope, dear, we really shouldn't go into this with

Madison present," Maude said once again, making me feel like a small child who needed protecting from this family drama.

"Why not? Isn't that the reason you asked her to come for a visit so you could heal the wounds within the family? I didn't want her to come, but she was set on it. So I prayed that you had changed in all these years alone in this house and that this would be a good thing for her to get to know her great aunts, but it may only have caused further division within the family. Maybe Madison's visit should be cut short. I don't want her regretting the Wyndam blood that runs through her veins."

I blinked, listening to what my mother was saying. She knew the secret. Had known all along, but had refused to tell me. My frustration boiled as I realized what had been going on all around me. It wasn't just my great aunts keeping secrets but my own mother. Had my father as well?

I stood up, placing my hands on both sides of my head. "Stop talking as if I'm not in the room or that I'm a child in need of protecting. I'm an adult who wishes that everyone would stop keeping this terrible secret from her."

I waited for them to say something more but they didn't. They just looked at one another, shocked by my outburst which in hindsight went against my claims of being an adult. I turned to my mother, but she shook her head and I saw the look of regret in her eyes for speaking at all. I couldn't understand why no one would own up to the truth. They speak of it, but they act as if the world would come to an end if they admitted what it really was.

"Fine. Keep your secrets to yourselves." I left the room feeling defeated once again. And this time I felt lower than I had before. I went out the front door and down the winding drive to River Road.

I walked without a destination in mind. All I wanted to do was put as much distance away from my family as possible. I wanted space from the reminder that I had a family who couldn't bear to speak of their past. And away from Wyndam House itself because it was within the walls of that house that the problem was buried. I wished I had left well enough alone because then I wouldn't dislike my family right now.

I began to regret coming to Charleston and if it hadn't been for my meeting Conner, I'd gladly walk into town and purchase a bus ticket back to Camden right now. But I didn't have any money in my pocket. I wondered if I told them I was a Wyndam if they'd grant me fare and bill my aunts? Isn't that what they'd done when we went shopping? Charged everything to their account to be billed later?

I kicked a stone with the toe of my loafer and

watched it skip along the dirt road before it disappeared off into the grassy field. Trees lined most of the road, giving shade from the hot summer sun. In the distance I heard the rushing water of the Ashley River. And then I heard a familiar voice coming from the ravine a small distance below the road.

"That does it, Duncan," Conrad Montgomery said.

"Now old man, don't go getting all huffy."

I smiled as I stopped walking and turned in the direction of their voices. I found a pathway that looked like it had been trampled by foot many times so I followed it down to the water.

"Grandfather, it isn't Duncan's fault."

Conner's laughter wafted up telling me I was getting closer and then I saw them only a short distance away.

"He's just an excellent fisherman."

"Excellent fisherman my foot." Conrad took his cloth-brimmed fishing hat off his head and threw it down on the ground. "He bribes those fish. Have you seen what he uses for bait?"

Duncan chuckled. "How do I do that?"

"You know good and well how you do it." Conrad was red in the face holding up the line of fish Duncan had caught already that day.

I found the scene I had stumbled upon amusing, but I didn't make a sound and they didn't notice my presence. I walked a short distance and disappeared into a small thicket of brush where I sat down with my back to a tree trunk and could listen to the three of them ranting about who caught the most fish.

It was comforting to be near them and yet not to be noticed. I closed my eyes and forgot about my troubles. I let my thoughts drift back to Camden and a time almost forgotten to me. I was ten, and I had begged my dad to take me fishing at the creek. There was a fishing competition being held, and I wanted him to take me. He was usually too busy to get away from his chores on the farm, but I kept on pestering him until he stopped and took me down to the creek like all the boys' dads did.

My father noticed that I was the only girl sitting on the bank with her father fishing and he'd given me a good look, but said nothing until we were on our way home. We hadn't caught the most fish, but that didn't matter. I'd spent the day with my dad just like my three male cousins had.

"You know, Madison." He swung his fishing pail in one hand and held mine with the other. "Most girls would rather be learning to cook and sew with their mother than going fishing."

"Maybe. But I'm not most girls. I'd rather be outside than trapped in the kitchen."

My father only nodded. "You like playing with your cousins don't you?"

"Yep."

"What do the other girls at school think of you being such a tomboy?"

"A tomboy?" I recalled saying that word as if it was dirty. "I'm not one of those. I'm not a boy and my name isn't Tom."

"I think you are a tomboy, Madison. You're all the time climbing trees and tearing your dresses. Getting scrapes and cuts on your legs, and your hair never stays neat in the braids your mother puts it in of the morning."

"So." I had looked up at him out of the corner of my eye. "You don't have a boy, you have me."

"Exactly." He let go of my hand and chucked me under my chin. "You're a girl, Madison, and maybe it's time you started acting like one."

I shrugged, scuffing the toe of my shoe in the dirt, thinking about this as we headed for our driveway. "Maybe."

I really hadn't seen why my dad had to go pointing out that I was a girl. I knew that. But, I also knew that he wasn't disappointed in who I was. He just wanted me to grow up right. He didn't want others ridiculing me. My father was very big on respecting other people's feelings. He said it didn't matter who we were, where we had come from or where we went because we were all God's creations and He didn't make anything bad. My dad had wanted others to come to that realization during his lifetime. He said if they did, it would make the world an easier place to live. And I had to believe he had been right. If my great-grandfather had come to see this, then maybe the Wyndam family would not be in the shape it is in today.

I don't know how long I slept in the bushes under that tree, but it was getting dark when I woke. The sun cast shadows over the Ashley and a cool summer breeze blew, giving me chills. I stood up and stretched, knowing that my mother was probably beside herself that I had not shown up at the house before now. I headed back up the path I had taken earlier, stopping short when a dark figure came out of the brush, causing me to suck in my breath.

"There you are." Conner sounded worried and he had a frown creased across his mouth with his hands planted on his hips. "Do you know that you scared everyone to death?"

"You and who?" my voice sounded gruff with sleep and annoyance.

"Me and all of River Road. When you didn't show up for dinner, Maude and Mossie called the police, claiming you'd been abducted or assaulted. And do you know where they came first?"

By his tone I didn't have to guess. "Montgomery House?"

"Yes and if my grandfather didn't know the police chief, I'd be sitting in jail right now. Your mother tried to talk sense into your aunts but they were adamant that foul play was involved and I was responsible. While they were arguing over this, I slipped out of the house and came looking for you. Duncan has headed up a search party of the neighbors, determined to bring you back home safe. Let's get you back to Wyndam House before someone finds us here together and thinks this is where I've been hiding you."

"I'm sorry to have caused all this trouble. I fell asleep listening to you fish."

"So you've taken up eavesdropping?"

"No. I just enjoyed your jolly banter with one another. It reminded me of days long ago with my own father." I stumbled going up the bank and he reached out a hand to help me. "How did my mother seem? Is she terrible upset?"

"No. In fact, she was heading out to look for you herself, but had to stay behind with your aunts. Those two have a pretty colorful imagination in what they were saying I had done to you."

"Conner!" My moth fell open, realizing what he meant when he said he'd be sitting in jail.

He laughed at my reaction. "What's wrong? Don't you think I have it in me to be Jack the Ripper? Or did you assume your virtue was always safe with me? After all, I have just returned from the South Pacific where I lived among savages. At least that is what the last rumor in town was about me."

I slapped him on the arm for making light of the situation. "I'm so sorry. I can't believe Maude and

Mossie would fabricate such a ridiculous assumption."

"It's okay Franklin. Your aunts are old and they've lived sheltered lives hidden away in that big house. They became bluenose, letting their imaginations run wild with them."

"That doesn't make it right. They can't go around making accusations at your expense or anyone else's. I won't be upset if you can't find it in your heart to forgive them. I know I am finding it harder and harder to overlook their refusal to answer my questions outright." I shook my head. "Sorry. I know I must sound like a broken record."

Conner didn't say a word. He just walked beside me and listened to what I said until I finished. Then he wrapped his arm around my waist, pulling me close to his side. "You'll be okay, and once they do tell you what you want to know, you'll no doubt be amazed that it really doesn't matter anymore."

I laughed. He was probably right. After all, hadn't Duncan said something similar the other day, that the root of the problem might not be of importance anymore?

"Family secrets usually are embarrassing. But maybe the Wyndam family secret is too petty to have caused such a rift and that is why your aunts can't find it within themselves to admit to it."

I sighed and nodded, kicking at a stone and sending it across the dirt road. "I have a feeling you are right on the mark. My only question is why they suddenly decided to open the can of worms by inviting me here? They could just as easily have taken it to their graves."

Conner shrugged as we came to the winding drive leading to Wyndam House. We stopped and stared at one another. I didn't know if he would be safe seeing me to the door and I could tell he was thinking the same thing as he rocked back and forth on his heels.

"I'll see you." In a swift motion, he kissed me lightly on the forehead and started on down the road.

"Conner, thank you."

He stopped and turned to look at me. "For what?"

"For putting up with me and my crazy aunts." In the dim light, I could just make out his Cheshire grin forming on his face.

"Awe, it's nothing. I fancy crazy." He took a few steps backwards before doing an about face and disappearing towards Montgomery House.

I crossed my arms and hugged myself before heading up the winding drive, not sure what I would encounter.

My mother was waiting for me in the foyer. She pulled me into her arms as soon as I walked in the door as if she had expected me to arrive at that very moment. "Madison honey, I'm sorry. I should have handled the aunts better. I've been so worried about you, but I knew you were okay. I knew you had to be."

"It's okay. I'm sorry I worried you. I went for a walk and sat down under a tree and fell asleep. I didn't mean to scare everyone to death. Did Maude and Mossie really believe Conner would harm me?"

"Yes, I'm afraid they did, but don't worry about that now. The sheriff didn't believe their claims once he found out who they were accusing. I'm just glad Conner was able to find you so quickly."

"How did you know?"

"How else would you have known about Maude and Mossie's claim? Besides, I was coming up the drive when I saw the two of you on River Road. Come to the kitchen. Bea left you a plate warming in the oven. I know you have to be starving."

I nodded and went to the kitchen with her. "Where is everyone?"

"Maude and Mossie were exhausted after the excitement so I sent them to bed after I told them you'd been found."

"Conner didn't deserve to be accused like that."

"No he didn't, and if I had known that was what Maude had told the police when she called, I would have stopped anything more from happening. As it was I didn't know until we were at Montgomery House. But don't you worry. I've given them both a stern talking to about making accusations that are unfounded."

"They need to apologize."

"And they will. I'll see to it." Mom set the plate on the table in front of me and took a vacant chair. She yawned.

"You must be exhausted. Why don't you go upstairs to my room and take a hot bath? I'll be up as soon as I eat."

"No. I want to spend time with you. I–" Her words were cut off by another yawn. She blinked. "Maybe you are right. A hot bath sounds glorious."

"My room is down the hall on the left. It was your mom's room."

"Okay. You know Maude and Mossie wanted me to sleep in grandfather's room." She made a funny face. "I told them I'd stay with you tonight until a room could be made up for me."

When she left, I ate quickly and went upstairs. I could hear humming coming from the closed bathroom door so I poured water in the wash basin and sponged off before putting on my night gown. I curled up in bed, closing my eyes, and waited for my mom to join me.

"Madison, are you asleep?"

"Hmm. No." I turned over and propped myself up on my elbow. "I was listening to your humming."

A puzzled look crossed my mom's face. "I wasn't humming. I thought that was you."

I sat up completely and an eerie feeling crept over me. I pulled my knees up to my chest and wrapped my arms around them, resting my chin on my knee caps. I didn't want to think about who could have been humming.

"Did you ever come to Wyndam House with grandmother when you were little?" I asked.

"We came for a visit in the summer. I'd spend most of my time in the nursery. They set up a bed for me there, and I had the largest room ever to play with my dolls. And then over the years, it became more like a studio for me."

"When did you stop coming?"

She looked at me as if I were leading her into a trap. "When I decided to go to college."

"Didn't great-grandfather approve of you going?"

"It wasn't that he disapproved. He felt art school would have been more appropriate than the university. You see, I drew just like you, but I stopped like my mother did and that disappointed him. He said I could have made something of myself if I'd applied myself more." She pulled her knees up to her chest like me. "Grandfather had been before his time in believing a female could pursue a career as an artist."

"What did grandmother think?"

"She wanted what I wanted. She didn't think I should live my life to please her father. She hadn't and she wasn't going to force me to either. You see, Madison, your grandmother was a very private woman. She was independent and strong. She didn't need a man to make her whole. She loved my father very much and when he was taken from her so young she vowed to live her life as if she was still married to him."

"So that is why she never remarried?"

"Yes. And that is why she remained in the house on the Battery even though her father wanted her to return to Wyndam House."

"Maude and Mossie told me about that."

"Did they also tell you that dressed in black my mother and I marched down the street behind my father's casket the day of his funeral?"

I nodded. "I can't imagine what she must have felt. She was younger than I am when he died."

"My mother was a remarkable lady, Madison. You take after her in many ways. Your father and I were so proud of that fact even if you were a tomboy growing up. We saw your potential to be as strong and independent as my mother." My mom yawned again and straightened her legs out. "I don't know about you, but I'm exhausted. Let's continue our talk in the morning."

"Good night." I reached and turned off the bedside lamp before slipping back under the thin coverlet. I didn't fall asleep right away, but I heard the soft sound of mom's gentle breathing indicating that she had. I lay awake thinking about what she told me. Why hadn't she told me these things before? There wasn't anything bad about what she had said. Yet, she had kept them to herself all these years. Was she just as private as her mother had been? As all the Wyndams seemed to be?

Chapter Ten

The next morning Maude and Mossie were waiting in the dining room for me and my mother to come downstairs. There was a grand breakfast of sausage links, country ham, scrambled and over light eggs, biscuits and gravy on the sideboard. Bea was pouring fresh squeezed orange juice into crystal goblets when I walked in.

"Madison." Mossie fluttered over to me in her sheer morning dress and gave me an endearing hug. "We are so thankful that you are safe and back home with us. We were so worried for you."

I patted her on her back and nodded, looking over at Maude, knowing she had to have been the one who planted those terrible thoughts into Mossie's head. "If you really are then I would appreciate it if you'd both apologize to Conner this morning."

Mossie looked shocked, but she didn't refuse and

went silently back to take her place at the table.

"Good morning all," my mother called when she walked into the dining room as if everything was fine. "I hope you all slept well. I know I did."

"Yes. I slept like a lamb." Mossie smiled brightly. "It was wonderful knowing that our dear Madison had been found unharmed."

"I was never in danger. I wasn't abducted, kidnapped, or assaulted. I went for a walk and fell asleep in the shade. I can't believe you called the police and said those things about Conner." I scooped up a big pile of eggs and placed them on my plate. "Whatever made you think that?"

"Young men have unsavory fantasies." Maude spoke for the first time.

"Yes, father always said you could never trust a young man with your virtue."

"You know nothing about Conner."

"We know enough," Maude said. "He isn't very respectful of you or he wouldn't sneak into our garden to see you. He'd have come introduced himself to us and waited to have been invited to call on you. That is what a proper young man would do, but then he is his father's son."

"Maude." Mom glared at her aunt. "Not now."

"What is that supposed to mean?" I asked. "First you say that about me and Mother and now you say that about Conner and his father. Is there something I should know?"

"It was so good to have you and Hope sleeping here last night," Mossie said looking dreamily at us. "It was as if this is the way it always should have been."

"Yes, Moss, it was good." Maude patted her hand. "We should have invited them both before now."

Good gravy. Here we go again. Mossie changing the subject.

"Yes, you should have."

Mom surprised me by her comment. I smiled, sitting back in my chair, waiting to see where this went.

"And since you and Mossie invited Madison here, I feel you owe her an explanation. We won't expect it right now, because you won't give one, but I would suggest that you both think long and hard about your response and be prepared to give her one by this evening."

"Th-that's a large request to make of us," Maude sputtered. "You act as if it is a simple task."

"You started this, not I. You were quite eager to get my daughter here and now that she is, I don't think you have the right to string her along like a puppet."

Maude was silent and I was glad. Yes, my mother was just the one to get the truth out in the open. I was going to have to watch her carefully while she was here. She could teach me the right way to handle our aunts.

Mossie daintily wiped the corners of her mouth with her cloth napkin and cleared her throat to get our attention. "I owe you each an apology," she said softly looking down at her plate. "Maude and I both agreed to tell Madison when she arrived, but I couldn't go through with it once she came. I feel she should know why there was such a rift in the family. I also feel that she should know that Wyndam House belongs to her as much as it does to Maude and me. Father may not have reached out to her during his life, but I can tell you both this. He did think of his only great-granddaughter."

My mother shifted in her chair, and I could feel her glancing out of the side of her eye at me to see how I was reacting. Knowing my great-grandfather thought of me during his life was little comfort now because he was gone. And I was beginning to accept that this was all I was going to get from him. As far as accepting that Wyndam House was part mine, only time would tell if I truly could do that. The only good that had come from my coming here was meeting Conner and perhaps that would be enough to endear this place to me.

"Mossie speaks the truth. We had both agreed to sit down with Madison when she arrived and I tried on more than one occasion to follow through, but Mossie didn't want to push the issue." Maude looked uneasy. "And the longer we waited the more difficult it became to do so. Madison wants so much to know about her family and I want her to know it all. I just don't want her to regret being a Wyndam when she does."

"Being a Wyndam isn't a dreadful thing," Mossie pointed out. "It's a complexity to life, but it's not bad. I think Madison was able to see that when she read father's journal."

My mother looked at me and her brows arched. "You read his journal?"

I nodded.

"What did you find?"

I reached for my orange juice and took a sip. "I found out he was a loving man for what all that was worth." I hated that I sounded cold and bitter, but I had reached a breaking point.

Mom smiled. "Yes, your great-grandfather was loving. He made sure his family was well provided for. He was a shrewd business man. He rebuilt this house after the war and kept his family from going belly up when so many of other plantation owners did just that during reconstruction. He was proud of his heritage and maybe that was something I was not."

"Oh, Hope. Don't feel like that," Mossie said warmly. "I don't think you denied your heritage by the choices you made. You just chose to be a Franklin."

I listened and tried to fit the pieces of all I had learned together. I still had many puzzle pieces to find before I could see the whole picture. But right now it looked as if everything kept going back to my mother and father.

"Didn't great-grandfather approve of father?" I asked.

Maude shifted in her seat and Mossie blanched whiter than the napkin she clutched in her hand. My mother sipped her coffee for a moment and then smiled at me.

"Your great-grandfather held strong to his beliefs, Madison. Approving of a person didn't always come easy for him," my mother said.

My mind raced back to the passages I had read in Richard Wyndam's journal. And it all made sense what she said.

The room grew quiet until Bea announced that Aunt Maude had a visitor.

"A visitor? Whoever would dare to call so early in the morning?" Maude pushed away from the table. "Is there a calling card?"

Mossie's eyes sparkled. "I wonder who it could be, Maude?"

"No ma'am," Bea said. "He wanted to wait on the portico until you finished breakfast and were prepared to see him. Should I show him to the parlor instead?"

"A male caller." Mossie took a deep breath in. "Oh, it has been ages since we've had a male caller."

A thrill of excited anticipation filled the room and Maude looked perplexed as to what she should do.

"Send him away."

Bea blinked. "Are you sure?"

"Yes. Yes. Tell him to go away." Maude clasped her hands together. "Never mind. I'll tell him myself."

We all watched Maude leave the dining room.

Then one by one we slipped over to the parlor where we could peep out of the window to the portico.

"This is most exciting," Mossie whispered loudly.

"It is, isn't it?" my mother said, touching my cheek. "Isn't that Mr. Claiborne that we met last evening? He did seem quite taken with her. Didn't you think so, Mossie?"

Mossie nodded, looking at me. "He seemed to know her, Madison. Like they had met before. But I'd have known if they did since we never go anywhere without the other."

Except when Maude came searching for me the other day.

"Actually, Aunt Maude followed me to Conner's last week. Duncan and Conrad were outside when she arrived and they brought her into the house." I recalled how Duncan had waited on her attentively and had even offered to drive us home. She had turned down the offer haughtily and I hoped she wasn't too harsh with him today.

"Well that explains why she was fit to be tied the other day then."

Mom and I looked at one another and she winked at me.

A few moments later the front door opened and closed. There were no voices in the foyer. The only sound we heard was a pair of slippers walking across the floor making tapping sounds. And by the timber of the tapping it didn't sound as if Maude was in a very good mood.

"Oh dear, I better go speak to her." Mossie shuffled out of the parlor.

When she was gone, Mother and I began to giggle.

"I think Maude has a suitor." Mother shook her head. "It's about time."

Mom and I went down to the gazebo later that morning. She was quiet for a few minutes as we walked around looking at the landscape. "Isn't it amazing how some things never change?" She ran down to the arched bridge and turned around to look at me. "You fell in love here didn't you?"

For a moment, I thought her question odd and I started to protest because I didn't consider myself in love with Conner, but then I saw how she lovingly caressed the foliage, looked at the swans as they glided across the pond and I knew what she meant.

"From the first moment Maude and Mossie brought me here."

"I knew it. I saw it in your drawing." She came back to the gazebo and sat down in the doorway. She leaned back on her elbows and closed her eyes as if mentally absorbing the solitude of the garden. Then she looked over at me as if she just thought of something.

"You won't be coming back to Camden with me."

Her voice was calm as if she was resigned to the idea.

"What?"

"You won't be returning to Camden. Grandfather has accomplished one thing from his grave. He has brought you home. It all makes sense now. That is why he allowed mother to come home before she died. He wanted his family back together after he was gone. He couldn't accomplish it before because of his pride, but through Maude and Mossie he can."

I sat down beside her wondering where she came up with this. "How can you say that I won't go back to Camden as if you are so sure?"

"I know my daughter. You love beauty and this is where you belong. You always have. Beauty has changed for you over time. When you were small, it was the freedom of being an equal with your male cousins. Running. Playing. Climbing trees. It didn't matter what they did, you could do it just as well, if not better. As you grew older, you developed a new love, a love for drawing. You have my mother's talent. A gift I didn't fully acquire, but then you've always had love in your life."

"You have too. I know you have. Grandmother loved you. Father loved you."

She nodded. "Yes, my mother did, but sometimes being loved by one parent isn't always enough, Madison. I never knew my father like you got to know yours. They were both taken away from us similarly, but my father's loss did more damage than when your father died. When Ronald Madison died it began something no one could have anticipated within this family."

"I don't understand." I wondered where all of this fit into the puzzle and why my mother was finally speaking of her past in such detail.

"You will, dear, in time." She patted my hand. "I'd tell you now, but I owe it to Maude and Mossie to finish what they started. Just promise me to be patient with them. I know they have frustrated you, but they've lived with this bottled inside for too long. We haven't begun to live life in their shoes and we should be thankful we won't have to. The world is evolving faster than we can ever imagine, Madison. Times are changing fast. Old principles are not as important as they once were. In a few years we won't even recognize ourselves. Look how much life has changed for us women. Before the Civil War, we were as much slaves to the men as those they owned. And now, we are on the verge of having the right to vote. Congress has passed the 19th Amendment and as long as it is ratified in August we will. It's exciting times, Madison. Just look how much life has already changed for you since you came here."

I still didn't understand everything my mother was talking about, but I knew that patience was one virtue that a Wyndam woman had to have. It was the only way to fully deal with our family members.

After our conversation, I took my mother for a

walk through the garden and showed her the path that Conner used when he came for visits.

"Tell me about him. I know he is very special to you."

"He's elusive and extremely charming." I pulled at the long weeds that had gotten about hip length now that summer was coming on. "He's a good listener and he helps put my thoughts into perspective even when I don't know I'm asking for help. He can read my thoughts and expressions and he tells me he can see clear to my soul when he looks into my brown eyes."

Mom nodded as we walked around the pond.

"He can be dramatic at times like when he brings me a bouquet of tiger lilies."

"So that is why you have so many of them in your room. You like him very much, don't you?"

"He's become my best friend.

"Those are always the nicest to have." She stooped down to smell the rose bush in bloom.

"Was father your best friend?"

She looked up at me. "It makes a marriage more special to be able to share everything with one another. Now that didn't mean we didn't have friends of our own sex because we did. And it doesn't mean we didn't spend time apart doing things we enjoyed either. But a friendship of that kind is like a magical communion of the souls. If Conner is truly your best friend, you will know what I mean in time."

I thought about the night we had danced in the

gazebo after the dinner party. I had felt a magical power that night, but I didn't think that was exactly what my mother meant.

"It doesn't hurt as much to think about father as it once did," I said out of the blue more as an observation than a question.

"No, it doesn't."

We walked back across the arched bridge to the gazebo where Bea was setting out lunch for us. I was still having a little difficulty becoming accustomed to having things done for me. It was odd to not have to ask for something because your every need was always anticipated by another.

"Thank you, Bea," mom said, taking a seat at the table inside the gazebo. "Do you think Conner will come by today?"

"I don't know. After yesterday's unpleasantness, I don't know if he'll ever want to come back here."

"But he will because he'll want to see you. Don't fret. We'll take Maude and Mossie over to apologize this afternoon and then everything will be back to normal."

I hoped she was right as I picked at my watercress salad. We usually spent the mornings together in the garden, but I hadn't seen him as mom and I took our walk. What if he had come by and overheard what I had been saying about him. Had I sounded moony?

Getting Maude and Mossie to go back to the Montgomery House wasn't easy. For one, they were ashamed of their behavior and another Maude didn't want to see Duncan Claiborne. I found the latter to be amusing and thought it was cute that at their age Duncan was interested in Maude. But then they say the heart wants what the heart wants so age didn't always factor into the equation.

My mother was relentless, and she finally persuaded our aunts to get into the car. It didn't take long for Godfrey to convey us the short distance to the Montgomery estate. Conrad and Duncan were sitting in the shade whittling when we pulled up. I didn't see Conner at first, but he soon appeared from the side of the house.

"Welcome, ladies," Conrad called, getting to his feet. "I didn't expect to see you again so soon."

"I hope you don't mind our coming without calling first?" my mother said. "But my aunts have something they want to say."

"Of course. Please have a seat." Duncan got up from the bench he was sitting on so Maude and Mossie could sit together.

Conner brought a few more lawn chairs over from the shed so Duncan and his grandfather could sit down too. I chose to stand with him to the side and mom stayed close to Maude to nudge her if necessary. But to our surprise, the apology came without them being prompted.

Conner graciously accepted, and we were invited to stay for watermelon.

The next day mom and I made plans to go into Charleston and see the old house on the Battery. Bea made a special lunch for us to take for a picnic at White Point Garden just like grandmother and I would do when I came to visit. Neither Maude nor Mossie wanted to come with us. They claimed the events of the last few days had been too much for them to venture from home again a third day in a row.

"As you wish," my mother told them before we got into our Model T Touring Car and headed to Charleston.

"I don't think Maude or Mossie like it too much that you insisted on driving."

"It doesn't matter what they like as long as we enjoy ourselves. Besides they know me well enough by now to realize that I would never agree to what they wanted easily." She slowed the car when we came upon a lone walker. "Why don't you ask him to come along?"

"Who?" I glanced out the window and saw it was Conner. My hands began to sweat.

Conner looked surprised when we pulled alongside of him and I asked him to join us. "Are you sure I won't be intruding?" He looked past me to my mom for her approval.

"You won't be intruding at all." Mom moved the picnic basket to the back seat so I could scoot closer to her and Conner could sit in the front with us. "We'd love you to come along if you don't have other plans?"

"No. I've got nothing pressing to do. I was only going for a walk." He opened the car door and got in.

The fit was a little snug, and I was quite conscious of his thigh pressed against mine all the way into the city. My mom talked the whole way about when she was young and came for visits to Wyndam House. If Conner was bored, he didn't show it. I on the other hand couldn't concentrate on what she was saying because I was too aware of the way he kept pressing his thigh against mine ever so often as if he were caressing my body with kisses. I felt perspiration forming above my upper lip, and it wasn't from the warmth of the summer day either.

I glanced over at him out of the corner of my eye and I found him watching me as he talked with my mother. I was certain she was not aware of what he was doing or how I was reacting to it. I tried to follow the conversation and say something intelligent, but words failed me.

"You've been quiet, Madison," mom said. "I don't believe I have ever seen you this way."

"I have." Conner spoke up; winking at me, reminding me of the day we met at the pond. "She has a tendency to let the cat get her tongue."

"Interesting." Mom turned the car onto Meeting Street. "I didn't know that Maude and Mossie owned a cat."

"They don't." I felt my cheeks warm. "That's not what he meant."

Mom ignored my comment and changed the subject. "Do you come into Charleston often, Conner?"

"No. Grandfather doesn't like the city much now that he is older. He prefers the privacy of River Road. He orders his groceries delivered and makes do with what he has at the estate."

"But the city is beautiful," I said, not understanding how anyone could stay away completely. But I had been to Charleston only once since coming to visit.

"It may be beautiful, but there are many things about its past that keeps one at bay." Conner looked out the window as we went by the many shops and businesses before we entered the residential part of the city.

I felt uncomfortable as we headed for White Point Garden. It was increasingly clear that I knew little about Conner other than what he wanted me to know. He didn't talk about his family when we were together, and other than knowing his parents live in Dalton, Georgia, I knew nothing about his past or his family.

All we ever talked about was me and my family problems. Did I come across as self-absorbed? I hoped not, because I wasn't…at least not normally.

My mom found a place to park and we got out of the car. Conner carried the picnic basket for us and we found a shady spot under one of the large trees in the grassy area of the park.

I spread out the blanket and Conner set the basket down.

"You both should take a stroll along the boardwalk while I set up lunch," Mom said.

"Shall we?" Conner asked, offering me his hand.

"Sure." I looked forward to spending some time alone with him. We hadn't really had a chance to talk alone since he found me down by the river the other night.

"You sure are quiet today," he said as we walked by the old Civil War cannons that decorated one end of the garden.

"I've had much to think about. My mom and I have had long talks and she's gotten more out of Mossie and Maude than I ever could."

"Oh. Good. I thought you were angry with me."

"Angry?" I stopped walking. "Why would I be?"

He shrugged and began to walk again. "I didn't come by yesterday and if you all hadn't shown up at the house…well…you might have thought I didn't want to see you because of what happened."

"Don't be silly."

There was an awkward moment of silence as we walked up the steps to the boardwalk and stared out over the Charleston Harbor. The water was a deep bluish-brown and the waves were choppy as they lapped against the rock barrier.

Conner pointed out to a structure on a small island that was barely visible in the bright, afternoon sunlight. "That's Fort Sumter."

"Did your grandfather take part in the Civil War?"

"No, he was too young." He smiled down at me. "But his father served under your great-grandfather."

"Oh. I didn't know that." I knew what that meant. The Montgomery family wasn't in the same social class as the Wyndams before the war. Had they been after? I recalled again how Duncan Claiborne had spoken about attending balls with my grandmother and her sisters. Reconstruction had opened up the social classes for migration of families in and out.

"The Civil War changed the South, Madison," Conner continued when I didn't speak. "Just like the World War changed the world. There is always going to be turmoil among people. Political and social."

"You don't talk about your time in the war much. Did you have to kill anyone?" I hoped I was not bringing up something he would be uncomfortable talking about.

"Yeah. I had to kill someone." He stepped away from me a little as he turned to look out over the water. "I had to kill more than I wanted to. It was either them or me and that wasn't a good feeling. I hope there isn't another war in my lifetime. I don't think I could live through it."

I felt his anguish and I stepped closer, wrapping my arm around his waist. "I hope there isn't one either."

"Being in the war is the loneliest place you could ever be." He turned to face me. "The loneliest and I won't go back there. Don't make me, Madison. Don't ask me about it."

I shook my head seeing the change in his cobalt blue eyes. They held coldness and pain. "I won't, Conner. I promise you I won't ask you about it again."

He crushed me against him, and we stood on the boardwalk for several moments. I could feel him trembling and I regretted bringing up the war, but I had needed to know how he truly felt about it. I needed to know about him and his life experiences. I needed to feel a part of his world more than I already did. This was of great importance to me.

"I'm sorry, Conner," I murmured inching my hand up his neck. "I'm sorry for bringing up the past."

He shook his head. "It isn't your fault. I made the choice to go. I went even though my family didn't approve." He pulled away and urged me to walk again. "I suppose that is why I want you to learn about your family history so much. In a way I feel if you can find peace with yours then I am making amends with my own."

I looked at him as we walked. I couldn't imagine his family not being happy that he had survived the war even though they hadn't agreed with his decision to fight in Europe. "Have you seen your parents since you returned?"

He nodded. "Yeah. I went home when I got back state side. They were glad to see me, but I didn't truly feel at home until I got to Grandpa's. That's when I knew this is where I belonged."

I smiled at him, recalling how my mother assumed I would not return to Camden with her. Conner was so sure that he belonged in Charleston. I only wished I knew I belonged here as well.

"Which house belonged to your grandparents?" He changed the subject as we headed along East Battery Street.

"The third one was the Madison house." I pointed it out to him. "My grandmother left instructions in her will for the house to be sold and the money divided between me and my mother after her death. That was before she became ill. Mom and I never saw a dime of that money because great-grandfather had her will declared invalid. The Wyndam estate assumed the sale of the house."

Conner was silent as we turned and walked back towards the park where my mom waited. "How could he do that to you?"

I shrugged. "He was very influential. All he had to do was prove that my grandmother had been ill when her will was drawn up. Her lawyer testified to the fact that she was and her doctor provided her medical records and that was all the proof the judge needed."

"Why would he do that?" Conner said shaking his head.

"I don't know. If I knew what made my great-grandfather do the things he did during his life then I wouldn't be so confused." I shook my head. "I'm sorry. I didn't mean to take my frustrations out on you."

"You have every right to be upset." Conner sounded annoyed himself. "I'm surprised you came to visit your great aunts when you did after what your great-grandfather did."

"I know. I think that is what made my mother so surprised that I wanted to come when I received their letter of invitation." We had reached the edge of the garden. "Don't mention this to my mother. We vowed not to think about this today. We haven't been here since the judgment."

"No, I won't." Conner squeezed my hand as we headed back to the blanket to join my mother.

"Did you have a nice walk?" Mom poured us each a glass of lemonade.

"Yes. We even saw the house."

"How does it look?" She dug in the basket for plates.

"The new owners have painted it."

"Mother always said it needed a good white washing."

"It is more than white washing. They painted it yellow."

Mom looked up from the food. "Yellow? My mother detested yellow."

I didn't say anything, and I could tell Conner was a little uncomfortable by the turn of the conversation.

"Well, we cannot do anything about that." Mom forced a smile. "Let's eat."

Conner took the plate she handed him and reached for a piece of fried chicken and piled a mound of potato salad on his plate. Mom and I dug in as well, enjoying the small feast that Bea had prepared for us.

When we finished eating, Conner stretched out on his side while mom and I put away the leftovers.

"What are you planning to do this afternoon?" he asked.

"I'm going to take Madison over to the house and see if the new owner will allow us to come inside for a look around." My mom got to her feet.

"Uh, do you think we should?" I asked.

"Why shouldn't we? If someone came to our home in Camden and wanted to have a look around because it was where they had once lived, I would let them come in." She picked up the picnic basket.

Conner's brows arched and he sat up. "I think it's a splendid idea."

His response surprised me. I could just imagine what Maude and Mossie would say when they found out about this. Good heavens! I was beginning to think and sound like them.

"Are you coming, Madison?"

I got to my feet and we quickly folded the blanket before we took it and the basket to the car. We proceeded to East Battery and then to the newly painted yellow house. My mom took her time inspecting the house before she knocked on the door. We waited a few moments and she knocked again. The door slowly opened and an old lady stood in the entrance way.

"Yes?" She clutched a thin crocheted shawl around her shoulders.

"Hello," my mother said. "My name is Hope Madison Franklin. My mother previously owned this house and I was wondering if I might come in with my daughter and her friend and have a look around. I know it is an unusual request, but it has been several years since my mother passed away and the house was sold."

The woman looked at my mother for a few moments and then her eyes enlarged. "Ellen. Ellen, come here."

A moment later a woman about my mother's age appeared at the door. She was finely dressed. "What is it, Mother?"

The old woman pointed a withered finger at my mother. "It is her."

The younger woman with silky blonde hair that fell down past her shoulders looked at us and a smile spread across her face. "Hope Franklin!"

Mom looked puzzled for a moment but then she smiled as well. "Ellen Barnard."

"It's Ellen Tidsdale now." She stepped out on the porch to hug my mother. "I told Harold, my husband, this house used to belong to your family. We heard that Madison was visiting the family on River Road, and I told him I hoped you'd want to see the house again."

"How long have you lived here?"

"About five years now. The couple that bought the house after your mother died moved north and Harold made them an offer. He has always wanted to live on the Battery. Please come inside."

"We'd love too," Mom said. "Ellen, this is my daughter Madison and her friend Conner."

Ellen shook our hands. "I'm so glad to meet you both."

We followed her and her mother inside to the parlor and she rang for tea. "I hope you don't mind, but I remember how your mother had the house decorated when we were growing up. I always loved her taste and I tried to replicate it the best I could."

"I'm flattered and I know she would be also. Do you remember it, Madison?"

I was surprised that Mrs. Tidsdale had gone to the effort to restore the house to how it had once looked. The furnishings resembled some of the same pieces that my grandmother had, and I wondered if she'd bought them when the house was first sold or had just been lucky to find them over the years.

"I even found one of your mother's paintings still in the attic." Ellen walked over to the wall and pointed to the picture of a little girl sitting in a swing in a garden that looked much like the garden at Wyndam House.

"Oh my." My mom's eyes began to glisten with unshed tears and she went to the painting for a better look. "I thought she had destroyed them all."

"I know." Ellen sighed. "I remember the day she got into that fit and took them all out to the back yard and had a grand bonfire with them. You'd just invited us all home for tea after the lecture at the college."

Mother shook her head and said softly. "I never understood what made her do it. Then I found out she'd had words with my grandfather."

"It was such a pity too. But I remember all too well how your grandfather could be."

Mom turned and motioned for me. "Madison, come look. You have her same style."

I left Conner sitting on the sofa and joined them at the painting. It was strange seeing the oil painting of the garden because it resembled some of my own sketches. "Is that you?"

"No. It's my mother as a child in the garden. She always said she dreamed of being a child in that garden again."

"But I thought grandmother gave up drawing

when she married?"

"She did, but she sometimes would close herself in the small room upstairs and paint for hours at a time. She started doing this when I went to college, but that didn't last long." Mom reached out and touched the frame of the picture.

Ellen's smile began to fade as if remembering something sad. "I know I should have written, Hope. I should have stayed in touch all of these years, especially after Edward was killed." She laid a hand on my mom's arm affectionately.

"I should have made an effort too, Ellen. So don't feel bad. We were too close as girls to let time and distance separate us the way it did."

"But this painting rightfully belongs to you. I want you to have it." She reached for the frame to remove it from the wall.

I held my breath as she did this, but my mother stopped her.

"No. The painting belongs in this house. It's all that is left of her here. This is where she was the happiest and so it should stay." She sniffed and cleared her throat. "My mother did not destroy this painting for a reason and it has stayed hidden in the attic for years for you to find. You keep it, Ellen."

Tears began running down Ellen's face at what my mother was doing and she hugged her tight. "You haven't changed, Hope. You haven't changed. We all thought you would when you married Edward and left

Charleston."

"Sh-h-h. It's all right. You have to stop crying or I'm going to start," my mother said blinking to get rid of the moisture.

The two turned and walked over to the curio cabinet and began admiring the small figurines that Ellen had collected over the years. From the corner of my eye, I caught Ellen's mother staring at Conner, I watched her for a moment, wondering what she found so fascinating about him. Turning back to the painting I tried to ignore her and focused on the most precious legacy my grandmother had left us, but my mother had selflessly given it away.

I couldn't help but feel regret because I wanted it. I wanted that painting more than I could imagine.

"Are you okay?" Conner asked, coming up behind me.

I nodded, still studying the painting. "She had talent." He wrapped his arms loosely around my waist and I leaned back against him.

"You have talent too," he whispered, running a hand up the side of my arm. Chills spread over my body in the wake of his gentle touch and I closed my eyes, picturing the painting as I memorized it so I wouldn't forget how it looked.

After tea was served and we visited a while, Ellen took us on a tour of the house before we left. She made plans with my mom to have dinner one evening next week. And despite seeing the house again and bringing up old memories for my mother, she seemed very happy as we headed back to the car.

She had reunited with an old friend and she was talking about staying in Charleston a little longer. Conner nudged me as we rode back toward River Road when she announced this. I suppose he thought that meant I would be staying in Charleston longer as well. He didn't know I would be staying on even when my mother left.

Yes. I was going to stay even if Maude and Mossie drove me to delirium with the incessant secrets about the family.

When we returned to River Road my mother dropped Conner and me off at the foot of the driveway so I could walk the rest of the way home with him. She seemed content to return to the house alone, and I could tell she had things on her mind.

"Today turned out to be interesting. I'm glad I came along with you." Conner picked a Tiger Lily growing by the side of the road and handed it to me as the car disappeared up the drive.

"I know and I'm glad you came with us."

"You don't sound all that happy." He pulled a foxtail from the weed patch we were passing and tickled me with it.

"Conner, stop! I don't feel like being tickled with a foxtail."

"Would you rather I tickle you myself? I can do that just as easily."

I backed up a few steps to keep him from doing it. "No. Please. Don't you realize this afternoon has been very enlightening for me? As well as emotional. Therefore I can't be jubilant all the time."

"True, but just think, one of your grandmother's paintings has survived after all these years."

I shook my head. "But what good does that do me? You witnessed my mother giving it away when I'd have rather brought it home with us."

"I know, but she felt it rightfully belonged to Mrs. Tidsdale now." He took a step towards me and grabbed my hand, pulling me along with him into the tall grass off the side of the road.

"Where are you taking me?" I asked, having difficulty keeping up with his long stride.

He didn't answer my question but kept walking further and further into the tall grass that was almost ready to be cut for hay.

"Conner, aren't we trespassing?"

"No." He began to run, pulling me along with him as the grass scratched my arms and legs. We soon came upon an old faded red barn and what looked to be a deserted farm house and then an old bridge that crossed a stream. When we were on the other side of the bridge, Conner stopped short at a nearby tree and I crashed into his back.

He finally let go of my hand when he sat down under the tree. I dropped down beside him. "Conner, what has gotten into you?"

He looked at me as we caught our breath. There was a seriousness in his eyes that made me afraid for him to speak. Did I really want to know what had crossed his mind to send him running like that?

He reached out a hand and cupped my face with it and leaned toward me, brushing his lips over mine. "I think I love you, Madison."

My heart skipped a beat. I closed my eyes and licked my lips, tasting the saltiness of his kiss. "Are you sure? We barely know one another."

"That doesn't matter. I know what I feel. Don't you feel it? Whenever we're together. That pull that makes you not want to be apart?"

I nodded. "My sweaty palms. You pressing you thigh against mine in the car making it hard for me to focus."

He laughed. "That's it."

My stomach muscles tightened and I had difficulty breathing. Was I in love with him too? How did one know? I leaned in and kissed him this time, pulling away just as quickly, laughing. "I think I might love you too."

His Cheshire grin appeared and he laughed, pulling me onto his lap. "I know." He gently brushed his lips against my ear lobe before his mouth found mine again. I relaxed into him, returning his kiss until we broke apart and I laid my head against his shoulder.

"Marry me."

My head was spinning and my heart was thudding so his question didn't register immediately.

"I'm serious, Madison. I don't want you going back to Camden. I want you to stay here in Charleston with me, forever. Marry me."

I sat up and stared at him. "You don't know what you're asking." I scrambled off his lap and got to my feet. "I–I have to go."

I hurried across the bridge, not daring to look back at him for fear I might say yes. It would be so easy to do because I definitely wanted to spend every day with him, but was I ready to get married?

"Madison, wait!" he called, running after me. "I do know what I'm asking. I've been thinking about it for days. Maybe right now wasn't the best time to ask, but life is too unpredictable. The past few weeks have been the happiest for me since we met. Aren't you happier when we're together than when we're apart?"

I turned around and found myself face to face with him. "Yes, but that doesn't mean we're meant to be married. We need more time to be certain."

"How much time will you need? I've got time. That's all I have."

"I don't know. I don't know what I want to do with my life. Maybe I should go to art school."

"You could still do that even if you become my wife. I wouldn't stop you."

I swallowed. He wasn't making this easy on me. "There's still the whole mess with the family secret. What if once I uncover it, you have a different opinion about spending your life with me?"

"I honestly doubt anything could make me feel that way."

"We're too young."

"Now you're grasping at excuses. How old was your grandmother when she married your grandfather?"

"Fifteen, but that was a different time. Girls married young."

"Girls still do. Whether you realize it or not, Franklin, you're on the shelf."

I swatted at him and he grabbed my wrist, pulling me to him. He stole a kiss and winked at me.

"I won't take no for an answer. So think about it."

I nodded. "Can I talk to my mom about this?"

"Sure. Just don't let her talk you out of it when I know you want to."

I laughed, shaking my head. "Why is this so important now? Why not have waited and asked me at the end of the summer?"

"Because I want you to forget about the Wyndam history. I want you to forget about your great-grandfather and all the pain he has caused you. You don't need Wyndam House. You don't need to suddenly become a part of a life you were forbidden to live. You need to be you. You need to be happy. Let me make you happy, Madison."

I smiled and gently touched his cheek. "You are wonderful, Conner, but marrying you will not solve my problems. They'll still be there. The answers lie with Maude and Mossie and I can't let any more time pass by without finding out the truth. Once they are gone the questions will be unanswered."

He started to say something but stopped. We walked back to River Road and he cut across a yard leading me to the garden at Wyndam House. He kissed me and left me at the arched bridge contemplating his proposal.

Chapter Eleven

I walked in the garden for over an hour overwhelmed by the day's events. First, going to the house on East Battery and seeing my grandmother's painting. Second, Conner's marriage proposal. I still got warm and tingly every time I thought about it. He wanted me. Out of all the girls in Charleston, Conner Montgomery wanted me to be his bride. He thought he loved me enough to ask me to marry him.

"I think I love you, Madison."

I could still hear him saying those words, but if he wanted me to marry him, then why did he only think he loved me? Or had he added the word 'think' because he was afraid he'd scare me away? And when I admitted the same to him, had that given him the confidence to pop the question?

I shook my head, crossed the bridge for the fifth

time before finally climbing the stone steps up to the house. I couldn't put off going inside any longer. I had to get ready for dinner. But if I went in the back, I'd disturb Bea as she cooked.

Maude was coming downstairs as I entered the front door and she hurried across the foyer, giving me a big hug. "Madison, I am so thrilled for you." She kissed me on the cheek then held me at arm's length beaming.

Before I had time to question what she was talking about, Mossie joined in congratulating me. And over their heads, I saw my mom at the parlor doorway with a bright smile on her face as well.

They knew! How on earth did they know about Conner's proposal already? I had never imagined Maude and Mossie would have reacted this way, not after accusing Conner of the unthinkable the other night. I had envisioned them protesting and refusing to let me hold the wedding at Wyndam House.

I placed a hand over my mouth and headed for the stairs. I wasn't ready to discuss any of this with them, especially when I hadn't even accepted his proposal.

"Madison, is something wrong?" My mother followed me.

"Yes, Maddy, you act as if something is bothering you." Mossie looked up at me puzzled as I climbed the stairs.

"Aren't you thrilled about your invitation?" Maude asked, holding up the card for me to see.

Invitation? How on earth had they already had invitations printed up?

I turned, gripping the curved railing and stared at my mother, praying she could explain what was going on. "What invitation?"

"The invitation to the Fourth of July Ball at Mayor Peterson's house. It came for you this afternoon." Maude held out the envelope for me to take.

I laughed and relief washed over me. They didn't know about the proposal. I'd overreacted. "Is that why you were congratulating me? Because I got invited to a party?"

"It isn't just any party, Maddy, it's 'the' party." Mossie shook her head, clearly disappointed in me. "Don't you remember, we told you all about it weeks ago?"

I nodded and sat down on the step, unable to stand any longer. My mother watched me closely, and I could tell she sensed more was going on here than a misunderstanding. She didn't say a word but took the invitation from Maude and handed it to me.

And as quickly as a mother worries over her chick, she placed her hand on my forehead and frowned. "Madison and I will be down for dinner shortly. I think she's overheated from being outside so long," Mom told the aunts and helped me to my feet.

"Oh dear." Mossie sounded worried. "I hope she isn't taking ill."

"Lying down with a cool cloth on her forehead

should help," Maude called.

Even with my mother's support, I held onto the railing the whole way up the stairs, not trusting my legs to support me. I was trembling and I felt like I wanted to cry, but that was absurd, wasn't it?

"What's going on?" my mother asked as soon as we were safely inside my room.

I laughed and shook my head, trying to shake off this silly reaction. "I didn't know what Maude was congratulating me about. I knew she couldn't have known, it didn't make sense how she could have found out so quickly."

"Found out what, Madison? You aren't making any sense."

"I know. Nothing makes sense. Nothing at all." I laughed at myself and staggered into the bathroom, not bothering to close the door before turning on the water to fill the tub. I needed a bath. A hot bath to wash it all away.

"Have you been drinking?"

"No." I pulled my dress off over my head and shimmied out of my underclothes, stepping into the tub.

"Then what is going on?"

I sank low underneath the water, not bothering to answer her until I resurfaced. I wiped the water away from my eyes and pushed my hair back. "Conner told me he loves me and he asked me to marry him."

"Oh." Mom turned off the water.

"So when I came in and Maude was congratulating me..." I pulled my knees up to my chest and wrapped my arms around my legs.

"I see. What did you say?"

"That I needed more time."

"And do you?"

I nodded, swallowing hard. "I don't want to rush into anything. I don't know that I'm ready to get married. I–it's too soon to be thinking along these lines. Don't you agree?"

My mother sat down beside the tub. "If you feel that way, then it is for you. Do you love him?"

"Yes...at least I think so. How do you know for sure?"

"That's hard to answer. I can't tell you if you do or don't, only you know how you feel."

I sighed. "Let's not mention this to Maude and Mossie. I'm not sure how they'd react and I don't want to deal with them until I've made up my mind on what to do."

"I think you already have, at least for now. Be honest with him on how you feel and if he truly loves you and wants to be with you, he will wait." Mom got to her feet. "I'll leave you alone to finish your bath, but don't take too long. Dinner will get cold."

She closed the bathroom door behind her, and I sank back under the water, laying there holding my breath for a few moments before sitting up again. I still felt like I wanted to cry, but not as much as I had earlier. I didn't have to make a decision right now or not even tonight. I'd sleep on it and maybe in the morning I'd feel differently.

Bea was placing dinner on the dining room table when I came down in a rose-colored sheer, sleeveless dinner dress with my hair slicked back. I took my place at the table as if the earlier episode in the foyer hadn't happened, and I hoped neither Maude nor Mossie would bring it up. And to ensure this I started the conversation.

"I was thinking I will need a new dress for the ball, won't I?"

"Don't worry about that," Maude said. "I've already called our seamstress and she has made you an appointment for tomorrow afternoon. You can't wear anything off the rack to the ball. It will need to be custom made."

I looked at my mother and she shrugged her shoulders as if to say *'when in Rome do as the romans do'.* "Were you ever invited to the Peterson's ball?"

"Yes, but the ball wasn't given by the current Mrs. Peterson, but her mother-in-law in my day."

"The Petersons have been holding this ball since we were girls," Mossie added. "It's a family tradition."

"I assume I can take an escort? The invitation said 'and guest'."

"Of course." Maude laid down her knife and fork. "And I think you should ask Thomas Whitfield, our friend Anna's son. You remember him from the dinner party."

I drank a sip of water. "Yes I remember him, but I was thinking of asking Conner Montgomery. We are closer in age and I enjoy being with him."

"But we've already told Anna you will ask Thomas and she was thrilled," Mossie blurted.

"You had no right to do that. You'll have to call her back and explain I will not be asking him."

"We can't do that. It would hurt Anna if we did," Maude said.

"Then Anna will have to be hurt." Mom joined the conversation. "Madison is right. It wasn't your place to speak to whom she will be asking to go with her. I don't know who this Thomas Whitfield is, but if Madison prefers to go with Conner, then the matter is settled."

"But Thomas is from the *right* family," Mossie said. "He will be a good match for her and more doors will be opened for them socially as a couple."

The right family?

Opening doors to us as a couple?

A couple?

No. I was not going to be paired with Thomas Whitfield. Not by Maude, Mossie, or Anna. The very thought make my stomach bunch into knots.

I pushed back from the table and stood. "Please

excuse me. I don't wish to continue this conversation. And just so you know, you'd better get to liking Conner Montgomery and thinking he is the right match for me because I'm going to marry him."

Crystal goblets clinked against the china as Maude and Mossie both let go of their glasses when I dropped that bombshell on them, and I heard my mother sigh. When would Maude and Mossie learn they could not run my life?

I was curled up on the window seat in my nightgown sketching when my mother finally came upstairs. She opened my bedroom door without knocking and came inside. "That was a dramatic exit you made. I don't think Maude and Mossie will get over your announcement easy. Not to mention breaking their precious crystal goblets from Romania. I hope you're not going to marry Conner because they made you mad. Marriage isn't a game and I thought your father and I taught you better than this."

"No. I'm not getting married because they made me angry. I may not give Conner an answer right away, but they don't have to know that."

"Madison, this is unlike you. I'm not liking what coming here has done to you."

I looked up from my sketch. "Are you saying I'm

becoming a Wyndam?"

She crossed her arms over her chest, evidence she didn't like my snarky tone. "Yes."

I sucked in a deep breath. "That will make Maude and Mossie very happy. That's all they've wanted since I arrived—for me to become a true Wyndam and take my rightful place within Charleston society."

"Is that what you really want?"

"No."

"Then stop this nonsense. Don't let them push you into being something you're not."

"What if it's already too late?"

"Then I'm taking you home to Camden. I won't stand by and watch you become someone I don't know anymore."

"But what about Conner? I can't leave him."

"You can't?"

I shook my head.

"That sounds like your feelings are more serious for him than you first let on when you came home today. Maybe you do love him enough to marry him. Have you thought of that?" She dropped her arms to her side and came over to sit in the window with me. "Love comes quickly and softly sometimes, Madison. Other times it rushes in. Don't overthink it. Listen to you heart. It sounds like that is what Conner was doing when he proposed to you, darling."

I thought about what she said, feeling conflicted again. Was it really that easy to meet your soulmate?

Who was I kidding? Conner and I had had a connection ever since we met in the garden that first time. I'd felt it. He'd felt it. That's the reason we'd spent so much time together since then. Maybe that was even the reason I had kept him a secret from Maude and Mossie as long as I could so they couldn't object.

I smiled at my mom. "I believe you are right, Mother. I've been trying to overthink my feelings. Letting doubt and fear keep me from seeing what my heart has been trying to show me. I do love him. I do want to be with him. And if we truly love one another, we'll be able to work out any obstacles that come in our way together. As one. As man and wife just like you and daddy taught me."

I hugged her tight, feeling the elation and love for Conner that had made me laugh after we'd kissed this afternoon.

She hugged me back and kissed me on the cheek when we broke apart. "You don't have to rush into a wedding right away. It's proper and expected of a Wyndam to have a lengthy engagement period. This will allow the two of you to get to know one another better."

"How long is lengthy? Surely not a year or two?"

"No. Six months to a year."

"What if—" She placed a finger at my lips, stopping me from saying more.

"Enough. Just enjoy the moment." Mom looked

out of the window as the sun was setting. "The view from here is lovely, isn't it? I think that is why grandfather gave my mother this room as opposed to one of the others. He knew she'd appreciate the landscape."

"Life is full of surprises, isn't it?"

She nodded. "I never thought my daughter would be making her debut into society, especially Charleston society after the way I left all those years ago."

"What about me? I'm more shocked than you."

"You did sound excited about getting a new dress."

"Oh that. I was trying to keep Maude and Mossie from talking about my near collapsing on the stairs earlier."

Mom patted me on the cheek. "Nice diversion. Distract them with dress talk so they don't discuss what you don't want to. Maybe I was wrong. Maybe you aren't becoming like them, you're much more cunning like my mom."

Now that was a compliment. I liked the thought that I was like my grandmother in that way.

We both stared out into the garden, not talking while the sun disappeared and the moon took its place, lighting the garden. What a perfect setting for a wedding. But would it be easily accessible to guests? If I knew Maude and Mossie well enough, they'd insist on inviting their peers and that meant the guest list could get rather lengthy with older folks.

"Do I have to have a large wedding? Or can I have a small, intimate one with only a few family and friends?"

"You can have whatever you want for the ceremony. The reception, on the other hand, may need to be large to appease our aunts."

"Hmmm...I suppose you are right. I can't prevent them from celebrating in a grand way. It would be expected. Of course, this isn't their wedding, but mine and Conner's. I'm sure he'll have his own thoughts on it too."

Mom smiled. "There's plenty of time to worry with the details. I think I'm going to bed now. It has been a long day."

"Yes it has. And tomorrow will be another long one. I have to visit the seamstress, remember."

"Yes, but we can have her make two dresses instead of one."

"We can?"

Mom nodded, slipping out the door.

Chapter Twelve

I have to admit that I was still trying to figure out why I'd need two dresses made by the seamstress as we drove to the appointment the next day. It seemed extravagant in my opinion and totally unlike my mother until she went into the fitting room with me for the seamstress to take my measurements and she began describing what I would need for one of the dresses. And then I felt like a ninny. Of course the second dress would take longer to make than the one for the Fourth of July ball. And it made perfect sense to take this opportunity to get started on my wedding dress even if I had not said yes to Conner yet.

After the measurements were taken, we went to the pattern room and took suggestions from the seamstress on what styles would look best on me for the ball and my wedding. I knew for the ball I wanted something loose fitting that would not be too hot for a July night. I'd worn a tube dress several times since we'd purchased dresses after my arrival in Charleston, and I liked the freedom it gave me to move. I thought that would be a perfect style for dancing.

"I've never made a ball gown in that style before," the seamstress admitted. "The tube is normally used for more casual dresses, but I can make you a dress more stylish with the same principle. You'll definitely make a statement. I've got the perfect material for it too."

The seamstress disappeared and came back with a bolt of pale pink chiffon and a bolt of slightly darker pink silk. "We can layer these two and with beading and sequins it will be a very flattering dress that will compliment your skin tone. Would you prefer a V neckline or a scooped?"

"V," my mother and I said at the same time.

"I agree. The dress should be sleeveless with a carwash hemline edged in beads and sequins so it gives the illusion of shimmering as you dance. Many of the other dresses I've made for this ball used fringe and with you being new to town you should stand out from the rest."

"Excellent." My mother smiled.

We followed the seamstress into the materials room where we looked at beading panels and sequins and found a design we liked for the dress.

"And for the second dress? May I suggest you

consider silk and chiffon for it as well? I have a lovely pearl white in both fabrics with matching beading and sequin that will pick up the glow of candlelight perfectly. The S curve looked excellent on you for the dinner party; we could copy that style but not do the waterfall hem. Instead if you want a train, we can make it a detachable one that can be removed after the ceremony. Did you have a sleeve style in mind?"

"I'm not sure yet." I admitted.

"Will it be an indoor or outdoor ceremony?"

"I was considering a garden ceremony, but—"

The seamstress nodded. "But you haven't decided. I can design the dress sleeveless with the ability to add them later. It will not be difficult to make them out of chiffon and attach under the beading."

"Thank you."

"I'll begin sketching a few ideas and have them ready for you to look at by the time you come back for a fitting on the Fourth of July dress."

"Perfect."

When we were finished with the seamstress on my dresses, I realized that Maude and Mossie had left us totally alone to do the shopping which was really unlike them, but I understood why when we found them sitting in the little waiting alcove while the seamstresses' assistant showed them a few dress choices that they might like for the upcoming holiday season.

"Did you get your dress?" Mossie asked when she

noticed we'd joined them.

"Yes."

"Excellent. You'll need a new pair of shoes for the party." Maude stood. "I don't want to hear no come from your lips, Madison. You got out of it on our last shopping excursion, but not this one."

"I agree." Mom nodded.

So off we went to the shoe store down the street. Mom and I saw the shoes on display as soon as we walked into the store. A pair of pink champagne Mary Janes with silver metallic inserts instead of cutouts. They felt like a dream on my feet and the heel wasn't too high for me at all. I walked around in them and then did a quick twirl to make sure I'd have no trouble on the dance floor.

"That was simple enough," Maude said when the purchase was made and we were back out on the sidewalk.

"Let's have lunch before driving home," Mossie suggested. "I feel as if breakfast was eons ago. And I'm a little light headed."

"Typical." Maude frowned turning to me. "Take your shoes to Godfrey and tell him we're having lunch at the Tea Room and he should meet us there in an hour."

"Is the Tea Room still open?" I heard my mother ask as I headed toward their car and to instruct the driver where to meet us.

By the time I traveled the half a block back to the

Charleston Tea Room, I saw them seated at one of the few window tables. Going inside, I was amazed by the Oriental carpets that covered sections of the hardwood floor and thick draperies that hung at the double windows in the front of the room. Small tables for intimate parties were spaced throughout and ornate marble columns divided the room. Crystal chandeliers hung throughout giving off light. Brocade and floral settees, low seated chairs in matching fabrics offered seating for larger parties. And on the interior wall a grand fireplace offered warmth during the winter months. A very fashionably dressed man sat at the piano playing concertos.

"What do you think?" Mossie asked when I failed to take my seat right away because I was looking around the room.

"Close your mouth, Madison. It isn't polite to gawk," Maude instructed.

"I thought the parlor and dining rooms at Wyndam House were spacious, but this tea room is absolutely spectacular."

"I know," Mossie cooed. "And the food is heavenly."

Mossie insisted on ordering for us and soon two, three-tiered stands were brought holding finger sandwiches, jellies and scones as well as miniature cakes, a china tea pot and four matching cups. It was a grand feast and the food was scrumptious just like Mossie said.

We were having a wonderful time until Maude smiled warmly at me. "You know, Madison. I can understand why you want to take Conner with you to the Fourth of July ball. He is the only young man, other than Thomas Whitfield, that you have met. What I can't understand is why you want to alienate yourself at your debut."

The bite of cake I swallowed lodged in my throat, and I reached for my tea, taking a drink. My spine tensed, and I felt cornered even though I knew my mom was on my side. I looked at her to make sure she hadn't suddenly changed her mind.

"Maude is right, Madison," Mossie began. "You really should reconsider who escorts you to such an affair. Conner is perfectly acceptable as a friend you spend time with in our garden, but for this type of an affair, you should chose a more appropriate companion. "

My lungs contracted, and I found it difficult to breathe while I tried to keep my temper in check. How dare they insinuate that Conner Montgomery was not acceptable? What gave them the right to determine this?

"I thought we already settled this matter last evening?" Mom laid down her fork and looked at them both.

"Yes. Yes. I know, but Maude and I agree that Madison should rethink her position on the matter."

"And of course you think I should ask Thomas

Whitfield."

"Yes we do." Maude laid down her napkin.

"No." I said flatly. "He is almost twice my age, and all he can talk about is his family's money. I find him a bore."

"Age has nothing to do with it. Your debut into society has to be perfect. Just like the dress and the shoes you have chosen to wear must be sophisticated. Who takes you to the ball will accentuate that fact."

"Conner is not an accessory in my life." I said loud enough so only they could hear. "And I find your opinion of him upsetting. He is a decent human being, and if you would ever stop long enough to invite him to join us for dinner, then I do believe you would see what I find so endearing about him."

Maude blanched. "Endearing? You sound as if you love the boy. Were you serious last evening when you said you were going to marry him? Has he asked you? Have you accepted?"

Her questions came fast, not giving me time to respond, but I wasn't worried about them. I was concerned with Mossie who grabbed hold of the lace tablecloth and began to breathe erratically before she slumped in her seat.

My mother who sat beside her began to pat her cheeks. "Mossie. Mossie. Can you hear me?"

Maude jumped up from her chair, turning it over. "Help! We need a doctor. Someone go get a doctor."

A waiter hurried over, sat the overturned chair

back on its legs and helped me calm Maude down. Another waiter came over with some smelling salts. That brought Mossie around. And once the doctor came he checked her pulse and blood pressure and assured us she had only fainted.

"Mossie, don't scare me like that every again." Maude hugged her and glared at me. "See what all this nonsense has done. You'll just have to forget the notion of Conner Montgomery."

"Like you try to forget what tore this family apart?" I retorted.

"Madison." Mom shook her head. "While I don't begin to agree with Maude and Mossie on this matter, you need to keep calm and not lash out at them in public."

In public.

Of course. That is why Maude brought the matter up again. She knew if she did so here in the tea room then I couldn't make a fuss. Or storm out of the room. It would not be good form to make a scene in public.

While I didn't doubt that Mossie had fainted at the tea room, I wouldn't put it past the two of them to try to manipulate the situation in their favor because of it. The car ride back to River Road was quiet. Mom tried a few times to start a conversation, but neither Maude nor Mossie said more than yes or no in reply. Were they sulking?

"I'm sorry," I finally said. "I shouldn't have said what I did. But you must realize that Conner means everything to me and I do not like you putting him down. We've grown extremely close in the last few weeks."

Mossie began fanning herself with her lace handkerchief.

"I hope you have not become *that* close," Maude quipped.

"I will not sit here and listen while you insinuate that my daughter doesn't know how to behave with a young man. Isn't it bad enough that you convinced the sheriff that Conner did something vile to Madison the night we couldn't find her? It's almost as if you derive joy in the thought of it."

"Now, Hope, dear, you misunderstand me," Maude said, changing the tone of her voice.

"No. Don't try and candy-coat your words and thoughts. I'm sure this is exactly what caused grandfather to dislike Edward."

I quickly looked at my mother and realized what she was saying. Is that why she had been so quiet? Had she gone through the same type of insurrection when she began seeing my father? Had Maude and Mossie been opposed to her relationship as well? Had all of this discussion brought back memories she would have rather kept out of her mind?

The car became quiet as Godrey turned into the winding drive and as soon as he stopped the car, my mother got out, not waiting for him to come around to open the car door for her. She didn't wait for us as she headed into the house either. I took my shoe box and hurried after her into the house and up the stairs.

I found her in my room standing at the bay window, staring down into the garden. I put my new box of shoes in my closet, but she still didn't acknowledge my presence. It wasn't until after I went into the bathroom and splashed cool water on my face that she spoke.

"Close the bedroom door, Madison."

I did as she asked and then went to the settee, hoping she'd join me. I watched her shoulders shaking and the slight movement of her arms told me she was wringing her hands.

"I'm sorry." I didn't know what else to say, but if I had done something to upset her on top of Maude and Mossie, then I wanted her to know I didn't mean it.

"It isn't your fault, honey." She turned and I saw moisture glistening on her cheeks. "It isn't even my fault for falling in love with your father. He was a very respectable man. I want you never to forget that, no matter what you learn from this visit. Edward Franklin's only fault was where he came from and even that isn't a sin in the eyes of God. We all cannot live in the low country. We all cannot be a part of the same society. And we certainly cannot all have money.

It's a damnable crime for money to do this to people."

I listened and tried to fit this information into the holes in my jumbled puzzle. It was suddenly taking shape and I regretted the fact that it was causing so much pain for us all. Maybe we would have been better off if we just forgot about the past.

"I know what you are thinking. It's written all over you face. But you are not to blame for coming here. You wanted answers and we couldn't go on trying to forget about the problem within this family. I think Maude and Mossie knew that when they wrote to you, but they weren't ready to admit to it either. So it is time to face the truth. I see that now. I was wrong in trying to protect you from the family. You were right to search for the answers. If we cannot solve the problems within our family together, then how can we expect society as a whole to solve the problems of the world?"

My mother was right. Future generations of our family were depending on us to straighten things out in our lifetime. If we didn't, then their lives would forever be affected by it. And, I was the sole heir to bring those generations into being. Whatever I decided to do with my life would affect us all. That was a heavy burden for me to carry. Was that the burden Mossie and Maude were referring to on my first night here?

My mother and I stayed in my room for the rest of the evening talking. Bea brought us up dinner trays and we ate while we discussed how I should wear my hair to the Fourth of July ball. We also talked about the possibility that I would become Mrs. Conner Montgomery and how I shouldn't allow Maude and Mossie to sway me. My mother supported me, and she'd support my decision to marry Conner even if they didn't.

I left her sitting on my bed looking at my sketch book while I went to take a bath. When I returned, she was staring at one of the many sketches I had done of Conner. "These are very good, Madison. You have captured him perfectly. Have you ever thought of trying to paint his portrait?"

"No, I haven't. I've never worked with acrylics. I'm not sure I'd be any good at it."

She stood up and walked to the door. "What are your plans for the future? Have you given it any thought? What might you do if you do not marry Conner right now?"

"I—I've thought about art school and Conner said he'd support my decision to go even if we were married."

Mom smiled. "And what are your feelings on the proposal today?"

"I'm leaning towards yes. The more I think about it, the more I think I'd be very happy spending my life with Conner."

"Why do you suppose you are hesitant?"

"It's a big decision. I don't want to rush into it and regret it later."

"Marriage is a two-person partnership. You have to give and Conner has to give. You work together, you talk it out. If it begins to feel like a tug of war, then something isn't right. Good night."

"Night." I turned down my bed and got under the coverlet, thinking about what she had said. I also considered what she had said during her outburst in the car. The more I learned from listening, the more I was beginning to suspect that my mother knew more about the family secret than she let on. It sounded as if her marriage to my father was the final thread that ripped the Madison branch from the Wyndam family tree in my great-grandfather's book.

This realization left me sad. I reached to turn off the bedside lamp and closed my eyes.

The next morning I had breakfast with my mother down in the gazebo. It was a beautiful late June morning and a cool breeze blew, keeping away the heat. "You've been awfully quiet since we came down here," my mother said, watching me push my fruit around in the bowl. "Do you want to tell me what is on your mind?"

"Nothing really. I've just been thinking. Do you

suppose father would have liked Conner?"

"I see. I can't speak for him of course, but knowing the qualities in a person that your father liked I'd have to say yes, I do believe he would."

"Really?"

She nodded. "And you know what else?"

"What?"

"He'd want to know what you're waiting for. Your father was a strong believer in seizing the day."

I smiled. Yes, he did believe in that. "I'm going to see Conner later this morning."

"Good. I have one other piece of advice for you. Always remember you're not living your life to please the Wyndams. You're living your life to make you happy. Happiness is all you should worry about, Madison, even if it does give others a few ulcers in the process. My mother told me the same thing when your father asked me to marry him despite how grandfather felt. We had twenty good years together. That was sixteen more than my mother had with my father. We aren't promised long lives so we need to live every day like it's our last. If you love Conner and he loves you and you feel he is the one to make you happy, then it's as simple as that. Marry the boy."

I took a deep breath, not sure I should ask the question that was eating at me, but decided to take a page out of my father's book and seize the opportunity. "How did great-grandfather feel about my father?"

Mom exhaled deeply and squeezed my hand. "Your great-grandfather didn't like the fact that your father wasn't from Charleston. He had a bias against anyone who wasn't from the low-country, but he wasn't alone in this opinion. Many from the low-country look down their noses at folks from the up-country. It also didn't help that your father's great uncle served under your great-grandfather in the war."

"I read about the difference of opinions between those from the up and low country in his journal."

"And really your great-grandfather may not have been so opposed to him if I had been more accepting of his criticism. Like most men of his generation, he believed young women should attend a finishing school or pursue the arts instead of extending their education. So we butted heads when I chose to go to the university instead of an art school."

"And what did you mean yesterday when you told Aunt Maude that you were certain she'd swayed great-grandfather's opinion of my dad?"

Mom's cheeks flushed. "I'm sorry, darling, I'm afraid I wasn't being a good role model for you yesterday. I chastised you for letting them rile you up and there I went and did the same thing."

"It's easy to do."

"But I shouldn't have let them get to me like that. Maude has always been a stickler for being prim and proper. And being a spinster didn't help that cause any. She would watch me like a hawk whenever mom and I visited as if she expected the worst behavior possible from me. And I always felt she told grandfather things in private about me that caused problems for my mom. I also strongly believe she told him things about Edward that weren't always true. So when she made that comment about how close you and Conner had gotten I—I couldn't stop from saying something."

"I understand. Believe me I understand. It's maddening the way Maude and Mossie can needle your nerves."

"Yes, it is. Now finish eating so you can go see Conner. I'm sure he is anxious to talk to you again."

I finished my fruit and then set out on my walk to the Montgomery House. Traveling the well-worn path, I saw gardeners working on landscapes and a few of the neighbors taking in the early morning by sitting in their yards. A few waved since they had become accustomed to seeing me and Conner traveling this way often. No one seemed to mind us cutting across their property, and it made me wonder why Conner had been so certain Aunt Maude and Mossie would have objected to my trespassing in their garden when we'd first met. Unless they'd caught him before...was that the reason he was hesitant to be seen there? Hmmm...was that also one of the reasons that they objected to my friendship with him?

Duncan met me on the path with a lovely bouquet of wild flowers. He was dressed in a white suit with a vibrant colored tie and a white hat on his head. He raised it slightly as we came closer to one another.

"Good morning, Madison."

"Good morning, Duncan. Is Conner at home?" I asked.

"Up and gone already this morning. He said he has things to do today. He took his roadster."

"Oh. I see."

"Now. Now. Don't look so long in the face. I'm sure if you go on to the house, he will return shortly."

I tried smiling, but the thought of idly waiting around for him to return started butterflies going crazy in my stomach. "Couldn't I just walk with you?"

Duncan shrugged. "Suit yourself, but I'm heading to Wyndam House."

"You are?" I glanced at the flowers clutched in his hand. "Are those for anyone I know?"

He smiled and he began to walk again. "Maybe."

"She isn't as difficult as she appears," I assured falling into step beside him. "It's more of a protective barrier that you have to get around."

"Is that so?" He glanced at me sideways. "You speak as if from experience."

I nodded. "I've had my bouts with her since coming to visit. You saw how she was the morning she found me in the kitchen with Conner and how she overreacted when I was missing. But underneath it all, she is loveable if she'll only let you in to love her."

"Has she finally told you what in tarnation

happened in the family all those years ago?"

"No."

"Stubborn woman." He shook his head. "It isn't my place to speak ill of people, but don't you get the feeling that they thrive on secrecy? It's as if they cannot go on living if the truth is known."

"I've felt the same way at times, but I believe I'm getting closer to finding out the truth. I fear it has much to do with my father. Apparently, great-grandfather didn't approve of him marrying my mother."

"Ah, yes. I remember the stink that was raised when he found out about their wedding." He pushed a limb back for me to pass ahead of him. "It was a shame too. Your mother was the nicest young woman. And you are just like her. Too bad I'm old enough to be your grandfather or I'd give Conner a run at courting you."

"Duncan!"

He laughed with a gleam in his eye. "Have you learned anything else?"

"Nothing that makes much difference to what I already know."

"Too bad because I was hoping that you'd discovered that the answer to the questions were right under your nose all along." He plucked a daisy from the bunch of wildflowers and gave it to me.

I stood smelling the flower while he crossed the arched bridge and climbed the stone steps up to the house. Were the answers to my questions already known, but I couldn't see them? I didn't think so. There seemed to be a big spot in the puzzle missing pieces.

Retracing my steps back along the path to Montgomery House, I thought about my great-grandfather's journal. He'd not been happy about being an officer in the war and he didn't feel he was doing the job his position required. He'd become annoyed with his fellow officers for ragging him about a particular man from the up-country who had the leadership skills he felt he lacked. Had that man been my father's great uncle? He didn't name names in his writings, but it'd be nice to know the identity of the man.

Mom had said many low-country folk disliked up-country folk so maybe great-grandfather's reasonings had nothing to do with a specific individual but a community as a whole. And if that was the case then how did one go around disliking others? It didn't make sense. None of this made sense.

I picked off a petal from the daisy thinking about what Duncan had said about my great-grandfather struggling after the war to prevent his name and family standing from slipping from the realm of those accepted in Charleston society. So did that mean when my mother married my father, he felt the Wyndam blood line had been tainted? Is that the reason he had disassociated himself with them? Is that the reason he didn't want me in his life?

My heart pounded within my chest, and I stopped in the shade of some trees where the neighbors had been sitting earlier. My legs seemed wobbly for a moment, and I wondered if I had finally figured it out. Was this the reason great-grandfather refused to let me sit on his lap at my grandmother's funeral? Had he feared touching me would make me real to him? But keeping me at a distance made it easier to pretend I didn't exist?

Absently I plucked the rest of the petals off the daisy until all was left was the stem. I tossed it to the side and stood once more forcing my legs to make it the rest of the distance to Montgomery House.

The sun was high up in the sky and beating down on my head by now, and I thought about detouring down to the Ashley for a swim. A cool dip in the running water would feel marvelous, but I didn't have a bathing suit or cap with me and the dress I wore was rather new.

"Well now," Conrad Montgomery said, bringing me back to the present when I stepped out from the tree line. "You are the last person I thought I would see heading this way. Isn't Conner over at the garden with you?"

I shook my head and took a seat in the vacant chair beside him under the apple tree where he was sitting, drinking iced tea. "I was hoping Conner was here."

"You saw Duncan?"

"Yes. He was heading to see a special lady."

"What makes you say that?"

I shrugged. "He had a bouquet of wild flowers."

"Ah." He chuckled and set his glass on the small wooden table. "I hate to say it, but that man has lost his head if he thinks that Maude Wyndam, after all these years, will give him a second look. No offense intended."

"None taken. I agree. I think Duncan has his work cut out for him. Maude is not an easy woman. She's got a very protective shell built around her. Both of my great aunts do."

"Comes from the type of life they grew up in," Conrad agreed. "But if anyone can wheedle his way through it, my money is on Duncan."

"Just like he bribes the fish?"

His brows arched. "So you were down there listening to us the other day. I thought I caught a glimpse of you. Why didn't you come and join us?"

"I needed to be alone, to think."

He nodded. "Is everything going well with you now? Especially since your mother arrived?"

"Yes. She's making it easier to deal with Maude and Mossie and get to the bottom of the family secret. As for adjusting to living in Charleston, I think I'm making the transition just fine."

"Sounds like you won't be going back to Camden."

"No. I think I'll be staying on."

"Then you've decided?" Conner asked coming up behind me. I jumped at the sound of his voice having not heard the car pull up in the drive.

I turned around and smiled. "Maybe."

"That maybe doesn't sound so tentative."

"Oh? How does it sound?"

"More like a yes." He grinned.

"You've asked to take on a very difficult task."

"Is that so?" He came around and knelt before me, taking my hands in his.

Conrad gave us both curious looks, but didn't ask what we were talking about. He sipped his iced tea and enjoyed the small breeze that stirred underneath the apple trees.

Chapter Thirteen

Conner pulled me to my feet and excused us from his grandfather's presence, leading me to the back of the house where we entered the kitchen and then went into a lovely solarium filled with tropical plants and a running fountain in the center of the room. The solarium was quite cool and despite the condensation on the window panes, I noticed two ceiling fans moving slowly to circulate the air.

Conner led me over to an iron and wooden bench in front of the fountain and we sat down. I felt a little awkward because I knew he was waiting for my answer to his proposal, and even though I had made up my mind, I wasn't quite ready to give it to him for some reason.

He squeezed my hand and turned it over so the

palm was up and he began to trace my life line. "You see how this line connects with that line?"

I looked closely at the creases on my palm and nodded. I was curious to see what he had to say about the tiny scar I had gotten as a child climbing trees with my male cousins, but what he said I did not expect.

"That line is me. It's proof that we belong together, Madison." He pulled out a tiny box and opened it, showing off the sparkling diamond ring inside. "Tell me you'll be my wife."

My heart beat so loud I could hear and feel the pounding in my ears. I looked down at my hand, and the scar he'd pointed out to me. He was wrong. He wasn't that scar. He was what would make me whole.

"Yes. Yes, I'll marry you."

He pulled me in his arms and whooped so loud I thought the glass panes would shatter around us. He danced me across the solarium and back and I began to laugh.

I hugged him and when we pulled apart, he slipped the ring on my finger. "This belonged to my grandmother, Madison. She gave this to me before she died because she wanted me to give it to my bride."

"It's lovely and I will cherish wearing it."

He gave me a quick kiss and then shook his head. "I thought I was going to die waiting for you to give me an answer. What took you so long to decide?"

"I think when a girl makes a decision that will affect the rest of her life; she should be able to take time to consider the proposal. I never in my wildest dreams imagined when I came to Charleston that I would meet you. I didn't plan on falling in love." I looked into his shining cobalt eyes and a warm feeling flooded my stomach. I was melting within and he had no idea he was causing it.

I sucked in a deep breath and continued. "But falling in love is what I did and I didn't even know it was happening until you said those magic words to me. And then it was like a vapor had vanished, giving me clear sight at a new world—one with me and you in it."

I could tell by his reaction that I had caught him off guard, but that was okay. He'd done that to me already.

He pulled me into his arms and kissed me so deeply my legs almost buckled. "You don't know how happy you've made me."

"I think I do. You've been showing me here in the solarium how happy you are."

"Are you saying that's bad?"

"No, but will you still be happy if I ask you to accompany me to the Fourth of July Ball at Mayor Peterson's."

He laughed and backed away from me. "Don't tell me you've been invited? Of course you've been invited. Sonya Peterson wouldn't dare leave you off of the invitation list. You're a Wyndam after all."

I didn't like his tone or his reaction to my question.

"Don't you want to go with me?"

"I'd rather not." He pivoted, doing a one hundred and eighty turn on his heels. When he faced me again he was smiling. "But what better place for us to announce our engagement."

"No. That isn't the place at all for it."

"Why not? It will save us from having to hold a party of our own. One less fancy dress you'll have to buy. One less time I'll have to dress up in a suit and tie."

I frowned and crossed my arms over my chest. "I see you don't really want to go and that's fine. I'm sure I can get someone else to accompany me. Maude and Mossie really want me to ask Thomas Whitfield. I'm sure he'd be eager to escort me."

Conner looked aghast, and he placed his hands on my shoulders. "Over my dead body. I'll wear a suit and tie every day and walk through hot coals to keep you from asking that bore to anything."

"How'd you know he's a bore?" I relaxed my arms, curious if I had mentioned this to him. I didn't think I had.

"You forget, I've lived around here longer than you have." He pulled me gently into his embrace and kissed me tenderly. He ran his hands up and down my back, sending tingles in their wake.

"Conner." I pulled back and he moved his lips from my mouth to my neck, which sent shivers throughout my body. "Conner. You're going to have to stop this."

"Why? Are you afraid what might happen?"

"No. I'm more afraid of someone seeing us. We don't need vicious rumors spreading about us. Not after Maude called the police—"

"Sh-h-h. Say no more. Let's go to the parlor and listen to some music. Grandfather has a phonograph and I picked up a few records in town."

We walked into the parlor, and he sat me on the sofa before going to the phonograph and putting on a record I had never heard before.

Mossie loved Mozart and we listened often to her record after dinner, but this composer was nothing like Mozart. He had a sense of youth and the changing of times.

"Who is that?"

"George Gershwin." Conner sat on the sofa, wrapping his arm around me. I snuggled against him as we listened, wondering if this might be the way we'd spend our evenings together, listening to the phonograph.

Conner jumped up when the music ended and put on another record. When he came back he offered me his hand and before I knew it he had us waltzing to one of the songs and when another one came on with a tempo beat he sashayed us into the fox trot.

"You're a good dancer."

He winked at me. "You sound surprised."

"I'm not that good. I can fake it if my partner is a

strong lead."

"You're doing fine. Stick with me, kid, and you'll go far."

I laughed and he twirled me around under his arm, bringing me back against his body so I was facing away from him. He wrapped his arms around my waist, and we swayed to the music until the record ended.

He turned off the phonograph and put the record back in its protective sleeve. "So I assume this party at the mayor's is formal?"

"Yes."

"I was afraid of that."

"You've lived in town longer than I have so you should know all about it. There's a formal dinner as well, and there will be dancing and singing. Aunt Maude said there is always a top orchestra hired to perform. Everyone who is anyone will be there."

"That explains why I've never been invited. I'm not considered anyone."

"But you are to me."

He stepped over to the window, staring out over the lawn. "Have you mentioned my proposal to your mother?"

"Yes."

"And what was her reaction?" He quickly glanced at me.

"She approves, but she told me it was my decision and that I was the one who knew if accepting was right or not. And she told me that if my father was alive that he'd have only one thing to say about it."

He turned toward me. "And what is that?"

"What am I waiting for?"

His Cheshire cat grin spread across his face. "I think I'd have liked him very much."

"I think you would too." I took hold of his hand.

"I'm sure Maude and Mossie had plenty to say on the matter."

"Actually, I haven't told them yet. They're not important in my decision. Plus, with the Fourth of July ball invitation arriving, they've had plenty on their minds."

He shook his head. "But you're wrong, Madison. They're very important. If they do not approve, that could drive a bigger wedge within your family when you're working so hard to heal it."

"Maude and Mossie do not have to give their blessing. Only my mother does. And she has."

"No. It's important that they give it. Just like it's important that my parents give theirs."

I pursed my lips together. Would his parents object? Could they possibly oppose his marrying me?

Conner walked me home a few hours later, and we said good-bye in the garden at the arched bridge even though I tried to persuade him to stay for dinner. He wouldn't because he wanted to be officially invited by Maude and Mossie before coming to the house. It was important that he do things proper where they were concerned. So I watched him disappear in the trees on his way back to Montgomery House before I headed up the stone steps. I was almost to the house when I heard sobbing. At first I thought it was the squawking of the swans, but the longer I listened the more distinct the sound was that of someone crying.

I turned back toward the gazebo and found Maude's monogrammed lace handkerchief lying in the doorway. The crying became louder, and I searched the surroundings, looking for her. That's when I saw her graying head bent in the doorway on the opposite side. I hurried to her, thinking she had fallen, but found her sitting on the step.

"Aunt Maude?" I called softly not the startle her.

She looked mortified that I had found her crying. Quickly she wiped the moisture from her face with the hem of her dress before standing. "Madison, did you come looking for me, dear?"

"No. I was returning home from spending the day with Conner. I thought I heard crying and then I found your handkerchief." I handed it to her and noticed that Duncan's flowers were scattered around where she'd been sitting. Things obviously had not gone so well between them.

"Is there something I can do for you?" I asked,

wondering if she didn't feel confused by Duncan's attention and might like to talk about it.

Maude used her handkerchief to finish drying away any signs of her crying. "It's nothing, dear."

"Are you sure? It looks like you might have fallen while picking flowers."

Surprise was etched on her face for an instant but she recovered quickly, pressing her lips together. "No." With her curt response, she stood tall and stepped on the flowers as she went around the gazebo to the stone steps.

I followed her, choosing my steps carefully to avoid squashing Duncan's flowers more than she already had. Neither one of us said a word as we went up to the house. I kept my hands behind my back so she did not spot the ring Conner had given me. It would only upset her further if she did.

"Aunt Maude, did you happen to see Duncan Claiborne today?"

She stopped at the back door and glanced over her shoulder at me. "That man is a menace. I do not wish to ever hear his name mentioned in my presence again."

Amused by her indignation with him, I bit back a grin. He really was getting to her. "Then you did see him earlier?"

I could have sworn she grunted as she opened the door and let it snap shut behind her before I could enter the house. Chuckling, I opened the door and went inside, not surprised to find that Maude hadn't lingered. It was just as well because this gave me a chance to see if Bea had spotted the scene in the garden while she prepared dinner.

"Can I help?" I asked.

"You mean, can I help you."

She handed me the tray of linens, and I followed her into the dining room as she went to set the table.

"What exactly do you want to know? Or do I even have to ask?"

I shrugged and placed the napkins around the dishes she placed on the table. "Maude seemed rather upset. I was just wondering if you might have caught a glimpse of why."

Bea nodded her head. "Just like I always know what is going on with you, but do I tell? No. That information never leaves my lips."

I understood her clearly. "Thank you for that, Bea. But I want to help Aunt Maude if I can. Could you at least tell me if the situation looks promising, or does she need a bee in her bonnet?"

Bea grinned, planting her hands on her hips. "A hornet might be better to get the job done."

"Do you really think extreme measures are called for?"

"Yes. After all these years a cannon wouldn't hurt." She took the tray and went back to the kitchen.

A cannon. Yes, an explosion usually did cause people to sit up and take notice, but before that could happen there needed to be much ground work laid. And who better to help with the task than Mossie.

I went upstairs planning my strategy. I liked Duncan and if he saw something in Maude that attracted his eye, then why shouldn't he be given a fair chance to court her? She had lived her life alone in a large house with her sister and ailing father. Shouldn't she at least have a few years of happiness with a male companion?

I found my mother and Mossie on the second floor in the large room that had once served as a nursery and was now used solely for a library. They were going through the many volumes of books on the shelves and dusting them off.

"Father loved collecting the classics." Mossie ran her hand over the delicate leather binding of one of the books. "He said a war makes one cherish the antiquity of life. He never really cared about reading before the war, but afterwards, he spent many hours reading when he could find the time. Maude and I saved our money and bought him a book each year for his birthday. Millicent sketched and painted small portraits of him."

"Where are they?" My mom and Mossie jumped at the sound of my voice, not seeing me come into the room.

"Where are what, dear?" Mossie placed the book back on the shelf.

"The small sketches and portraits my grandmother made for her father."

Mossie smiled weakly. "Gone. Father destroyed those years ago in a fit of rage. He didn't want any reminders of the daughter he no longer had." She shook her head. "Of course he regretted doing so once Millicent was truly taken from us. He suffered greatly before he died. He called out for Millicent and mother to forgive him. It was sad watching him in agony, because he knew he'd never have their forgiveness."

Mom patted Mossie on the shoulder. "I wish there had been one or two that were overlooked. It would have been nice to have them now."

"Yes it would." Mossie put down her dusting rag and walked over to the bay window, sitting down. "Father was always diligent. If he was going to do something he did it right. He didn't leave loose ends to be tied later."

Hmmm…her opinion of him was far different than his opinion of himself. Obviously she hadn't read his journal about his time in the war.

"I think our lives are proof he knew how to tie things up in a knot."

They both looked at me shocked.

Mossie slowly nodded. "Yes, our lives are like a knot, but there is still a link to father that is unknown and will be told to you shortly. Your twenty-first birthday is in September, it is not?"

I nodded wondering what that had to do with anything. I looked at my mom and found she looked as perplexed as I felt.

"We shall celebrate it in style. You shall have the kind of party anyone of your station should have." Mossie rattled on, going over to the many volumes of books on the shelves and ran her hand over them until she came to one shelf in particular. She pushed on it, revealing a smaller chamber inside. She turned with a sly smile on her face and motioned for us to follow her.

My mother and I slowly followed her down the narrow corridor. I couldn't believe how mysterious Mossie was being at the moment and I could tell that my mother had never seen this kind of behavior from her aunt either.

"You must promise me that you will not let Maude know I showed you this," Mossie whispered. "This is father's private room. All of his valuables were kept here after the war. It's storage of his legacy now."

"Mossie, if this will upset Maude, do you really think you should be showing this to us without her approval?" My mother squeezed my hand as we walked to a closed door that Mossie slowly turned the handle to open.

"It's fine. Maude is too fragile right now. Besides, I'm the oldest. Father left me in charge. And I say it is time."

The door opened onto a room with a single

window that had a dark drape blocking the light. Mossie pulled it to one side and the room filled with the evening sunlight. The room was filled with trunks stacked upon trunks against one wall. More books lined a small shelf against the interior wall and fragile crystal and china were displayed in a glass cabinet. And then, my eyes caught sight of a portrait I'd never seen before, yet it was of me. It was of me as a young child sitting on a blanket at White Point Garden. So my great-grandfather had known what I looked like. He had kept a portrait that surely my grandmother had painted of me hidden away all these years.

"I always wondered what happened to this." My mother left me standing in the doorway and went over to the portrait. "Mother had been working on it before she became ill. She had planned on giving it to Madison on her birthday but she didn't live long after she started it. I assumed she'd been too ill to finish it once she came here."

"Your mother brought it with her and set up her easel in the library where she worked a few hours each day until it was completed. Father fell in love with it and insisted she allow him to keep it until he could give it to Madison himself."

"But he didn't!" Renewed anger and frustration with my great-grandfather boiled inside me. I couldn't believe that he'd kept yet another part of my grandmother from me all these years. She had painted this for me and he had selfishly kept it. I ran from the room, but not before I heard Mossie say, "Oh dear, I fear I have upset her."

"Madison. Madison, wait." Mom called following me back into the library. Mossie was a few steps behind her.

"Why did he hate me so much?" I cried.

"He didn't hate you, Madison. He loved you." Mossie put an arm around me. "I didn't mean to upset you, dear, but you must be satisfied in knowing that there are many treasures he left behind for you. It's his way of reaching out to you."

His way? His way was peculiar. His way made no sense except to make me angry and to hurt me deeper with each painful discovery. What good had his way produced?

I shook my head and stepped away from her, unable to bear having her touch me. "I don't care to know about these treasures. I don't want any part of him. Richard Wyndam has done nothing but cause me pain. I was wrong to want to know about the Wyndam side of the family. I shouldn't have wanted to go back into the past when the future is before me. My future with Conner is taking shape before your eyes and you don't even see it."

"Don't feel that way dear," Mossie attempted to touch me again, but I hurried out of the library to my room. I needed to be alone so I could sort things out.

Chapter Fourteen

Crying would not help anything. I knew that, but it sure made me feel better. I lay on my bed playing with my ring and bawled. I didn't know why I let this last bombshell bother me so bad, but it did. Everything I had learned about the family secret and my great-grandfather told me I shouldn't have expected any less from the man and his foolish pride.

Mossie claiming I shouldn't be upset because this was just her father's way didn't console me. But I couldn't expect her to feel differently. She'd worshipped the ground he walked on. It was clear by the way she would go on and on about things he said.

When my tears ran out, I got up and went into the bathroom, splashing cold water on my face. My eyes were red, but that was okay. I doubted Maude would notice since hers would be too. However, when I got down to the dining room it was only my mom and Mossie. Maude had asked for a tray to be brought to her room.

Dinner conversation was strained. Two or three times during the meal, Mossie would start to say something then think better of it and sigh heavily. Afterwards, she didn't retire to the parlor for dessert and music but instead went up to her room.

"Poor dear," Mom said. "You need to apologize to her, Madison. I know finding the portrait upset you. It upset me, but darling, Mossie is right. No one could change Richard Wyndam. He was set in his ways. And I'm sure when he told my mother he'd give you the painting himself, he meant it."

"Don't make excuses for him. He had more than enough time to do so."

"One would think, but his health began to fail shortly after mother passed."

I sat down on the sofa and she came to join me. "What are we going to do about Maude?"

"Nothing. She'll deal with it."

"Really? Do you think she's strong enough to do that? Look at what happened after they invited me to come visit. They apparently were resolved to tell me everything and Mossie objected. Maude followed her lead."

Mom placed her hand over my left one. "We have to trust this will be different."

"We need to help Duncan."

"No, we don't. We need to stay out of it."

I sighed.

"You don't like Maude and Mossie sticking their nose in your business. So show them the same courtesy."

"I get your point, but even if it is for Maude's own good?"

She chuckled. "We might think it is, but we can't be certain. Let her make her own decision."

"Okay."

"Now show me that ring you've been flashing about all evening."

My cheeks warmed and I pulled my hand out from under hers so she could have a better look. "It belonged to his grandmother. She gave it to him before she died so he could give it to his bride."

"Lovely." She pulled me to her and hugged me. "So it's really going to happen. My baby is getting married."

"We haven't discussed dates yet, but yes, I accepted his proposal today."

She released me. "We should celebrate. If we were at home, I'd invite Conner's family over, but we're here. And with how Maude is behaving…I don't know if that would be the best plan at the moment."

"Conner's family lives in Georgia so it may take some arranging to get them here."

"Then I shall write them and express how pleased I am about your engagement. Can you get me their address?"

"Yes."

"Good. I think we've all had enough excitement for one day. I'm going to retire for the evening."

"Good night."

She kissed me on the cheek before leaving me in the parlor alone. Even though I was tired, I wasn't ready for bed yet. I went over to the phonograph and searched through the record collection, but all I found was Mozart and a record of various classical composers. So I listened to a few songs before going to bed, determined to pick up a modern composer the next time we went into the city.

Maude kept to herself for the next few days. She stayed in her room for most of them, only coming downstairs for the evening meal and a short visit to the parlor before retreating back upstairs. I watched her closely and I sensed she was afraid, a behavior I had never seen or expected to see from her. This worried me greatly.

My mother assured me it wasn't anything unusual for Maude to become withdrawn. She'd seen it often in the summer whenever they visited Wyndam House when she was growing up.

"Mother and Mossie took Maude to see a doctor once and he diagnosed these spells as a result of the trauma she felt losing her mother during the war."

I wanted to protest that this spell wasn't about that but had been brought on by Duncan coming to call on her. I hadn't told my mother about finding Maude down at the gazebo crying or how Duncan's flowers were strewn on the ground and she'd purposely walked on them. He hadn't been back to visit either and that made me wonder if something had happened while he was here that day to cause her sudden withdrawal.

Determined to find out anything that could help Maude through this episode, I went to see Duncan. He was his usual self, greeting me before I reached where he sat whittling alone under the apple trees in the Montgomery yard.

"Well, Madison, what brings you out our way?"

"I wanted to see you. Is that all right?"

"Certainly. Have a seat. I'm afraid Conner isn't around. He took Conrad into Charleston."

"Oh? Is anything wrong? Conner told me Conrad preferred staying away from the city."

"True, but he has to see his doctor once a year. And today is the day."

I nodded, taking the empty chair beside Duncan. "How have you been the last few days?"

"Fine. What about you?"

"Good, but a little worried about Maude. She hasn't been herself."

He stopped whittling, his knife barely touching

the wood. "I hate to hear that."

"Did anything happen when you saw her the other day?"

He looked up at me, and I noticed he had a dark shadow around his eyes like he hadn't been sleeping well. "She was her usual curt self when I was there."

In other words she turned him down. Had she thrown his flowers on the ground in front of him? "I see."

"That woman can be insufferable." He went back to whittling.

"Yes she can. I'm sorry."

"All I asked is if we might have dinner one evening together or even lunch. But she said that was absurd. A woman at her age didn't do that and I shouldn't come sniffing around when she had nothing to offer."

"Sniffing around?" I almost laughed, but he stopped whittling again and looked at me.

"Companionship. Someone to talk to other than Conrad once in a while. That is all I wanted. I thought she would enjoy getting out of that house and to talk to someone other than Mossie."

"You're right. She does need to get away from home more often, but Mossie is not only her sister, but her dearest friend. Maybe she found your suggestion offensive, like you wanted to take her away from Mossie."

"Never. And if she thought that I'm sorry." He

resumed his whittling and we sat there in companionable silence for a while. I thought about the situation between them and tried to come up with a solution.

"I'll try to talk with her. I can't make any promises and my mother has warned me to stay out of it, but I did encourage you so I feel responsible for what happened."

"It isn't like there aren't other women in the area my age that are widowed whom I could spend time with," Duncan said. "But you've seen my collection in the shed. I like the peculiar, the unique. I'm not saying that is Maude, but she is different from other women her age. She's like a new flower about to bud and experience life. That makes me want to watch her experience it, protect her from being crushed."

I thought that was the sweetest thing in the world, him wanting to protect Maude. She needed someone to care for her in this world. She needed someone to be there if Mossie were to go before her. She needed to seize this opportunity before it passed her by. If only I could help make it happen for her.

"Then I'll do my best." I stood. "I better get back. Tell Conner I dropped by."

"I will."

The walk back to Wyndam House was delightful as usual. I always enjoyed walking the path and admiring the flowers that grew in the yards or the wooded area. When I entered the house, I stopped in the kitchen long enough to get a glass of water before heading upstairs. I was halfway up the winding staircase to see if Maude would see me when a knock came at the front door. I turned to come back down to get the door when Bea came from the dining room to answer it.

Thomas Whitfield waltzed into the foyer with a bouquet of roses in his hand, asking to see me. Bea turned and gave me a startled look as she announced my visitor. I swallowed hard; my pulse raced for a moment and I wished I'd gone on upstairs instead of waiting to see who was there.

"What on earth brings you by today, Mr. Whitfield?" I asked, trying to act pleased by the surprise.

"I hope you will forgive me for showing up here so unexpectedly, but I just returned to Charleston after a short trip abroad and my grandmother said I should come pay a visit." He pushed the flowers toward me.

"You really shouldn't have, but I'm sure Aunt Maude will adore these. Do thank your grandmother for us. We had no idea that word had spread about Aunt Maude being under the weather." I smelled the roses and handed them straight to Bea, giving her specific instructions to place them in water before taking them upstairs.

Bea gave a little nod. "Shall I bring tea to the parlor?"

I turned my attention back to Mr. Whitfield and

found him a little pink around the collar. "Would you like to have tea?"

He awkwardly nodded, watching after Bea who carried the flowers away.

I hid my smile, feeling awfully devilish and a little ashamed of my behavior as I led the way to the parlor. But I knew what his impromptu visit meant. Maude and Mossie had not called his grandmother back and informed her I would not be asking him to escort me to the mayor's ball. This would turn out to be an awkward visit for both of us.

I was grateful when he chose to sit in one of the cream colored Queen Anne chairs instead of on the sofa with me. He still looked puzzled by my sending his flowers off to Maude, but if I was going to pull this off, I didn't need to allow him a moment to regain his composure. He needed to stay off-guard if I was going to tell him I already had an escort without offending him.

"You said you just returned from a trip abroad? Was this a trip for business or pleasure?"

"Uh bus-plure," he mumbled tongue-tied. He flushed again, tugging at his shirt color. "A little of both. Grandmother has investments in England that I regularly check on. I enjoy the theatre so I spend my evenings there."

I nodded, thankful that Bea brought in the tea service. The last thing I wanted to hear was an updated recitation of his grandmother's finances.

"Thank you, Bea." She set the tea on the small coffee table and poured us each a cup.

"Will there be anything else?" she asked.

I smiled at Thomas and looked at Bea. "Yes. Do not let me forget the time. I am to sit with Aunt Maude in twenty minutes."

She nodded, her brows arched, before she left the room.

"Is your aunt terribly ill?" Thomas asked.

"Not in body. I think it is more a matter of the soul. She just isn't herself lately. That is why I was surprised when you showed up with the bouquet of her favorite flowers. I didn't realize Mossie had spoken to your grandmother about Maude. Do thank her again for the flowers."

Thomas nodded, clearing his throat and adjusting his tie as if he wanted to correct my misunderstanding. "I hope your aunt recovers soon. The Mayor's ball is approaching. Everyone who is anyone will be invited. You did receive an invitation, didn't you?"

"Oh yes." I dropped a sugar cube into my cup of tea and stirred it before taking a sip. "And I have had the best fortune in finding a suitable escort for the evening. Have you also had the same fortune?"

Thomas paled and looked across the room. He nervously popped his knuckles, a trait I was certain vanished in men of his character at an early age.

"No. Not yet. My trip has prevented me in making my request with haste." He glanced back at me and smiled. His eyes lingered on me before quickly looking away. "Do forgive me, Madison, but I must be going." He stood abruptly not even touching his tea. "I just remembered an appointment that I made before leaving for England. I can't believe it completely slipped my mind."

I set my cup of tea down and stood. "Of course." I shook his hand and walked him to the door where we exchanged parting pleasantries that I doubted he meant.

When I closed the door and turned around, I found Bea giving me an amazed look.

"You handled that like a professional actress, Miss. Have you ever thought of performing on stage?" Bea clapped her hands quietly.

I sighed, finding it hard to believe that I had actually prevented him from asking me to the ball. "I was rather spectacular, if I do say so." I laughed and Bea joined me, but we quickly sobered as if on the same way length.

"My aunts must never know. They would have coronaries if they learned of my behavior because of their friendship with Mr. Whitfield's grandmother."

"Of course, Miss. I won't say anything." She nodded and looked at the grandfather clock in the foyer. "Miss, it's time to sit with Maude."

I looked at the clock as well. "Indeed it is."

Aunt Maude welcomed me when I knocked on her door and I could tell that whatever had been bothering her wasn't weighing as heavily on her mind by her smile. The flowers I'd sent up were sitting on the little table in the sitting area of her room.

"How are you, Madison?" she asked, not bothering to get up from her rocking chair.

"I'm good. Do you like your flowers?"

"Oh they are lovely. Wasn't it so nice of Anna to send Thomas over with them? He's quite the gentleman, don't you agree? Such class. That's the type of young man you should be looking for."

"Conner is a gentleman."

"If you say so, dear."

I let her comment slide by. I hadn't come to argue with her. "I wanted to check in and see how you are feeling today. I went for a walk this morning and saw Duncan Claiborne."

"You did?"

"Yes. He was looking fit as a fiddle. He asked about you."

"He did?" She stopped rocking.

I nodded. knowing he'd only done so because I had brought her up, but Maude didn't need to know that. "He's a very nice man. Don't you agree?"

Maude didn't get to respond because Mossie came shuffling quickly into the room with a letter.

"Can you leave us, Madison? I need to talk to

Maude," she insisted.

"Of course." I left the room wondering what on earth could have been so important or private that they needed to meet in secret. I went to my room to collect my journal and colored pencil box before going down to the garden. I had stopped in the kitchen for a sandwich when my mother came in.

"Madison, there you are."

She wore a frown and I wondered if she'd overheard me in the parlor with Thomas Whitfield or if she'd walked by Maude's room and heard me mention Duncan Claiborne. In either case she'd most likely not be pleased by my behavior.

"Is something wrong?"

"I'm still waiting on an address so I can mail my letter to Conner's parents in Georgia. Have you gotten it yet?"

"I'm afraid not. He wasn't at home this morning when I walked over. He'd taken his grandfather to the doctor."

"Oh? I hope Conrad isn't ill."

"Duncan said it was an annual appointment. I'll go over again this afternoon if I don't see Conner soon."

"That may have to wait. The seamstress called earlier, and she has sketches for us to look at as well as a dress for you to try on for the fourth of July. I told her we'd drive to town this afternoon. So after you eat go freshen up, and I'll let Maude and Mossie know we'll be going to the city today."

"Okay."

"I just wish you and Conner had set a date so we'd have a time frame of when we'll need the wedding dress to tell the seamstress. We also need to consider when we should announce your engagement and how to handle that."

"Conner wants to do it at the mayor's ball."

"No. You can't do that. It would be seen as bad form. You don't announce something like this at another's party. If you don't want to make a big fuss, then we can take care of it easy enough and in an acceptable way. You and Conner need to have your photo taken together and we'll have a write up in the society pages. I'll call the paper and see if the society reporter and a cameraman can drop by one afternoon soon to take care of it."

"The society pages. I don't know if Conner will like it, but he doesn't want a big party either. I'll talk to him about it."

"You need to do it soon if you are going to be wearing that ring. Someone is bound to notice sooner than later."

She was right. There were details we needed to take care of about our engagement. Conner would have to accept it being a big deal; after all, he was going to marry into the Wyndam family.

I finished my lunch and went into the little nook off from the foyer where the telephone extension was located. I asked the operator to be connected to the Montgomery extension and soon I heard ringing on the line, but no one answered on the other end. I thanked the operator and hurried upstairs to get ready for our visit to town. When I came back down, my mother was putting on her hat.

"Can we drop by the Montgomery's? No one answered when I called, but they could be outside. Both Conrad and Duncan enjoy spending their days outdoors. I don't think they keep a live-in housekeeper, but someone who comes once a week. At least I've never seen one there when I've been to visit."

"Certainly. And I can get the address I need."

So we left, leaving Maude and Mossie behind. They didn't seem at all interested in my dress for the mayor's ball, not after that letter arrived. I wondered what could have been in that letter to have them both locked in Maude's room.

Godfrey took us down River Road to the Montgomery's, and he appeared happy to have something to do with his afternoon. It had to be a lonely job waiting around for Maude and Mossie to go somewhere. Since I'd come to Wyndam House, I noticed he washed and waxed the car at least once a week, if not twice. And the chrome shined brighter than a new nickel whenever he finished. Yet most days the car sat in the garage with the door down, and Godfrey sat at the window of his room above, reading a book.

Some liked to read, but I found his job boring and if it was up to me I'd find something for him to do around the place other than drive a car that went nowhere most of the time.

I leaned toward my mom and whispered. "What do you know about the driver?"

She glanced at me with a puzzled look. "Why do you ask?"

I shrugged. "He has a boring job. He gets paid to do nothing."

"Oh." Mom nodded and smiled. "He does more than you know."

He did? Hmmm...she didn't say more on the matter and I really wondered what he did that wasn't obvious. I planned to ask her when we were not in his presence.

Soon he pulled the car into the long drive leading up to the Montgomery House. Before we pulled to a stop I saw Duncan, Conrad, and Conner sitting under the apple trees, but they weren't alone. A man and a woman were there and an unfamiliar car was parked in the drive.

"Looks like they have company. Maybe we shouldn't intrude," mom said.

"We can't not stop. Conner has seen us and is waving."

By the time Godfrey stopped the car and got out to open the door, Conner had crossed the lawn to greet us.

"Madison, Mrs. Franklin. I'm so glad you came over. I called, but Bea said you'd left to run an errand," Conner said.

"Really? We must have just left then because I tried calling here but no one answered," I explained, taking his hand. "How was your grandfather's doctor appointment?"

"Fine. He said he should live a nice, healthy life. Just keep doing what he's doing."

"What's that? Enjoying his days, taking it easy?"

Conner nodded.

"I see you have company. We don't want to intrude," Mom said.

"Company? No. Well, yes, but not really." Conner grinned. "That's my parents."

"Your parents?" I looked at mom. "Looks like you won't have to send that letter after all. I've been supposed to get their address from you, but I keep forgetting."

"I wanted to write to tell them how pleased I am about your engagement."

"Good thing you didn't because I haven't told them yet. Come on and I'll introduce you and we can tell them together."

We crossed the lawn with him, and the men stood when he reached the apple trees. His father, a tall man like himself, had a darker shade of blond hair, but they shared the same cobalt blue eyes. Mr. Montgomery looked shocked when he saw us approach and he came forward.

"Hope? Hope Madison, is that you?"

My mom stopped walking and looked a little stunned. "Seth Montgomery?" She blinked and shook her head. "I should have realized Conrad was your father. How have you been?"

I looked at Conner but he was staring at his father. It really wasn't at all surprising that our parents would have known one another from their youth. I thought this was a good thing, but the frown on Conner's face told me he didn't.

"I've been good. And you?" His dad reached us and shook my mom's hand. "How long has it been?"

"More than twenty years I know."

"You two know one another?" Conner finally asked.

His father grinned and I saw the same dimple as Conner had in his cheek. "One summer when we were…sixteen… I guess?"

Mom nodded. "You ran around with Buddy Jacobs that summer. He was a trouble maker."

"Yes, that's right. And you brought a friend from the city out with you. What was her name?"

"Ellen Barnard. She came out for my summer visit that year. Goodness. I haven't thought about that summer in years."

Conner's mom came over and protectively wrapped her arm through her husband's. She had shoulder length brown hair with a slight curl to it and brown eyes, a pleasant smile. Immediately, she extended her other hand to my mom. "I'm Irene Montgomery."

Mom shook her hand. "It's a pleasure to meet you, Irene. I was just telling Conner that I had wanted to get your address to write you both a letter, and here you are."

"Why?" Irene asked.

"Mom, dad, this is Madison Franklin. I've asked her to marry me."

His parents looked stunned by the announcement, but Conrad and Duncan eagerly came over, hugging us and giving their approval.

"Married?" Seth said, looking from my mom back to me and then at Conner. "How long have you two known one another? You just returned from the South Pacific after you ran off and joined the war. Now you say you're getting married?"

Conner's mother smiled at me, but I felt her eyes as they slowly looked me up and down. "You are a pretty little thing to have caught my boy's eye."

"I know this must seem so sudden," mom said. "But if there is one thing about love, it happens when you least expect it."

"Exactly." Irene let go of her husband's arm. "Look at Romeo and Juliet. No shorter courtship could there have ever been."

"That's Shakespeare, Irene. Not real life." Seth frowned and I didn't like his tone. It made me wonder if he spoke to his wife like that often in public or worse in private. "Do you want our son marrying a Wyndam?"

"A Wyndam? Is that who you are, dear?" Irene cooed, stepping closer to give me a hug. "If Conner loves you then I'm sure I'll love you too. Don't pay Seth any mind. He gets his temper from his mother's side of the family. She was Scottish."

"What is wrong with being a Wyndam?" Mom demanded. "You had no problem with it when we were teenagers. In fact, you were quite chummy with my grandfather as I recall that next summer."

Seth glared at my mom and she smiled. There was a story there. I just knew it, but Irene was saying something about my ring so I couldn't watch them.

"Have you set a date yet?" Irene asked.

"Not yet. That was something else I wanted to talk to Conner about today."

"Long engagements are best," Seth said, going back to where Duncan and Conrad were seated under the trees.

Irene shook her head and laughed. "Don't listen to him. I had the hardest time getting him to settle on a date. But you know, now that we've had the World War, I say why wait? We don't know what tomorrow will bring."

"That is so true," mom chimed in. "However, Madison is a Wyndam and I would suggest at least a six-month to a year engagement period to keep the gossips at bay."

Conner's mom nodded. "So true. It would never do for folks to think our babies are in the family way before they married."

"But we aren't." I felt my face warm.

"No one is saying you are, but gossips might." Irene placed her hands on Conner's cheeks. "I couldn't be happier, precious."

"Thanks mom."

"Don't just stand there, Irene, invite the ladies over to have a seat," Conrad called. "Conner, go get a few more chairs from the shed."

"Thank you, Mr. Montgomery, but I'm afraid we can't stay. We were on our way to the city for Madison to try on her dress for the mayor's ball. But I would love to have more time to visit with you. How about we plan on a dinner at the house tomorrow night?" Mom suggested. "That includes you, Mr. Claiborne. I won't take no for an answer. I'm sure Aunt Maude and Mossie will love meeting Irene and Seth."

"Are those aunts of yours still living?" Seth asked.

"Yes. My grandfather just recently passed."

Seth nodded. "I remember father telling me about that. We'd love to come to dinner."

"Excellent. We'll be expecting you around seven tomorrow evening then." Mom opened up her purse and took out the letter she'd written and handed it to Irene. "I really am happy that Madison has met Conner."

Mom and I said a quick goodbye and Conner walked halfway back to the car with us before we parted ways.

"I'll see you later tonight in the garden," he whispered before running back to his family.

The fitting with the seamstress went well. The dress she'd created for me fit like a glove and the pale pink material made my skin look sun kissed even though I hadn't spent hours in the sun. I was certain I could shimmy and shake doing the latest dance moves with ease. The sketches of the wedding dresses she'd drawn for me were wonderful. And each showed a different outcome for the basic dress to give me more options once I set a date.

"You'll need to come back by the first of next week so we can do the final fitting and then your dress will be ready for the party. And perhaps you'll have set a date by then?" The seamstress said walking us to the door.

"Perhaps." I thanked her for the lovely dress ideas and we left.

Mom and I had gone only a short way down the street when we ran into her friend Ellen Tidsdale coming out of the tea room with a few other ladies.

"Hope. It's so lovely to run into you and Madison.

If I'd known you were in town I would have invited you to have tea with us. Ladies, this is Hope Franklin and her daughter Madison. They're in town visiting family for the summer. Hope, this is Shelbie Humphries and Joy Clymer."

"Nice to meet you both."

Mom shook both their hands and I nodded back when they acknowledged me. They exchanged what I considered polite chit chat with us before excusing themselves to run errands before heading home for the day. Ellen stayed with us and we walked down the street toward where the driver waited with the car.

"You'll never believe who is in town," mom said.

"Who?"

"Do you remember Seth Montgomery? We ran around with him and Buddy Jacobs that summer you came to Wyndam House when we were sixteen."

Ellen stopped walking and looked pale, turning a little green around her mouth. Then she laughed, shaking her head. "No. I'm afraid I don't."

"Really? He remembered you."

"How odd, but I don't remember lots about my childhood. Mother talks about it often and I can't seem to remember." She began to walk slowly and I watched her, certain she was lying. Why else would she have paled at the mention of Conner's father?

If my mom noticed she didn't show it. In fact, she shocked me when she invited Ellen and her husband to join us for dinner the following evening.

"I'd love to, but Harold is out of town on business and I don't like to leave mother alone for very long in the evenings. She gets so forgetful these days."

"Bring her with you," mom insisted. "I know Maude and Mossie would enjoy visiting with her. We're eating at seven sharp. You do remember how to get to the house don't you?"

Ellen nodded. "If not, I'm sure everyone on River Road knows where the Wyndams live."

"Good. We'll see you then."

Mom and I waved and headed to the car. Godfrey stood outside the car waiting for us and opened the door, closing it once we were inside.

"Do you think Maude and Mossie will be cross with us for inviting so many people to dinner without checking with them first?" I asked.

"No. After all, didn't they say they wanted us to feel like Wyndam House is our home?"

Mom had a point. But I had a funny feeling Maude and Mossie wouldn't see it that way.

Chapter Fifteen

When we pulled up into the driveway at Wyndam House, there was an unfamiliar blue Model T touring car parked under the portico. A man dressed in a dark business suit came out the front door and tipped his hat when Godfrey let us out of the car. Mom frowned.

"I've seen that man before."

"You have?"

She nodded and hurried on into the house. I followed her into the parlor where Maude and Mossie were sitting with the remains of tea.

"Who was that man leaving here?"

Mossie stood with her hands clasped in front of her. "A business associate of father's. Why dear?"

"Because I know I have seen him before. In fact, I'm certain he's been in Camden more than once." Mom removed her hat and gloves, sitting down in one of the armchairs. "Now that I think of it, he's been in the store where I worked a few times."

"Worked?" I asked.

She looked up at me and smiled weakly. "Don't worry. I'll find another job once I go back to Camden. I didn't know how long I'd be visiting and my boss felt it was best to give notice. He'll hire me back if he can when I return, but if he can't I'm sure I can find something."

"This is my fault. I should have returned home instead of you following me here."

"No it's not." Mom touched my arm giving a little squeeze. "I needed to come here."

"And we're so glad you did," Mossie added.

"Then tell me who that man was?" Mother insisted. "Grandfather didn't have business associates. He hired people to do things for him."

"Yes, he did." Maude poured more tea in her cup. "And if you must know that man was a private investigator."

Mom stood up. "A private investigator? And he was in Camden watching me?"

"Not just you dear. He watched Millicent for father after Ronald died. And he went to Camden on occasion to check on you after Edward passed. Father, Mossie and I wanted to know everything was going well."

My mind raced back to those wonderful letters they would send when we were at our lowest. It seemed like divine intervention and yet it was really only because they'd hired a man to keep an eye on us. Mom must have thought the same thing because her back stiffened.

"How could you?"

"We didn't mean any harm, Hope," Mossie said taking a step toward her. "Really. All we wanted was to know you and Madison were doing well. And if you weren't then we tried to do something to help."

"Help? You mean you interjected yourselves into our lives. I should have known that bonus I received at work wasn't for being a great employee. You sent money to my boss to give to me, didn't you?"

"What if we did? You needed it. And you sure weren't going to ask for help. And we couldn't send you money. All we could do was send letters of comfort." Maude sat down her tea. "You survived, didn't you?"

"But I thought I was doing it on my own. Don't you get it? I thought Madison and I were standing on our own two feet."

"And you were, dear." Mossie reached out and patted her on the arm. "You were."

Mom turned away. I saw the hurt written all over her face. Maude and Mossie may not have intended harm by their actions, but they had taken away my mom's pride in being able to provide for me on her own. I hugged her and she wrapped her arms tightly around me.

"It's okay. You deserved a bonus for all you do. Does it really matter that it didn't come from your boss? I'm sure he would have given it if he could have afforded it."

"It's the principle." She cried into my shoulder and I patted her back. I could see nothing I said would make it any better. There was no excuse to take the sting out of what we'd just learned.

My mind went back to the fact that man was a private investigator. If mom and I were here with them, then what can they have needed that man to do? I released my mom and stepped to the side so I could look at my aunts.

"Why was that man here?" I asked. "Have you hired him for something?"

"If you must know we did." Maude looked me in the eye. "We asked him to investigate Conner Montgomery."

"Why?"

"Because there is too much we do not know about that boy. He's very aloof and if you are serious about having him in your life we wanted to know all there is about him."

Mom took a handkerchief from her purse and wiped her eyes, blowing her nose. "And what did you find out?" She turned around to look at them.

"That boy is a scamp," Mossie smiled. "Quite adorable. Acting like he has no care in the world."

I found her comment puzzling. "Is that good?"

"Of course it is, Madison. He's perfectly respectable. He stands to inherit Conrad Montgomery's estate when he passes. Far more money there than the Wyndams have."

My legs began to wobble at what she was saying. I didn't understand. Conner always talked about not caring about money. Mom sat me down in the arm chair and fanned me with her hat.

"But he doesn't care about money."

"It's easy to say that when you've got it," Maude said. "But we found out more than that in our investigation. While Conner is to inherit, his father isn't. Apparently Conrad wrote Seth Montgomery out of his will decades ago."

"Oh?" Mom said. "How did you learn this? Aren't wills sealed until after the person is deceased?"

"Yes, but you see, Seth has a friend who works at the county courthouse where the will was filed. He informed him about changes being made and that's when Seth petitioned the court to have his father declared...well...you know." Mossie looked uncomfortable. "Most of it was hearsay anyway."

"We've asked for more information on the matter," Maude said.

"You shouldn't. That's prying." I didn't want them sticking their nose in where it didn't belong. It was Conrad's choice who he left his estate to, not ours. And I didn't want to not like Conner's father before I even got to know him.

"We have a right to know why Seth Montgomery has been disinherited. He'll be your father-in-law if you decide to marry Conner."

"He seemed perfectly fine to me," I said. recalling how I didn't care for his temper or the way he spoke to Irene. And then the way Ellen Tidsdale reacted to the mention of his name this afternoon made me wonder what on earth had gone on between them when they were younger. Maybe poking into his past wouldn't hurt.

"You've met him?" Maude asked.

I nodded. "This afternoon. Mom invited them to dinner tomorrow night."

"I hope you don't object. I thought it would be nice to have dinner and get to know Conner's parents while they are in town. I included Conrad and Duncan Claiborne as well. Oh and while we were in Charleston, we ran into my old friend Ellen Barnard. She's a Tidsdale now and I included her and her mother. Her husband is out of town."

"Well, that is a large party, but I'm sure Bea can add a few courses to the menu and do a respectable meal. I better go inform her." Maude hurried from the room.

Mom followed her out, saying how she'd be happy to help Bea cook.

Mossie smiled. "Did you get your dress for the mayor's party?"

"Not yet. There's one more fitting and then I can

bring it home. It's so pretty. The pale pink makes me look like I have a sun tan," I explained.

"Oh, how exciting. I can't wait to see you in it." Mossie motioned for me to follow her. "Did you notice how Maude didn't bat an eye when Hope mentioned including Duncan Claiborne in the dinner invitation. I think she's coming around."

"Maybe." I climbed the stairs behind her, stopping halfway up when she did.

"I'm sorry I upset you when I showed you the hidden room. I thought it would help you to see it, but I suppose Maude and I kept our distance from you far too long. We've made mistakes. Big ones. And we keep making mistakes where you are concerned, Maddy. For that I am terribly sorry."

When she talked like that I found it hard to be angry with her. And I wasn't surprised when she took me back into the library and opened the passage way in the wall again.

"Maude and I have agreed that you should have the portrait now. So if you'd like to take it to your room, feel free to do so. Also, there is something else we'd like for you to have. It belonged to Millicent."

She opened the door to her father's private room and showed me an old steamer trunk that sat in the corner of the room. There was a lock on it, but she had the key in her dress pocket and handed it to me. "Go on. Do the honors."

I knelt down and put the key in the lock, turning

it. Lifting the lid I found layers of tissue paper and when I removed them a delicate white dress. I looked up at Mossie and she was smiling with tears running down her cheeks.

"Is this her wedding dress?"

"Yes. Your mother eloped so she never got to wear it, but Millicent brought it here when she came home before she died with explicit instructions for us to give it to you upon your engagement. It's yours if you wish to wear it."

Mom obviously didn't know about the dress or she wouldn't have taken me to the seamstress to have one made. Now I really didn't know what to do. Wearing my grandmother's dress would make it feel like she was sharing the day with me.

I carefully lifted the dress out of the trunk and let it fall down in front of me. I turned around looking for a mirror, but there wasn't one. I carefully carried the dress to my room and Mossie followed close on my heels. Once there I stood in front of the cheval mirror and stared at my reflection, taking note of the scalloped bows about three inches from the hemline and the many gathers all the way up to the waistline. Unable to decide, I laid the wedding dress on the bed and slipped my day dress off before putting the other on. Mossie had to help me get it on since there were so many layers to the dress.

When we finished positioning me in the dress so the cascade of flowers from the right shoulder to the waist was in a diagonal, she made sure the bustle in the back was puffed enough. Then she placed the lace veil on my head securing the beaded comb into my hair correctly. Finally, I stepped in front of the mirror again. I couldn't believe how a simple dress…well there wasn't anything simple about this dress…could transform a plain girl like me into a princess. This had to be my wedding dress. It just had to be.

"Simply breathtaking. It's a little out dated, but I'm sure you could have the seamstress in town update it."

"I don't think there is anything out dated about it. It's perfect. And it fits like it was made for me."

"It should. It's a Worth all the way from Paris."

I'd heard that designer's name before and was impressed. I slowly turned to the side and looked at my reflection from over my shoulder. The only change would be the cascade of waxed flowers that could be updated to silk ones.

I heard mom and Maude coming upstairs so I picked up the shirt of the dress and rushed over to the door and out into the hallway, careful not to snag the train on the doorframe.

"What is this?" My mother said looking me up and down. "Where'd you get that dress?"

"It was Millicent's. She wanted Madison to have it." Maude smiled. "And we thought it was time she had it if she's talking about marrying that boy."

"I thought the dress was lost when she moved."

"What do you think?" I asked.

Mom smiled and touched my cheek with her hand. "I can tell you love it. And if this is what you want to wear I have no objection."

"It is. I'll have my grandmother's dress and Conner's grandmother's wedding ring. What more could make our wedding special?"

After dinner, while mom, Mossie and Maude picked out linens for dinner the next evening, I slipped out the back door and went to the garden to wait for Conner. It had been several days since we'd met in the garden after dinner, and I missed our time alone. I saw him before I even reached the gazebo. He was standing on the arched bridge tossing what looked like flower petals into the water.

The swans glided away as I approached and he turned, smiling at me. "Hi." We spoke at the same time. He opened his arms and I stepped into his embrace and he held me close.

"I've missed you," he said, softly against the top of my head.

"I've missed you. Did you know your parents were coming to visit?"

He let me go, stepping away and shook his head. "It was a surprise to us all. Grandfather and my dad don't actually get along most of the time. It's been years since they've seen one another."

"Oh?"

"I know. Small world, right? Here I've been pushing you to get the answers to the questions to make things right in your family when I've got something like this going on in mine."

"No family is perfect. I've seen that first hand, but what I do know is when a member needs help the others come together despite the problems."

He grinned, looking over his shoulder at me and stooped down to pick something up lying on the bridge. "I normally bring you flowers that I pick, but I hope you don't mind. I went into town and got these before coming over."

He handed me a large bouquet of yellow roses, jonquils, pink snapdragons and orange tiger lilies tied together with ribbon, lying in tissue paper.

"They're beautiful, Conner. Thank you."

"I thought they were too and since you are a 'pretty little thing' as mom called you, I thought you deserved them." He tipped my chin up with his bent finger and brushed his lips across mine.

"Do you think your parents liked me?"

He shrugged. "They didn't say they hated you. And they didn't try to talk me out of marrying you once you and your mom left."

"But would they with your grandfather and Duncan present? Your dad did seem opposed to the idea."

"Yeah, but he always reacts that way." Conner took my hand and led me over to the gazebo and we sat down in the doorway. "For years I'd do what he wanted when he opposed, but I realized he was controlling me that way. So when I decided to go to the war I didn't back down. I went anyway even though he objected. I'm not going to back down about you either."

"Good. Because I have my dress."

"You do?"

I nodded. "It belonged to my grandmother."

"Can I see it?"

"No. It's bad luck to see the dress before the wedding."

"Seriously?"

"Yes."

"Will you turn into a pumpkin if I do?"

I laughed. "No."

"Then what will happen if I see it?"

"I don't know. I just know you aren't supposed to."

"That's silly."

I shrugged, getting to my feet. "I better go in. See you tomorrow night. Thanks again for the flowers."

"Wait." He stood as well. "If you got your dress then we better set a date."

I really wasn't in a hurry to do that, but it wouldn't hurt to talk about it. And he was eager to do so, more than Irene said his father had been. "Do you want a long engagement?"

"Not really. What about you?"

"Mom said it would be expected for us to have at least a six-month engagement and that we need to announce it soon. She said we don't have to have a big party, but we could have a write up in the newspaper. And I'm sure if we do that, then we'll have to announce the date."

He nodded. "Christmas?"

I thought about that for a moment. It would be six months away, enough of an engagement period to suit folks. And grandmother's dress wasn't the type you'd wear in a garden setting, but a church filled with flowers and candles. I could already picture the ceremony in my head. I slowly nodded. "I think that would be perfect."

"Then the Saturday before Christmas." He pulled me into his arms and kissed me. I wrapped my arms around his neck and returned his kiss.

The Saturday before Christmas I'd be Mrs. Conner Montgomery.

Chapter Sixteen

Ellen Tidsdale and her mother Sady Barnard arrived for dinner the next evening before the rest of our guests. Mom showed them into the parlor and introduced them to Maude and Mossie. Bea served refreshments and I waited on pins and needles for Conner to arrive. Maude and Mossie had received another call from their private investigator earlier this afternoon, but they wouldn't tell us what he'd said. And I feared the worst after learning Seth and Conrad did not get along with one another. I just prayed they wouldn't bring up the subject during dinner.

Finally the doorbell rang and I went to the door.

"Are you expecting others?" I heard Ellen ask.

"Yes. Conner's parents are in town visiting and this is the first time we've had an opportunity to meet. My baby is getting married."

"How lovely. I simply adore weddings." I didn't recognize that voice, but assumed it must be Mrs. Barnard.

I took a deep breath, put a smile on my face and opened the door. Conner was there smiling on the other side with Duncan and Conrad right behind him. "Good evening. We've been expecting you."

Irene hugged me as she came inside and Seth shook my hand.

"Oh this is a lovely home. I hear it is full of history," she cooed, walking around the foyer, stopping at the staircase and running her hand along the dark wood banister. "You'll have to tell me all about it sometime."

"I'd like that. Please come and join us in the parlor for some refreshments before dinner is served. Everyone is already there."

"I saw a car out front. Are there other guests?" Seth asked.

"Actually yes. Mom invited her friend Ellen. You recall her."

He nodded and offered Irene his hand, leading her into the parlor. Conrad and Duncan followed them, but Conner held back, pulling me to him for a quick kiss.

"I've missed you," he whispered near my ear.

"Come on, you don't want to miss the fireworks." I saw his puzzled look before I caught up with the others. My mom was already doing the honors of introducing everyone.

Ellen came over to me and gave me a hug. "Congratulations dear. Why didn't you and your mom tell me yesterday about the engagement?"

"Conner and I hadn't set a date yet, but now that we have, we'll be placing the announcement in the society pages."

"Of course." She smiled as Conner joined us and shook his hand. "I wish you both the best."

"Thank you, Mrs. Tidsdale," Conner said.

"I can already tell you take after you grandfather more than your father." She walked over to join her mother who was talking with Maude and Mossie.

I turned to Conner, not sure what to make of her comment and he was nodding as if he agreed with her. I decided not to ask. He'd tell me later if I needed to know.

"Would you like a cup of punch?" I asked.

"No. I'm fine." He wrapped his arm around my waist and I leaned back into him. "I looked up the date for the Saturday before Christmas."

"So did I."

"December 18th it is then."

"At three o'clock in the afternoon."

"The church is available. I called earlier today."

I turned around. "It is?"

He nodded.

"What is all that whispering about over there?" Maude said loud enough so everyone stopped talking and was looking at us.

I mouthed 'sorry' to Conner.

"Oh leave the kids alone," Irene said. "They'll tell us if they want us to know."

"As long as it isn't any more nonsense about them getting married," Seth said.

"Now hold on," Conrad objected. "Conner is a grown man who knows when he's found the right one."

"That's all fine and good, but the boy doesn't even have a job. How's he going to support a wife and a family?" Seth said.

Conner moved closer to where his father stood. "I do have a job. I start once the plant reopens after the two-week summer shut down."

Seth looked surprised. "Well, well. The plant. And what type of job will you being doing?"

"I'll be a supervising manager. Looks like my college education was good for something after all."

"That is wonderful, honey." Irene stood and hugged him.

"Yeah. That's great."

Seth didn't sound happy at all and I couldn't figure out what wasn't right. He didn't get along with his father and he was down on Conner, not bothering to keep his feelings hidden in company.

Ellen sighed and her mom patted her hand.

The room stayed quiet as if no one knew what to say and I was very glad when Bea appeared to announce dinner was served. Like the dinner party before, Maude and Mossie had placed name cards at each seat. So instead of sitting beside Conner I was between Seth and Duncan. Ellen was on Seth's other side and Irene on Duncan's. Across the table Conner, Mom, Mrs. Barnard, and Conrad sat across from us while Maude and Mossie sat at the ends of the table.

I did think it was good planning on Mossie's part to put both Duncan and Conrad at the same end of the table as Maude. I looked at Mossie and raised my brows. She winked in response. Yes, she had played that rather nicely.

Thankfully the meal went off without a hitch. The dinner conversation was pleasant and the food exceptional. Bea was a very good cook and it didn't seem that any surprises could be thrown her way that she couldn't handle.

Coffee and dessert was served in the parlor again and on the way there Seth stopped me in the hallway. "I want you to know that I do not oppose you marrying my son if that is truly what you both want. I only want to be sure he will provide for you as he should. That he won't up and run off, joining another war."

"I know you didn't agree with him going to Europe and fighting, but the world is at peace now. And so should you and your son."

Seth grunted. "Naiveté is the folly of being young. Your eyes will be open soon enough."

I stood there trying to fathom his cynicism. He was a very complicated man. It was hard to believe he was Conner's father.

"Is anything wrong?" Conner asked, coming out of the parlor looking for me.

I shook my head not wanting to put a damper on the evening, but I didn't really want to go in to have dessert either. "Can I show you something?"

"Sure."

"Follow me then." I led him back to the foyer and up the stairs. "You recall the painting that Mrs. Tidsdale found that was my grandmother's?"

"Yes."

"I found that it is not the only one that has survived all these years."

"It isn't?"

"No. This house is full of history and hidden treasures," I said, taking him into the library. I walked over to the bookshelves and stood in front of the moveable shelf. "To our eye this looks like a library and a play room. But it is more."

I made the shelf move and I heard Conner suck in a breath behind me. I motioned for him to follow me down the hallway.

"This was my great-grandfather's private room. He kept things that meant a lot to him here."

"Like that painting of you?"

"Yes. Like this painting. He promised my grandmother that he'd give it to me one day, but he passed before he did. I was angry when I discovered this, but after thinking about it, I'm glad he didn't. I may not have cherished it as much otherwise. Maude and Mossie tell me I can remove it from here and take it to my room, but it is heavy and I'm afraid I'll drop it on my own. Would you do the honors?"

"Certainly." He took a step further into the room, but stopped, staring at the open steamer trunk. "What was in that?"

"Another treasure that I can't show you right now, but I will later."

He grinned. "Will I like it?"

"I think you will."

I helped him carry the painting out of the room and we were almost back to the hidden doorway in the corridor when I heard angry voices. We carefully sat the painting down, leaning it against one wall and moved to the opening. I saw my mother and Ellen come into the library and I quickly pulled the bookshelf closed to give them privacy. But all it did was conceal our presence in the dark corridor. Their voices could still be heard.

"I can't believe you invited me here tonight without telling me you'd invited Seth Montgomery and his wife. Nor did you tell me that Conner was Seth's son."

"Calm down, Ellen. Please, lower your voice or they'll hear you downstairs. I'm sorry, but I don't understand why you're so upset. You told me yourself that you didn't remember him."

"Should we let them know we're here?" Conner asked.

"I don't know. I don't want to eavesdrop, but it might frighten them if we suddenly appeared in the room."

I heard the door to the library close before anyone spoke again. And I wished we could have gone back down the corridor into another passage way, but as far as I'd seen there wasn't another way out.

"I lied. I lied about not remembering him. I've tried for years to forget the boy he was and the girl I was that summer I spent here with you."

"Why?" my mother asked. "Did something happen I didn't know about?"

Afraid of what we might overhear I pushed on the shelf and made the door open wide so we could step out. Both Ellen and my mother looked at us stunned by our appearance just as I thought they might, but there was relief on Ellen's face too that she hadn't said more.

"Sorry to startle you. We were getting my painting to take to my room and the doorway must have closed."

"Do you need any help?" Mom asked.

"I've got it, Mrs. Franklin." Conner carried the framed piece across the library and I closed the hidden passage way back, hurrying to open the library door for him. Once we were safe on the other side I closed the door back.

"That was awkward," Conner whispered.

"I know. I feared something was up by the way Ellen reacted yesterday when mom mentioned your dad's name. Whatever happened must have been bad."

"Knowing my father it would."

I frowned at Conner's remark. The more I was learning about Seth Montgomery, the less I liked and I could see this could be a problem for us. We had not reached my room when the library door opened and Ellen hurried out.

We turned and watched my mother follow her down the stairs. I heard the front door open and close twice.

Conner carried the painting into my room and leaned it against the wall. "Where do you want to hang it?"

"I don't know. I hadn't really thought about it."

"Well, I can return when you do."

"Swell."

We went back down to the parlor and found Irene, Maude and Mossie trying to console Mrs. Barnard, who had noticed her daughter's absence.

"Maddy, dear, please, will you go find Ellen." Maude looked up with pleading eyes.

"Sure."

Conner had joined the men and was eating his dessert so I went in search of my mom and Ellen alone. They weren't in the front of the house so I walked around toward the garage where I saw the driver in his window seat, but he wasn't reading. He was watching something down in the garden below.

I hurried down the stone steps and saw my mother and Ellen in deep conversation, crossing the arched bridge. Once again I was about to interrupt them, but I feared for Mrs. Barnard's health if I didn't. So I approached the bridge slowly, hoping to give them enough time to finish.

"We were foolish, reckless," Ellen said.

"I don't understand."

"We hid our relationship from you and Buddy. We thought we were being so clever acting like we could care less about the other during the day, but at night, we'd meet down in this garden. There are so many secret spots down here. He could come and go without anyone the wiser. See, here is the pathway that leads to his father's place."

Conner's and my pathway.

"But I never knew…How'd you sneak out of the house without waking me?"

"There's a secret passage that leads out to the back of the house. I found it by accident when I was exploring the house after we arrived and I used it to sneak in and out. No one was the wiser until your grandfather caught me coming in that last night we were here. So he wasn't surprised when I paid him a visit a few months later."

"What do you mean, Ellen?"

I took a step onto the bridge but the plank creaked

and I quickly stepped back, afraid they'd catch me eavesdropping.

"What do you think I mean, Hope? A silly naive girl fooling around with a boy can only end up one way."

Mom shook her head. "And you came to my grandfather for help? Why him?"

"I was scared and I knew he had to have suspected why I was sneaking in the house in the middle of the night. He only asked one question of me. Who was the boy? Afraid of what he might do to me if I didn't answer him, I told him the truth. He promptly sent his driver to go to the Montgomery House and bring Seth over."

"And what happened then?"

"He denied it. He denied all of it."

I raked my fingers through my hair and hurried up to the gazebo. But the early evening was still and the swans weren't making any noise so their voices carried.

"And?" Mom asked.

"Your grandfather took matters in his own hands. He found a place for me to go so no one would be the wiser. He even arranged for the baby to be adopted."

"And your parents never suspected?"

"No. He was your grandfather after all. He came to them with a wonderful opportunity for me, a two-year all-expenses paid scholarship to a private girl's school where I could study literature and languages."

"I remember now. It was so sudden. You left before winter break was over that year."

"Yes."

"What did you have?"

"A boy."

"But you and your husband never had children."

"No. There were complications with the delivery which made my conceiving again impossible. Unfortunately I didn't find that out until after Harold and I were married."

"I'm so sorry, Ellen. I'm glad you told me."

"I felt you needed to know since Madison will be marrying Conner. What Seth did and didn't do as a teenager has no effect on the man Conner is, but I felt you should know anyway. And it's why I can't come to their wedding so please don't invite me."

Having heard more than I should, I left the safety of the gazebo and began to call out in search of them. "Mom. Mrs. Tidsdale."

There was no sound from them, but I knew they were in the small clearing on the other side of the bridge.

"Mom. Ellen, it's your mother. She needs you."

Finally I saw my mom lead Ellen toward the bridge. "What is it, Madison? What's wrong?"

I rushed to the bridge. "She noticed Ellen was missing from the room and she's agitated. They're trying to calm her, but she really wants her daughter."

Ellen nodded, rubbing her eyes. It was obvious she

had been crying. I felt so sorry for her. What pain she must have gone through. What burden she must have carried all of these years knowing she had a child somewhere in the world that she'd never see.

"I better go and take her home." Ellen started walking up the slope still holding my mom's hand.

Feeling guilty knowing what I did, I hung back and let them climb the stone steps alone before I started up them. Now that I knew did I tell Conner? Or did I keep this secret to myself?

By the time I reached the front of the house, Mom was watching Ellen's car go down the drive. She smiled at me, but I could tell she was troubled by what she had learned. And I wasn't sure what to say without letting on that I knew too.

"Will Mrs. Barnard be okay?"

"Yes. Old people get forgetful. She's much older than Mossie, having had Ellen later in life. But she'll be just fine." Mom wrapped an arm around my shoulders. "We've been away from our guests far too long. We better go back inside."

There was a hearty conversation going on in the parlor when we got back. Conner seemed to be in the middle of it all. He looked in my direction as if to say 'help me' and shrugged his shoulders.

"What's this?" mom asked.

Irene came over to us. "Conner said they have settled on a date, but he won't tell us. Not until Madison returned. So when will the wedding be?"

"December the 18th."

"At three o'clock in the afternoon," Conner added.

"That's a week before Christmas," Maude said. "What if the church isn't available?"

"I've already talked to the pastor and it is," Conner told her.

"Well," mom said. "It sounds like you have everything planned out. But before we go further I want to know whether Seth has any final objections to your union?"

Everyone looked at Conner's father.

"Now, Hope, I—" Seth started to speak, but stopped. He looked down at his shoes and then back up at my mother. "I don't."

"Are you sure? Because you've made comments like 'she's a Wyndam', and questioned whether Conner could support them. I want to make sure there are no other reasons why they shouldn't get married before I give my blessing."

I looked at Conner and then back to my mother a little shocked by her statement. I thought she'd already given her blessing to us. But I guess after learning what she had about his father, it was making her doubt that decision.

When Seth didn't say anything else, mom walked over to Maude and Mossie. "And what about you two?

Do you have any objections? Because if you do then you best speak it now because I don't want to hear it after today."

"Well, I—" Mossie stammerd.

"No. We approve." Maude asserted.

Mom turned to the others. "Conrad? Duncan?"

"Like I told Madison, if Conner didn't snatch her up I would," Duncan said.

"Oh, you did?" Conner said. "Isn't it bad enough you catch all the fish?"

The two laughed and then Conrad hushed them.

"I knew the first time Conner brought Madison over to visit that she was a special girl. That she was the one for him and I couldn't be happier that they've realized this too. I not only support their marriage, but I give them a place to live afterward if they need one."

"Grandfather, you don't have to do that," Conner said.

"I can and I am. That house is too big for just me and Duncan to rummage around in. It needs new life if the two of you can put up with us for a while."

Maude cleared her throat. "That is awfully nice of you, but that won't be necessary. They already have a home."

"They do?" Mom asked.

"Yes, dear, they do," Mossie said.

I looked at my aunts. "Where?"

"Well here, Madison. This house. The land. The car. The money. It all belongs to you. Father left it all to you except for an annual allowance for me and Mossie." Maude came over with a document that I hadn't noticed her holding earlier. "That's why we had you come here. We wanted to tell you in person, but then Moss, she got cold feet, and the longer we waited the harder it was for us to tell you."

"We wanted to make sure you were ready to care for this burden. And with you and Conner marrying, we know you can."

I was certain I had misheard them. Surely they hadn't just said what I thought they did. My great-grandfather had left me his entire estate? I began to have difficulty breathing and the room seemed to go black.

"Madison. Madison." Conner patted my cheeks.

"Here, try this," Maude said.

The next thing I knew I smelled something awful and my eyes opened again.

I gasped for breath. "What happened?"

"You fainted." I saw my mom smiling down at me.

"I did?"

Conner lifted me off the floor and carried me to the sofa. I tried sitting up, but everyone insisted I lie back. I did for a few moments, but then I recalled what I heard before I fainted. I sat up despite their protests.

"Is what Maude said true?"

"Yes, it is." Mom held the document. "You are the sole heir of the Wyndam estate."

"How? Why?"

"I know it doesn't make sense, Madison," Mossie said. "But father did love you even if he had difficulty showing you."

"That's just the way father was," Maude added.

"But what about you? Didn't he think about how this would displace you or hurt you?"

"Hurt us? No. He provided for us. He gave us an annual allowance to live on and we are to live right here until we pass on, if that is fine with you."

I nodded. "Yes. I wouldn't want it any other way. There are more than enough rooms in this big house."

"Well," Conrad said. "It looks like you'll have two houses to care for one day."

"Hopefully that day is not anytime soon," Conner added.

"Not according to my doctor." Conrad turned to his friend. "Duncan, let's head back home. This has been a little too much excitement for one night."

Duncan nodded to both Maude and Mossie. "Thank you for a wonderful evening, ladies."

"I think we should be going as well," Seth said.

"Yes, we should," Irene agreed. "Are you coming, son?"

Conner hugged me. "Talk to you tomorrow?"

"Yes."

Maude, Mossie, Mom and I walked them to the door. When my mother closed the door, she leaned back against it and looked at me with a relieved expression. For a moment I thought she was going to break out into laughter, but she shook her head instead.

"I don't know about you, but I'm exhausted."

"Good night dears," Mossie said as she and Maude went upstairs.

"Tonight was rough," I agreed once they were out of sight.

"Yes. And I fear I've upset my friend Ellen greatly."

"But you didn't know you would when you invited her to dinner."

"Oh, yes I did. I know you had to have seen that look on her face yesterday when I mentioned Seth Montgomery to her."

I nodded.

"A better friend would have realized she didn't want to be reminded about him. Instead, I invited her here because I wanted to know what that look had been about. My behavior was despicable. It was no better than anything Maude and Mossie have done to you or me. Really, I'm no better than my grandfather for that matter."

"Don't say that, mom. If you do, then I must admit I'm just as bad. When I was hunting for you both earlier, I eavesdropped down in the garden. What little I couldn't help but overhear upstairs, I had to know more. So I listened instead of interrupting you both to let Ellen know her mom was disturbed by her absence.

I knew it was wrong of me, but I had to know what Mr. Montgomery had done to her."

Mom hugged me and then steered me upstairs to my room. She shut the door behind us. "I have to tell you I fear that maybe Maude knew something about his behavior years ago and that is why she made those accusations against Conner."

I gasped, but then that made so much sense. "Do you suppose she saw Ellen sneaking in and out of the house through that passageway?"

"It would explain why she was always watching me like a hawk whenever I was here visiting. Maybe if she'd known about Ellen, she was afraid I'd end up the same way." Mom sat down on the settee. "Fear can be our own worst enemy. It can cause us to do things with a skewed judgment."

"Mossie told me that they'd made many mistakes where I was concerned. And I feel bad for getting upset with them like I did, but now that I know them better, I think I can handle living in this house with them."

"Are you sure you and Conner want to live here with them in the beginning? You need your privacy as a newly married couple. Perhaps you should rent a small house for a year and then move into Wyndam House."

"Maybe you'll sell the place in Camden and move here. Stay with Maude and Mossie while Conner and I live in town? Especially if I go to art school. I saw in the paper an advertisement for a new program they are starting at the College of Charleston."

"Maybe I could."

Chapter Seventeen

The phone rang early the next morning waking us. I pulled on my wrapper and hurried downstairs when Bea called up that it was for me. Maude and Mossie stood in their bedroom doorways with their hair up in curlers and my mom barely had her eyes open, holding her forehead against her hand and leaning against the doorframe.

"He-l-l-o," I croaked into the receiver.

"Madison, come quick. It's Grandfather. He's had a stroke."

"A stroke? Conner…oh my goodness. But his doctor just said he was—"

"I know." There was a pause on the other end of the line and I heard him take a ragged breath. "I know. It doesn't make sense. But he's hanging on. The doctor is here now. Duncan found him lying on the kitchen floor where he fell in the middle of the night. We don't know how long he lay there before he was found."

"I'll be right there." I hung up the phone and turned around to find my mother standing behind me. Seeing her worried expression, I began to cry. "Conrad had a stroke. Duncan found him on the kitchen floor."

She pulled me to her and held me while I cried. "I'm so sorry to hear this. I'm sure his doctor will do all he can for him."

I nodded, sniffling. "I've got to go. I told Conner I'd be right over."

"Go change and I'll make you some breakfast. Bea and I'll make enough breakfast for everyone and we'll bring it over."

I hurried upstairs, splashed water on my face and blotted it dry. I couldn't believe this had happened. Conrad was just here last night having dinner with us. He'd visited his doctor the day before and been given a good report. How had things changed so quickly for him?

I put on a clean dress and a pair of flats, fixed my hair and hurried downstairs again. I was halfway down the stone steps in the garden when I heard a siren. I quickened my pace running across the bridge and into the bushes to the well-worn path. Neighbors along the way were outside trying to figure out what the siren was for. One man stopped me.

"Has something happened?" he asked.

I nodded, slowing down only long enough to

respond. "Mr. Montgomery had a stroke."

"I'll be praying for him," the man said and he hurried toward his neighbor's house to spread the word.

As I feared, an ambulance had arrived at Montgomery House. The doctor walked out and then two men carried Conrad out on a stretcher.

"Oh Madison, isn't it horrible," Irene cried, hugging me. "They don't know if he'll make it."

"I still don't understand how this could happen. He was perfectly all right yesterday."

"I know." She shook her head, wiping her eyes with her handkerchief. "Even last night after we got home he didn't show signs of anything being wrong. We had a nice chat before he retired."

"If they're taking him to the hospital, I need to call my mom. She was preparing breakfast to bring over to you."

"Bless her, but that won't be necessary. We're all too upset to eat right now. But do go on in the house. Conner should be down shortly from changing. He can show you which extension to use."

I went inside and used the phone in the kitchen since I knew where it was. Bea answered. "It's Madison. No need to make breakfast. Mr. Montgomery is being taken to the hospital. I'll call once I know more."

"I'll tell your mother. Please give the family our best."

I hung up the phone and went back to the foyer and waited for Conner. He appeared shortly, dressed to go into town. He hugged me. "Thank you for coming."

"Of course I'd come. Where's Duncan? How is he taking it?"

"He's in his room, getting dressed. We're all going to the hospital. Will you come with us?"

"Yes."

"None of this makes sense, Madison." We walked to the parlor and he sat on the arm of the easy chair. "Something had to have happened to have caused the stroke. The doctor said a stroke is normally caused by an increase in blood pressure."

"Is that what the doctor believes happened?"

"He wouldn't speculate a cause until he can run some tests. But that could take a day or two to get results. Until then they'll monitor him and determine if there is any paralysis."

"I'm so sorry." I stepped closer, leaning my forehead against his. "I wish I could do something to make it all better, take the pain you are feeling away."

"Your being here with me helps," he said.

"Conner, we're ready to leave," Seth called from the foyer, interrupting our solitude.

Not wanting to keep the family waiting, we followed his father out to their dark green Buick touring car. Irene and Duncan were already inside. Conner opened the back door and I climbed in to sit between him and Duncan. The drive to the hospital seemed to take forever because no one spoke. Irene softly cried in the front seat, but if Seth noticed, he didn't make an effort to comfort her. Conner stared out of the window and so did Duncan on his side. Their thoughts had to have been on Conrad's condition. I couldn't get the image of him lying on the stretcher, lifeless, out of my mind.

Finally Mr. Montgomery pulled the car to a stop at the hospital on Calhoun Street. Conner exited the car and reached his hand inside for me to take as I got out. As soon as we rounded the car, Duncan called him over and I went on ahead to speak with Irene who was still dabbing her eyes with her now wet handkerchief.

"Are you okay?" I asked.

She nodded, biting her lower lip as we walked toward the entrance. "I'm sorry. I should be stronger, but I just adore Conrad. He's been like another father to me since I lost my own."

"I know. He's easy to like."

"Yes, he is. So is Duncan. He's my uncle, you know. I was glad the two decided to move in together to keep the other company when their wives died. It made us living so far away easier, knowing they weren't alone."

"Duncan is your uncle?"

"Yes. Didn't he or Conner tell you?"

I shook my head. I wonder why neither mentioned it? Conner rarely talked about his parents when we were together. But Duncan was the opposite. He talked about everything. "How'd you and Seth meet?"

"We knew each other as children. I always came out to visit Uncle Duncan and Aunt Ramona in the summers. Then as we got older we dated, nothing serious until the summer I was seventeen. All of a sudden Seth was anxious to get married and start a family."

I found that odd, for many reasons. "I thought you said he was reluctant to agree on a wedding date."

"Yes. That's true. It didn't make sense at first, but then all grooms get cold feet. He finally agreed and we married."

"When did you move away from Charleston?"

"Soon after Conner came along. We were closer to my folks that way. And Seth had a job that took him all over Georgia so it made sense to move there."

"Irene, are you coming?" Seth called, holding the door open for us.

She smiled and hurried along. I did as well, not wanting to upset my future father-in-law. I knew his gruffness today had to be because he was worried about his father. Once we were inside the building I looked back and saw Conner still at the car talking with Duncan.

I went ahead with his parents to the main desk. Seth told the woman who we were there for, and she advised us to have a seat until the doctor could see us. We settled in the chairs provided in an alcove off to the side and waited. It wasn't too long before Conner and Duncan finally came in. I noticed Conner looked tense. He didn't sit down; instead he went over to the window and stared out.

"How are you, Duncan?" I asked when he sat in a chair next to me.

"I've been better, Madison. I've been better. I don't care for hospitals. But I'm glad we have them for when they are needed."

"I'm glad you didn't have a spell finding Conrad the way you did."

Duncan glanced at me as if startled by my comment. "I wish it had been me."

I patted him on his back.

Seth got up from his seat and walked over to where Conner stood. He said something to him and tried to touch his arm, but Conner pulled away, clenching his fist. I saw his jaw twitch before he left the waiting area.

Not sure what had just happened, I knew it wouldn't do for Seth to follow him. I looked at Irene. "I better go after him."

She nodded and fresh tears streamed down her face.

I found Conner outside in a small courtyard between the two wings of the hospital. There was a fountain and a few benches under tall shade trees. He sat alone with his elbows propped on his knees staring blankly at the water that spewed from the fountain.

"Can I join you?" I asked softly, not sure how he would react.

He looked up and nodded.

"Is everything okay?"

"No. Nothing is okay. And nothing will ever be the same ever again." He got up and walked over to the fountain with his back facing me. "Madison, maybe we should call off the wedding. You don't want to marry me. I was fooling myself to think you would when I asked you."

Stunned by what he said, I tried to make sense of it and I wondered where it was coming from.

"What has gotten into you? What makes you think I don't want to marry you? Or that I'd change my mind so easily?"

He turned around. "Because I'm not who I thought I was, that's why. I don't know who I am anymore."

Hmmm… Hadn't I said something similar to him when he first proposed? And he'd quickly assured me I was the person I'd always been. Whatever Duncan had said to him out in the parking lot must have been bad for him to be reacting like this.

"What makes you say that?"

He pulled an envelope out of his front pant pocket. "Duncan gave me this. He said he found it clutched in my grandfather's hand this morning when he found him in the kitchen. I believe this may be what caused him to have the stroke."

I took a step toward him. "What is it?"

"A copy of my birth certificate and a letter from your great-grandfather."

My great-grandfather?

I swallowed, almost afraid to breathe. Why would my great-grandfather have had Conner's birth certificate? Had he given it to Conrad?

"Wh-h-a-a-tt does the letter say?"

He pushed the envelope toward me. "Read for yourself."

With trembling fingers I opened the envelope and took out the letter, almost afraid of what I'd find within.

> *Dear Conrad,*
>
> *I should have written sooner with congratulations for your son on his marriage. Please forgive me for not doing so. It would have been the neighborly thing to do. We haven't always seen eye to eye and I know you understand what I mean, especially after the incident last summer. However, I believe I can be of help to your son now if he will allow it.*
>
> *I hear he and his bride are having trouble starting a family. Yes, Irene's suspected barren state has already reached the gossips' lips, such a pity. But you know what they say, where there is a will, there is a way.*
>
> *As I said, I believe I can be of help. I*

know of a child that needs a home. He was abandoned by his father not too long ago when he had a chance to do the right thing. It is not too late for him to take that opportunity. The mother was forced to go into hiding so she would never be the wiser. This can remain our little secret as long as your son and his bride leave Charleston for several years. I can make the adoption possible.

I'll be awaiting your answer.
Respectfully,
Richard Wyndam

I read the letter through twice and I knew what it meant. My great-grandfather had gotten Seth Montgomery to adopt his own son. He had done a good thing and a bad one at the same time. Seth had been given this opportunity, while Ellen suffered in silence all these years. I didn't know whether to be angry or glad for what my great-grandfather had done. But, I knew that if it had not been for my great-grandfather I might not have ever met Conner.

I carefully folded the letter and slipped it back inside the envelope, choosing my words carefully before I spoke.

"Conner, this letter proves you are who you've always believed you are. You're Seth's son. You're Conrad's grandson. Nothing has changed except Irene isn't your mother by blood, but she's your mother because she raised and loved you."

Conner stared at me as if he didn't know who I was anymore. "You think that makes this all okay?"

I nodded and wondered if I'd feel differently if I didn't know that Ellen Tidsdale was his mother.

"You have no problem with your great-grandfather doing this to my family?"

"He didn't do anything except try to help a frightened young girl when the boy wouldn't step up and take responsibility. Instead that boy finds another to marry him and attempts to try to replace the child he didn't want. When Irene told me how your dad was so eager to marry only a year after you were obviously conceived I was shocked, but it all makes sense now. He wanted a child to replace you. What he didn't know is fate allowed him to have you."

Conner stared at me with dark eyes. The pain he felt showed as he tried to understand it all. "If he wanted me, he sure hasn't treated me that way. It's as if he's despised me for being alive."

"Maybe that is because he doesn't know your true parentage. We don't know how things went. Did Conrad tell him about the letter or did he agree with my great-grandfather for the adoption? Conrad could have told your parents about the baby and left it up to them to decide what to do, so your father was never the wiser. We don't know if your grandfather told him the truth about the baby or not."

Conner shook his head and walked to the other

side of the fountain.

I pulled out the birth certificate. "Did you even look at the other piece of paper in the envelope?"

"No. Why should I."

"Aren't you the least bit curious as to who your mother really is?"

"Should it matter? She gave me away, didn't she?"

"I think it should. I know if it was me I'd want to know." I walked over and handed him the paper. "But realize she only gave you away because she couldn't keep you."

He looked down at his birth certificate and back up with me. "You knew didn't you? But how?"

"Not all, darling, especially nothing about the baby being you. But I did overhear mother and Ellen in the garden last night when she was telling her about what happened when she was sixteen. Sixteen and with child. Alone and frightened. My great-grandfather saw that she was cared for during that two-year period. He made sure the baby was taken care of until it was adopted."

"Why didn't he make my father marry her? If my grandfather knew then why didn't he?"

"I can't answer those questions for you. All I know is that Ellen said Seth denied he was responsible."

"What did Seth deny?" Irene's voice made us both turn around. She was standing there holding Duncan's hand. "What are you talking about? Ellen who?"

If Duncan gave Conner the envelope, then he

surely had opened it and looked at what was inside. I didn't understand why he would bring his niece out here when he had to have known we were probably discussing the contents.

Conner went to her. "It's okay, mom. There is nothing to worry about."

"Don't lie to me. Your father has done enough of it over the years." She looked down at the paper he was holding and snatched it from him.

"Mom, no."

He tried to stop her, but she turned away. I saw the crushed look on her face as she realized what she held in her hands. She let the paper go and if floated to the ground. Conner grabbed it.

Irene didn't speak. She walked over to a bench and sat down.

"It will be okay," Duncan said, sitting down beside her.

She shook her head and looked up at Conner "Where did you get that?"

"Apparently grandfather had it clutched in his hand when he was found this morning."

She licked her lips and turned to her uncle. "If you found Conrad, then you gave it to him?"

Duncan nodded. "He's a grown man. He has a right to know."

She placed a hand over her chest and patted the spot over and over as she began to cry. "What about me? What about my feelings? Didn't you think I had a right to know you were doing this? Didn't I have a say in you telling my son he's adopted. Isn't it bad enough that I couldn't give my husband his own child?"

Duncan pulled her to him. "But you don't understand. That birth certificate proves that Conner is Seth's child. That is why he and Conrad fought all those years ago. That is why the two have been distant. Conrad must have been planning to discuss this with Seth before his stroke."

Irene pushed him away. "No. No. I don't believe it. He wouldn't…they wouldn't have lied to me so I'd adopt Seth's child. They couldn't have been so cruel."

I walked forward and handed her the letter that was in the envelope. "It appears they did."

She read over it and handed it back to me, shaking her head. "No. I won't believe it."

"But this is my great-grandfather's handwriting. I've read his journal. I'd know his script anywhere."

She left the bench and hurried back inside the hospital.

"Conner, you have to stop her. If she confronts Seth no telling what might happen," Duncan said getting to his feet.

Conner left us to follow her and I walked with Duncan in the small courtyard until he was ready to go back inside.

"Seth never deserved her, but I stayed quiet all these years because of my friendship with Conrad. I should have put my foot down when they decided to marry, but Irene had been so happy and so in love. I foolishly thought Seth would make her happy."

"Did you know about—"

"No. I knew they adopted the boy, but nothing more. Irene miscarried several times during their first year of marriage. And after they adopted, she even carried to five months once, but lost the child. A little girl. They eventually stopped trying."

"Why didn't you tell me she was your niece?"

"It never crossed my mind, really. I sure wasn't keeping it from you, dear. I really don't talk about Irene much because of Conrad's falling out with Seth. And the way Seth has always treated Conner infuriates me."

"Why do you suppose Seth is so hard on Conner? Doesn't he realize he is his child?"

"I'm sure he had to have known. They adopted him before he was six months old. Conner has a birthmark just like Seth's in the same spot on his upper left hip. He would have seen it when changing the boy's diaper."

"I suppose he can only answer for his reasons. I just don't want to see Conner hurt by it any more than he already has been."

"I'm afraid that's a sore spot that may never heal," Duncan said as we approached the door to the hospital. "I think we've stalled enough. Let's go back in."

When we reached the seating area, Irene sat with

Conner on one side of the alcove and Seth sat on the other. If they'd had words it wasn't clear and I really didn't want to stir the pot more by asking. Thankfully the doctor arrived behind us so we didn't have to wait long to find out how Conrad was doing.

"How is he?" Conner asked, coming to where we stood.

The doctor motioned for Seth and Irene to join us before he spoke. "We have him stable. He's responsive now. It doesn't look like he will have a speech impediment and I have not found a sign of paralysis yet. So we may be lucky and he won't need any physical therapy. I'd like to keep him here for observation until we rule out any permanent damage."

"Do you know what caused the stroke?" Seth asked.

"Not yet. We'll continue running tests." The doctor smiled. "We have him in a room if you'd like to see him now. Only two visitors at a time, but for no more than five minutes each half hour. He's asking for Conner and Madison."

"Of course." Seth nodded.

Conner and I went down the corridor and up a flight of stairs to the second floor to the room the doctor said. Conrad was propped up in the hospital bed and it looked like he was sleeping when we entered the room, but he opened his eyes immediately. He reached a hand out to Conner.

"Grandpa," Conner said, taking his hand and

sitting on the side of the bed. "You scared us."

Conrad grinned. "But not Duncan. He's thinking I'll kick the bucket before him now, I bet."

"No. He's worried." I stepped closer to the bed. "We all are about you."

"Don't be. I'm fine. Just a silly fall where I must have hit my head. I lost my balance and couldn't get up."

Conner looked at him closely. "Are you sure that's all that happened. The doctor believes you had a stroke."

"Doctor's don't know everything." Conrad pulled his hand free of Conner's and reached for mine. He placed it on his grandson's. "Promise me you'll always be true to one another. And you won't allow the years to turn you against the other the way Seth and Irene have."

"Grandpa."

"Listen to me, Conner. I know what I am saying. I was on my way to talk to you last night when…when I fell. I wanted to give you something."

Conner looked at me and I knew what he was thinking. He stood, reached into his pocket and pulled out the envelope. "Is this what you wanted to give me?"

Conrad leaned his head back and closed his eyes. "You've seen it?"

"Yes."

"I shouldn't have kept it from you for so long,

especially when you returned from the war and your father was still angry that you went. I thought if you knew why he was angry with you all the time it might help."

"What do you mean?" Conner asked.

"You have principles. You stand for what is right. You're a better person than he was all those years ago."

The door to the room opened and a nurse came in. "Your time is up. You can come back again later, but now he needs his rest."

I leaned down and kissed Conrad on the cheek. "Get better."

"Thank you, dear."

Conner was hesitant to go, but I finally tugged his hand to make him follow me out. "I'll be back."

He was silent as we went back downstairs to where his family waited. Seth stood as soon as he saw us.

"How is he?"

"Hanging in there. He said he didn't have a stroke. That he only fell."

Seth nodded. "That sounds like him."

"What's that supposed to mean?" Conner's back stiffened.

"Just that he dismisses the obvious where his health is concerned."

"Really?" Conner stepped closer to his father. "Like you really care. When was the last time you've come to check on him? You wouldn't have come this time if you hadn't been passing through and mom wanted to see me. You don't know the first thing about being a family."

"Now wait here, son. I think you better calm down."

"Conner, please. You don't want to make a scene here," I whispered, touching his arm.

He flinched and I backed away. "Maybe you can explain this." He held up the envelope and Irene rushed over and tried to snatch it, but Conner wouldn't allow her to have it.

"What's that?"

"The truth about me." Conner turned and walked out of the hospital toward the parking lot.

"Irene, do you know what he is talking about?" Seth asked.

She began to cry and covered her face with her hands.

"Madison, can you tell me?"

I shook my head, wrapping my arms around Irene and patted her back until she stopped sobbing. Duncan came over and we convinced her to try to eat something, so Seth agreed to drive us to a diner not far from the hospital since no one else could see Conrad for at least a half hour.

I watched for Conner as we drove down Calhoun Street toward King, but he wasn't among those traveling by foot. Maybe he'd caught the trolley. But where would he go? I thought about our visit with my mother and the picnic we'd shared at White Point Garden. Maybe he'd go there or to walk on the boardwalk to clear his head. Or maybe he'd go to East Battery and see Ellen Tidsdale.

"What's wrong?" Duncan asked when we got out of the car at the diner.

"I'm worried about Conner. He's so upset right now."

"The boy can take care of himself. He went to war and came back without a scratch on him."

"This is different, Duncan. He's had his world turned upside down today. Don't you understand that?"

"I know he has, but he's strong. He can handle it."

I didn't feel as confident about that as Duncan did, but I knew he was trying to look at it on the positive side. We went in and I ordered a sandwich and a cup of soup. The others did the same, but they had pie with coffee. I excused myself and went to the bank of phone booths to call my mom.

Bea answered and I asked for my mother.

"Madison, is everything okay?"

"Conrad's resting. The doctor still believes he had a stroke, but Conrad said he only fell. So they are keeping him for observation while they do some tests. Conner and I got to see him for a few minutes."

"How did he seem to you?"

"Like always, but tired. Mom…something has happened. Can you pick me up and I'll tell you more about it?"

"Of course."

"I'm going to catch the trolley to White Point Garden. I'll meet you there and then I'd like for us to go see Ellen."

"Ellen? Madison, what has happened?"

"I don't want to get into it on the phone. I'll explain everything when I see you."

"I'll be there as soon as I can."

After hanging up I went back to the table. "I'm worried about Conner. I'm going to go see if I can find him. I've called my mom to come into Charleston to pick me up. If we find him, we'll bring him back to the hospital. If I don't, I'm sure he'll come back here himself."

"Thank you," Seth said.

I smiled at Irene who I could see was about to begin crying again, but she blinked her eyes repeatedly to clear away the tears.

"Here," Duncan handed me some coins. "You might need that for the trolley."

"Thanks."

I left the diner and hurried down the street to the next trolley stop, keeping my eyes open for Conner among those out and about. I didn't expect he'd be at White Point Garden when I got there, but it was a good place to start.

I had gone about a block when I heard my name being called.

"Madison?"

I turned and there was Thomas Whitfield with a pleasant smile on his face. He wasn't alone, but with a young woman closer to his own age.

"Hi."

"What brings you to town?" he asked.

"An errand."

He glanced at his companion. "Miss Harper, I'd like for you to meet Miss Madison Franklin. My grandmother and her great aunts are friends. We had the occasion to meet a few weeks ago at a dinner party. Miss Franklin, this is Miss Ida Harper. Her father is on the city council and we have just recently become acquainted through the Library Society. We're both enamored with literature."

I nodded and reached out my hand, realizing in my haste this morning that I hadn't put on gloves. But Miss Ida Harper didn't seem to mind; she eagerly put her gloved hand in mine and shook it.

"It's a pleasure, Miss Franklin. Do you hail from Charleston? I don't believe I've had the fortune of meeting you before."

"No. I'm from Camden. I've only recently come to your fair city."

"Are you a lover of books too?" she asked.

"I do like to read, but my passion is with art. Drawing, sketching."

"How fascinating. I'd love to see your work some time."

"Perhaps you can," I offered to be polite. "Thomas, if you and your grandmother come out to visit the aunts, please be sure to bring Miss Harper along."

Thomas looked enthralled to be invited. "I'll do that. I'll do that for sure."

I heard the chime of the trolley and knew it was near. I didn't want to miss it and I had at least a half a block to go. "I hate to dash off, but I do have to be on my way. Will you be going to the Mayor's Fourth of July ball?"

"Yes." Miss Harper stepped closer to Thomas. "Mr. Whitfield just asked me to accompany him."

"Wonderful. I'll see you both there then. Good-bye."

The crowd had thinned so I was able to reach the stop before the trolley and once on board it did not take near as long to reach White Point Garden. I walked the oyster shell path until I came to the bandstand gazebo in the center, but as I had feared I did not see Conner. I took a different path toward the boardwalk and searched for him down East Battery before doubling back to White Point to wait for my mother. I was sitting on a wooden bench near the spot we'd had our picnic only a week or two ago when I heard whistling. I turned and there he stood, rocking back and forth on his heels with his hands shoved in his pockets and that Cheshire cat grin on his face.

"Conner!" I jumped up and wrapped my arms around him, relieved to have finally found him. "I've been worried. I didn't know where you'd gone or if I would find you."

"Why? Did you think I'd throw myself in the river?" His voice was soft, but the thought of him doing something like that had not entered my mind, until now.

"You wouldn't! Don't say something so crazy."

"Sorry. I don't know why I said it."

I pulled back and looked at him. "Are you really okay?"

He nodded.

"For certain?"

"Yes, Madison. I'm okay. The shock has worn off now."

"I wish Duncan had kept that envelope to himself. Today, of all days, wasn't the right time. Not after Conrad's fall and possible stroke."

He caught me under the chin with the crook of his finger and tilted my head so I was looking up at him. "Don't be angry with Duncan. The timing might not have been right, but he wanted to follow through with whatever my grandfather had started last night. I don't fault him there. And you shouldn't either."

He took a deep breath and a slow smile formed, making his dimple show. "Actually, finding out has liberated me. I feel like the cocoon that has been smothering me all these years is gone. I love Irene. She has been a great mom, but I always sensed something was missing. And if my dad didn't know he'd been saddled with his own bastard, well, I'm okay with that too. Serendipity can be a kick in the head. And no one deserves it more than him."

"Oh, Conner," I hugged him again. "It will be okay, won't it?"

"It's going to be fine." He returned my hug. "As long as you don't think Maude and Mossie will have an issue with me if they learned about this?"

I laughed. "According to them you are perfectly respectable, but a scamp because you stand to inherit more money from Conrad than the Wyndams have."

He tensed and dropped his arms from around me. "What did you say?"

I closed my eyes and thought fast. I guess I had said more than I should have. He didn't need to know what the private investigator had told them about his grandfather's will because it wasn't public knowledge.

"Madison, how do you know this?"

"I'm just repeating what Maude and Mossie said."

"But how would *they* know what is in my grandfather's will? I don't even know."

I glanced at the ground and licked my lips before looking back up at him. "Because it's public record since your father took Conrad to court."

"He what?"

I winced at his tone. *Keep your mouth shut, Madison. You're only making things worse.* But I couldn't keep this from him. "Maude and Mossie have this guy that looks into things for them. He once worked for my great-grandfather too."

He rocked back on his heels again. "They had this guy look into me?"

I nodded. "They did it without my knowing."

He raised a finger and started to say something when a horn blew and we both turned in the direction the sound came from. My mom got out of her car and waved to us.

"I hope I didn't take too long to get here. I came as fast as I could." She gave Conner a hug. "How is Conrad?"

"Resting, but his coloring looked good. He wasn't pale like he was this morning."

"That's a good sign then." She hugged me next.

"I'm glad you came, Mrs. Franklin, but you didn't have to come into town on my account."

"Of course I did, Conner. I couldn't stay away after Madison called and said something terrible had happened and I needed to come get her so we could go see my friend Ellen."

"Oh." He looked at me and I shrugged.

"So what has happened?"

I moved away from the bench. "Mom, I think you'd better sit down."

Chapter Eighteen

My mother listened to everything I had to say and Conner showed her the envelope with the birth certificate in it and the letter from my great-grandfather. She was quiet for a long time afterward as she read over the letter again and looked at the official document. Then she looked up at Conner.

"I'm so sorry you've had to learn this today, of all days, Conner. This is a lot to digest. I admit it was a lot for me to comprehend when Ellen told me last night and now to learn the baby she gave up is you." Mom covered her mouth with her hand and shook her head. "I'm so sorry if my grandfather's actions have caused you pain. I'm sorry I wasn't a better friend that maybe if I had been, I would have seen what was really going on all those years ago. Maybe if Ellen had confided in me—"

"It isn't your fault, Mrs. Franklin. It isn't anyone's other than my parents. And I refuse to believe I was a mistake any more than Madison was."

"And we know she wasn't," my mother said. "So what do you want to do with this information? Do you want to see Ellen and share this news with her?"

Conner turned and stared over at East Battery where the large houses sat. "I thought about that earlier. I walked down that street and back at least a dozen times, but I changed my mind each time I passed her house. Does she need to know? Would that knowledge make her happy? Would it cause her more pain?"

"I don't know." Mom reached for my hand and gave it a squeeze. "I'd want to think if it were me, I'd want to know my child was so close at hand and that I might have a second chance with him."

"I heard how upset she was with you last night when you both came into the library. She was hurt and didn't like being forced into a situation where she had to see my father again. What if we go over there and she takes one look at me and slams the door in my face?"

"Why would she do that? She doesn't even know you are hers." Mom stood and placed a hand on his arm. "If you want to see her, then I will not let her refuse to see you. I give you my word, Conner."

I waited silently to see what he decided. It was his choice after all. I didn't want to say the wrong thing again.

"What do you think, Madison?"

His question came out of nowhere and my heart skipped a beat that he would ask my opinion. "I think you should go see her. Tell her the truth. No more secrets."

He smiled. "No more secrets. I like that."

"Good." Mom smiled too. "I called her before I left River Road and told her we'd be stopping by."

"You did?" I asked.

"Yes. We couldn't just drop in again like last time. That would be rude."

We climbed into mom's car and she drove us over to East Battery.

Ellen greeted us at the door. Her smile faltered when she saw Conner though she tried to regain it so we didn't notice, but I'd seen. I wondered if she suspected. Now that I knew, I saw a resemblance in more than the color of their hair.

"How are you?" Mom asked.

"I've been better. Please, follow me. Mother's napping so I thought we'd have tea out in the garden so we won't wake her. She didn't sleep well last night. I've never seen her so agitated."

"I'm sorry to hear that," Conner said.

"Thank you." Ellen looked at him as if she were surprised he'd say it. "Hope told me your grandfather is at Roper. I hate hearing of older people taking ill."

He nodded.

Ellen stopped short of the patio as if she had lost her train of thought. "Please, have a seat and excuse me while I go get the tea."

"Can I help you?" Mom asked and followed her even though she said no.

Conner shoved his hands in his pockets and walked around the small flower garden, while I took a seat at the shaded table. I knew this was hard on him. It was an awkward situation. How did you tell an almost perfect stranger that she was your mother? That you were the child she gave up for adoption over twenty-two years ago? He was keeping his emotions in check.

Deep down I wished this was all a horrible nightmare and I was still in my bed, fast asleep and dreaming. Then the phone call wouldn't have waken us this morning and Conner wouldn't have been on the other end of the line telling me the bad news that his grandfather had had a stroke. If none of this had happened, then he wouldn't have found out he was a baby no one wanted. And we definitely wouldn't be here now, confronting his birth mother with the truth.

"Here we go," Ellen announced, coming back out of the house with the tea tray. My mom carried a three-tiered plate holder with small sandwiches and tiny cakes. "Conner, I hope you feel like eating."

He slowly walked over to the table and took the

seat beside me. "Yes ma'am, I do."

"I thought you might be hungry." Ellen smiled. "So Madison, your mom said you have a date, a dress, and the church reserved. It sounds like your wedding plans are almost finished."

I nodded. "We need to decide on a reception location and a guest list, but then that could change, I suppose."

"Change?" Ellen poured tea in the four cups and passed them around the table. "What could possible change?"

Conner cleared his throat. "I think what Madison meant is everything is in place as long as family issues don't get in the way."

The table was silent except for the clinking of our spoons against the china as we added sugar, lemon, or crème to our tea.

"I do hope that your grandfather does recover. It would be a shame for you all if he were to miss the wedding," Ellen said.

"Yes it would," Conner agreed and looked directly across the table at her. "It would also be bad if my mother were not there."

I sucked in my breath and held my tea cup tightly, afraid it would slip from my fingers. I glanced at Ellen when she did not respond and saw she was staring at Conner as well. I quickly looked at my mom and saw she was sitting very still.

"I'm sure Irene will be there. Nothing could keep

her away." Ellen reached for the bowl of sugar cubes and dropped another in her tea cup, stirring vigorously without sloshing any of the hot liquid over the side.

"I'm not talking about her." Conner's voice was firm; it didn't falter. "I'm talking about the woman who gave me life. The young girl who did what she thought was best for me."

Ellen's eyes enlarged and she glanced at my mother then back at Conner. "Whatever do you mean?"

"I think you know perfectly well what I mean." He reached for the envelope and took out the birth certificate. Carefully unfolding it, he laid it on the table in front of her.

She glanced down at it and then back up at my mother, clasping her hands together on the table in front of her, as if she were afraid she'd pick the paper up. "What is the meaning of this, Hope? Is this some kind of cruel joke?"

"No, it isn't a joke." Mom placed her hand over Ellen's. "I know it does seem cruel. So many years after it happened, you finally tell someone your darkest secret and then the next day you find out you've already met your grown son."

Ellen shook her head back and forth as tears began to stream down her face. "Are you telling me Seth has had our child all these years raising him as his own? After he denied he was the father, he got to raise our child?"

"I'm sorry, Ellen, but it looks like it."

Ellen pulled her hands free from my mom's hold and covered her face, sobbing. "No. No. No. That isn't fair."

Conner hastily removed the letter from the envelope. "Mrs. Tidsdale, everything is explained right here in this letter to my grandfather. Whether my father knew the truth or not, Richard Wyndam arranged for my adoption. I only learned about this this morning. I'm as shocked as you. If my grandfather hadn't been found with the envelope clutched in his hand when he was discovered in our kitchen, then the truth may never have been uncovered."

I set down my cup of tea, untouched. "We didn't come to upset you. We only wanted you to know the truth. No more secrets. Conner and I do not want that in our lives."

Conner rose from the table and went around to where she sat crying. He knelt beside her chair and wrapped his arms around her. "No one has to know the truth if you do not want them to. We can go on living like we were, but I would like to get to know you. I cannot make up for what my father did."

Her sobs grew louder as she wrapped her arms around him too, pulling him closer in her embrace.

Mom and I sat there silent. I was glad Ellen had not thrown us out when he told her. Though she still could once she stopped crying, but maybe she wouldn't.

Finally her crying grew softer and she pulled away, reaching for her napkin. She dried her eyes and dabbed at her nose. "I'm sorry. Do forgive me."

"It's okay."

She smiled at him, though her pain showed on her face. "Yes. It is okay. I see you are the good parts of Seth and I rolled into one. But I …I don't know that I can do this. I can't suddenly be your mother. I—I have a husband who doesn't know I had a child. I—I don't know how he'd react if I sprang the news on him."

She pushed her chair away from the table and stood. "I do want to get to know you and you know me, and I know we can do it through Hope and Madison, but I don't think I can offer you more than that."

Conner nodded. "Like I said, no one has to know the truth if you don't want them too."

"What about Seth and Irene? Will they accept that?" Ellen asked, turning to my mother.

"Ellen, we do not even know if Seth knows he adopted his biological son. All we know is Conrad had this letter telling him about a baby available for adoption."

"Irene knows now because of this envelope, but she is denying that it is true," I explained. "So I don't see her readily admitting she isn't Conner's mother."

Ellen shook her head. "I don't know what I'd do if Harold ever found out. To know I had a child by another and wasn't able to have one with him."

"Then you need to tell him," mom said. "Don't leave it to chance that he might learn the truth. Don't keep a secret from him like this any longer."

She sat back down in her chair. "I know I should. I knew I should have years ago, but I was afraid I'd lose him."

"The truth hurts, but also sets you free." Conner walked back to his chair and sat down again. "It makes you feel relieved. It makes you feel complete, like the missing piece of the puzzle was finally put into place."

Conner helped himself to a few of the sandwiches and began to eat. "It gives you back your appetite."

We all laughed softly as he enjoyed the food. I took a tea cake off the plate and finally took a sip of my tea. Ellen looked as if she had finally relaxed again when we heard her mother calling for her.

"Ellen. Ellen."

"I'm sorry, please excuse me."

"Maybe we should go?" mom asked.

"No. Don't leave. Not yet. I'll be right back." Ellen hurried into the house.

I didn't know about Conner or my mom, but the toll of the day's events had left me feeling drained. Maybe it was the heat, or maybe it was all the emotions that had been running high, but I wanted to curl up like a cat in Ellen's porch swing and take a nap.

"You've been very quiet, Madison," Mom said.

"That's because I don't know what to say or do to make this situation better. I'm ill equipped with the knowledge of how to handle it. I have no sage advice to give. I can only be present and give my support that way."

Conner reached for my hand. "That's all I need for you to do right now. Being with me is enough."

Inside the house, a door opened and closed and we could hear footsteps. A man in a three-piece suit appeared in the doorway to the patio where we sat. He smiled. "Hello. I'm Harold Tidsdale. Have you seen my wife?"

"Harold, it's so good to see you again." Mom stood and went to him. "I'm Hope Franklin. It's been years since we've seen each other so you may not remember me. This is my daughter Madison and her fiancé Conner Montgomery. Ellen is upstairs checking on Sady."

"Of course, Hope. I remember you. It has been years, but I don't believe you've changed a bit." Harold hugged her and then looked at me. "And you say this is your daughter. She's the spitting image of you when we were in college."

I felt my cheeks warm.

He came over and offered his hand to Conner. "It's a pleasure to meet you, Mr. Montgomery."

"Harold? Harold, is that you?" Ellen called coming back downstairs. She hurried out the door to his side. "It is. Oh, I'm so glad you are home."

He turned and pulled her to him for a quick hug. "I've missed you too. These business trips are good for the company but not good for my heart. I've been so homesick on this trip."

Ellen blushed. "You say that after every trip."

"But I mean it more each time." Harold frowned and touched her on the cheek. "What's wrong, dear? You look like you've been crying."

She looked away. "Mother isn't doing well. She had a terrible spell last night and she isn't doing much better today."

"I'm sorry, darling. But I'm here now to help." He pulled her into his arms and kissed her on the forehead.

I looked at Conner who was smiling at them. I'm sure it had been a long time since he'd witnessed a couple who truly cared about one another like Ellen and Harold did.

"I think we really should be going," Mom said.

"No. Don't rush off on my account," Harold said.

"Yes. You have been away from your wife and you need to spend time together. We have to be going back to the hospital where Conner's grandfather is to check on him. Thank you for the tea, Ellen," Mom said.

"Thank you for coming by." Ellen went to my mom and hugged her. "Do let me know if I can help with any of the wedding plans."

"Thank you, that is very kind of you to offer," I said before she hugged me.

"Yes, thank you," Conner said, hugging her before she walked us to the door.

Conner reached for my hand and entwined his fingers with mine as soon as we were settled in the backseat of the car. He leaned over and kissed me on the cheek as my mother pulled the car onto East Battery heading back toward Calhoun Street and the hospital.

"Are we okay?" I asked him.

He nodded.

"I'm sorry my great-aunts investigated you. I would have stopped them if I had known. You know that, don't you?"

"Yes. I just find it amusing that is all."

I shifted in the seat toward him. "Why? Because you don't think there is anything that interesting about you to find out about? Obviously that PI isn't that good. He didn't discover that you were adopted."

"Unless Maude and Mossie already knew."

I felt my eyes enlarge at his statement. If great-grandfather had been involved then one or both of them might have known as well. Thinking about how tangled this web of deceit might go was more than my tired mind could take in one day. I leaned back in the seat and laid my head on his shoulder.

"Let's hope they don't. Let's hope for once they aren't involved in this."

He wrapped his arm around me and held me close until my mother pulled into the lot and parked the car.

Once inside the hospital, Irene was the first to see

us as we neared the waiting area. She was leaned back in the chair where she sat, but she straightened her posture and slowly got to her feet before rushing over to us. She hugged Conner and then kissed both of his cheeks. "I've been so worried about you. So has your father."

Conner looked over to where his father sat with Duncan. "Has there been any news?"

"No." Seth got up and came over to us. "I saw him for a few minutes and then your mother and Duncan went to see him after that. Hello, Hope. It's nice of you to come."

"Of course. We'll be family soon. It was the least I could do. Can I do anything for you while you're here to help?"

"Yes," Seth said. "Can you take Irene and Duncan home? I'd like to stick around and see what the doctor has to say when he checks on my dad tonight."

"I can stay, Seth. I don't have to go," Irene protested.

"Listen, you're tired. I can see that. It will be best if you go back to his house and wait."

"No. I don't want to go." She shook her head. "He's my—"

"Irene."

She clamped her mouth closed and stepped back, looking hurt.

"Come on, dad. You can't order her around like she's your property. She can stay if she wants. Why are you trying to push her away? Is there something you don't want her to know?"

Seth glared at Conner. "I don't treat her that way and I'm not trying to push her away. I'm concerned for her well-being. It's been an emotional and draining day. You're one to talk. Did you care for either of us when you joined the service and went to war?"

Conner turned away from him, running his fingers through his hair. He walked down the hallway toward the stairs.

"Don't go away angry," Seth called.

I hurried after Conner catching up to him before he went through the double doors to the stairwell. "He doesn't understand me. He refuses to accept that I did what I had to do. I couldn't sit here while others my age fought in the war."

I nodded and followed him up the stairs to the second floor. "I can see the subject is still a raw one for you both. You may never see eye to eye on it. And I know you are angry with him for many reasons right now, but can you try not to take offense to everything he says or does right now. It won't help you get through your grandfather's illness. And I'm afraid your grandfather will sense the strife that is going on between you and your father and that won't help him either."

Conner stopped with his hand ready to pull open the double doors at the next floor. "I hear you, and I understand what you are saying, but I don't think that will be happening. Maybe my dad was right about one thing. Today has been emotional and draining. You need to go home with your mom when she leaves."

He went through the door and left me there. As the door swung closed behind him, it felt like a slap in the face. He was shutting me out when all I was trying to do was be helpful. Uncertain whether I should ignore his request to leave and follow him to Conrad's room or not left me shifting my weight from foot to foot. I so wanted to follow him, but in the end I went back down to the waiting area.

"I'm ready to go when you are," I told my mom. She looked concerned but I shrugged. "He needs time alone."

Mom nodded. "You're more than welcome to ride back to River Road with us, Irene. We've plenty of room."

She looked at Seth, but he didn't say anything more about whether she should go or stay. "I think I will. Uncle Duncan, are you ready to go?"

He nodded, getting to his feet. He slapped Seth on the back. "We'll be seeing you. Call if Conrad's condition worsens."

Chapter Nineteen

The night was hot and humid and after the long day we'd had it didn't make for an ideal sleeping condition. After spending some time tossing and turning, I ended up running a lukewarm bath and soaking for a while, trying to let my mind go blank so I could fall asleep. But it didn't help. When I got out and dried off I was still wide awake so I decided to go for a walk down in the garden. I slipped on my gown and sheer wrapper, a pair of shoes and tip-toed down the stairs, letting myself out the back door.

The sticky heat of summer was so thick it almost took my breath away, but I was certain it would be cooler down by the pond. Fireflies flickered here and there like low floating diamonds in the night sky as I carefully took the stone steps down to the garden. The moon shone bright down on the white arched bridge and I saw a lone figure standing down there. I instantly recognized that silhouette and it made me smile. I also felt a peace wash over me that I hadn't felt since I left the house earlier this morning.

"Conner, what are you doing out here?" I called, but he didn't turn toward me.

"I've always loved this garden. You know that? Even though I knew it was wrong to come here, I always found a way."

"And I'm glad you did, or we wouldn't have met. Remember how the first time we talked you warned me I was trespassing when it was really you?"

He nodded.

"I think I know why you love the garden so much." I stood beside him and leaned my head against his arm.

"You do?"

I nodded. "You were conceived here."

He didn't say anything for the longest time and then he stepped away from me, shaking his head. "Well, how do you like that?"

I didn't know how to respond so I changed the subject. "What brings you over here tonight?"

"I wanted to be alone, yet close to you. Forgive me, Madison. I shouldn't have asked you to leave. It was foolish of me. I knew it the moment you didn't follow me into grandfather's room."

"It's okay. I needed to come home. You needed space."

He turned toward me and an amused look crossed his face when he saw what I was wearing, making me feel self-conscious. "I never need space from you." He pulled me into his arms and kissed me with an urgency that hadn't been in his kisses before. At first I found it nice, but his kiss deepened and before I knew it he had the belt to my wrapper undone and his hands were inside, running up my body, leaving tingles in their wake.

Heat rushed all through my body like I'd never felt before and it scared me. I pushed him away, pulling my wrapper closed. "I-I need to go back in the house. And you need to go home and get some sleep. Goodnight, Conner."

"Don't run off!" he called, but I didn't stop or look back.

"Madison, come back. You can't leave me out here."

Maude was in the kitchen when I slipped back inside the house. She jumped when the door shut and turned around with fear in her eyes. "Madison, what on earth were you doing outside at this hour and in your nightgown?"

"I couldn't sleep. I thought a walk in the garden would help."

"And did it?"

"No. It's so hot and humid outside I think I'll have to soak in another cool bath."

"You need a glass of lemonade. Sit down and I'll get you some." She went to the refrigerator and pulled out the pitcher and poured me a glass. On her way to the table she stopped at the kitchen window. "Someone is out there."

"It's probably Conner."

"What's he doing here so late?"

"Thinking. He said he loves our garden and he always liked to come here even if he was trespassing."

Maude sat the glass down. "Trespassing you say."

I nodded.

She pulled out a chair and sat down as well. "Now that you mention it, a long time ago we had trouble with a young boy who liked to lurk in the garden during the summer months. He even tried to fish in our pond." She softly laughed. "We told him there were no fish in it, but he kept coming back with his pole. Mossie and I tried to discourage him, but then Father said to leave him alone. And do you know what he did?"

I shook my head.

"He took his own bamboo pole and went down there and fished with the boy, but they never caught anything."

"Do you think that boy was Conner?"

She shrugged. "It may have been. I haven't thought about that time in years. Father said the boy was a talker and he enjoyed listening to him. He also said it didn't matter if they caught a fish or not, the boy still loved to come and fish. You know, Father thought of putting fish in the pond the next summer just for the boy, but he didn't come. And the next year Father was house ridden and couldn't go down."

"Did the boy ever come back?"

"If he did, Madison, Mossie and I didn't notice. We were too busy taking care of father." She yawned and then smiled. "Sweet memories. I miss him."

I finished my lemonade and went to the sink to rinse the glass out. Talking to Maude seemed to help and I suddenly felt as if I could go upstairs and sleep.

I didn't hear from Conner for two days because he spent most of his time at the hospital with his grandfather. Conrad was still the same, but the doctors had confirmed it was a stroke, a mild one, but a stroke nonetheless. Mom and I went to the hospital to see Conrad on the evening before visiting hours were over, but Conner had already left for the day.

Even though I missed Conner, I didn't have too much time to think about it because we were busy working on wedding plans. Irene came over to help since she and Seth had cancelled their trip to the coast because of Conrad's illness. And it was nice working with her on the wedding and getting to know her better as well.

We had finally narrowed down a workable guest list for the wedding when Maude and Mossie came in with a list of additional names.

"We really think you should include these people in the guest list," Maude said, sitting down at the dining room table where we had been working over lunch.

Mom looked over the two sheets of paper and then up at Maude. "There is no way we can include everyone on your list. The church can't possibly hold that many if they all come."

"Where there is a will there is always a way," Mossie said, pulling grapes off the bunch from the bowl of fruit. "Besides, these are the families of father and mother's friends. We simply cannot have a wedding without inviting them. They must be invited."

Mom shook her head. "Out of the question. We've already made room for the one's you insisted on earlier and I appreciate your desire to honor these, but you must remember this is Conner and Madison's wedding. It should be about celebrating them. And besides, the wedding is the week before Christmas. We cannot expect folks who live out of state to alter their family plans and travel during the holiday."

"Well if you feel that way then maybe Maude and I shouldn't come either." Mossie stomped from the room and Maude pressed her lips together in a tight pout and hurried after her.

Irene and I began to giggle. It was hard to keep a straight face when the aunts got their feathers ruffled.

Mom sighed. "I don't mean to be insensitive to their feelings, but how many people do they think we can invite?"

"We have Anna and Thomas Whitfield on the list don't we?" I asked.

"Yes."

"And all the public officials they requested like the mayor and the banker?"

"Yes."

"Then that should make them happy. Besides, Conner and I wanted something small, but we have agreed to go larger within reason. And if that isn't acceptable to them, then we'll have a private ceremony at the church with only family present."

"It would be such a pity for you to do that. A wedding is a time of celebration just like the birth of a child," Irene said. "When will the write up about your engagement be in the paper?"

"The reporter and photographer will be here on Tuesday at two in the afternoon," Mom said. "Irene, please remind Conner he needs to be here for that. I know he is preoccupied with Conrad right now so it could slip his mind."

"Say no more," Irene assured us. "He will be here ready for the interview and photograph."

The phone rang, one of the few times it had since I came to Wyndam House. It wasn't long before Bea appeared in the doorway. "Miss Madison, it's for you."

The last time I'd received a call it was from Conner telling me Conrad had had a stroke. I feared it was bad news again. Mom and Irene watched me as I slowly rose.

"I'm sure it is nothing, dear," Irene said.

I hoped she was right as I walked to the telephone in the foyer.

"Hello."

"Madison, it's Conner, but I guess you already knew that."

"I had a feeling. Is everything okay?"

There was a prolonged silence on the other end of the line, but I heard him breathing. "Grandpa just had another stroke. It was worse this time."

"How bad? Were you with him?"

"No. I had gone to get some lunch. Dad was with him. The doctors and nurses came right away and began working with him."

"Do you want me to come? Your mom is here. We can be there within the hour."

"No. You don't understand, Madison. He's…he's gone."

The handset of the phone slipped through my fingers and dangled a foot off the floor. My knees buckled and the next thing I knew I was sitting on the floor, leaning against the wall. I was positive I hadn't heard him correctly.

"Madison? Madison, are you still there?"

Tears ran down my cheeks as I reached for the mouthpiece again. "Y-yes. I'm here. Are you sure? Maybe he's only sleeping?"

I heard him take a deep breath and clear his throat before he spoke again. "I wish you were right, Franklin, but he's gone. Dad and I will be back on River Road shortly. We'll stop by to pick up my mom. Will you break the news to her?"

I nodded. "Yes. I'll tell her. This is so unfair."

"I'll see you soon."

The line disconnected and I inched my way to a standing position before putting the handset back on the receiver. I felt horrible. Here we'd been making wedding plans, enjoying ourselves while Conrad had been dying.

Walking slowly back to the dining room I breathed in and out preparing myself to break the news to mom and Irene. I didn't want to break down crying even if that was all I wanted to do.

Mom lost her smile when I returned. "Madison?"

I looked at Irene who had been the happiest I'd seen her since we met. I hated breaking the bad news to her, but it had to be done.

"Conrad passed away a little while ago. He had another stroke. Conner…he said…he said it was worse than the first one and even though the doctors and nurses were there when it happened they couldn't save him."

Irene nodded. "And Seth?"

"He was with Conrad when it happened. Conner had left to get lunch."

"I need to go to them." Irene stood looking around the room for her purse. She rushed over to where she'd left it on the sideboard.

"There's no need to leave. Conner said they are both coming here and he asked we wait for them."

"Wait? I can't just sit here and wait. Duncan! I have to tell Duncan. He's at the house alone. He shouldn't be alone right now."

"Irene, it's okay. Take a deep breath. I'll send our driver, Godfrey, over to get him," Mom said wrapping an arm around Irene's shoulders. "Let's go into the parlor and have some tea. Madison, give Duncan a call and let him know a car is coming for him."

My mom was always good under pressure and I was so glad she was here with us for this. I would not have known how to handle Irene. I picked up the phone and asked the operator to connect me with the Montgomery extension. The phone rang several times before it was finally answered.

"Hello?"

"Duncan, how are you? It's Madison."

"Fine. And you?"

"I'm good. Listen, we are sending our driver over to pick you up to come to Wyndam House. Can you be ready when he gets there?"

"I suppose so, but you know I can walk over just as easily."

"True, but it is extremely hot out there today. We'd feel better if you allowed our driver to pick you up. Besides, he doesn't have an awfully lot to do in my opinion and this would help him out. Life in the garage has to be awfully boring."

Duncan chuckled. "I'll be ready when he comes."

"Swell. See you soon."

I hung up the phone and walked out to the garage. I found the driver cleaning the windows on the car even though I was certain they were spotless as they were when he finished them the day before. "Can you drive over to Montgomery House and pick up Mr. Claiborne and bring him back, please?"

"Certainly."

"Thank you." I started to go back in the house, but I felt a tightening in my stomach at the thought of Duncan riding alone in the car. Immediately I did an about face.

"Is there something wrong, Miss?" he asked coming back from putting away his cleaning supplies.

"I think I'll ride over to get Duncan, if you don't mind."

"Of course, as you wish," he opened the back door for me to climb inside.

We were on our way down River Road in no time and even though I had ridden and walked down the road before, it seemed different this afternoon. I began to softly cry and I sank down low in the seat so my head was lying against the backseat cushion. I could still look out the window at the passing scenery, but it didn't give me joy. My heart was heavy with grief for the loss of Conrad. I knew if I was feeling this bad then Duncan and his family would feel worse. I feared the grief would hit Conner the hardest since he loved Conrad the most.

Duncan was standing outside of the house in the shade of a nearby tree when the car pulled to a stop. Godfrey got out and opened the door for him to get inside.

"Hello, Madison," he said getting settled. When I didn't answer he looked at me closely. "Why are you crying?"

His question made the tears come harder and I hugged him. "I'm so sorry."

"Sorry for what? Has something happened? Is Conrad—"

My crying grew louder and he patted me on the back.

"Sh-h-h it's gonna be all right. We all have to leave this world sometime whether it's after a long illness or sudden like. That's why every day has to be spent loving one another and with those who matter the most." He pulled away and reached into his pants pocket for a handkerchief. He dried my eyes with it and then he looked out of the car window.

I scooted back into the car seat and tried not to

shed any more tears, but it wasn't easy. My heart was breaking. That's when I noticed Duncan's body was shaking and he covered his face with one hand.

By the time the car turned off of River Road and took the winding drive up the hill to the house Duncan had composed himself again. We went into the house and found Mom, Irene, Maude and Mossie in the parlor having sherry instead of tea.

"Can we get you one, Mr. Claiborne?" Maude asked, going over to the drinks cart where an assortment of bottles sat with a bowl of ice and several small glasses.

"Do you have anything stronger?" he asked.

"Father was a scotch man when he chose to have a drink, which wasn't often. I believe we have an unopened bottle here."

Duncan picked up the bottle. "Single malt. Very nice."

"Do you prefer ice?"

I walked over and sat down on the sofa with mom and Irene. They both patted my hand when I joined them.

"I figured you'd gone with Godfrey to get Duncan when you didn't come back into the house," mom said.

I nodded. "I couldn't imagine him riding over here alone. I guess I needed to break the news to him."

Irene sipped her sherry. "It's so hard to imagine how he will get along now without Conrad. I hope he doesn't decide to move back to his farm."

"Oh?" I said recalling the farm Conner had taken me to the day he told me he loved me. I'd been concerned we were trespassing on someone's land, but he'd said we weren't. Had that been Duncan's?

Irene sighed. "Seth and I might just have to move back here to help him if he does."

"To help who?" Duncan asked coming over with Maude from the drinks cart.

"You, Uncle Duncan. I'm worried about what this will mean for you. Where will you live?"

"I can assure you, Irene, that is the least of my concerns right now. Conrad and I had an understanding with Conner about what should happen when one of us goes. So there is nothing for you to worry about."

"But what do you plan to do with your farmland?" Irene asked. "And your house? It's been sitting there vacant all these years ever since you moved into Montgomery House."

"I really don't see that that is any of your concern. But if you must know, the house hasn't been empty that long. I rented it for several years, but a year ago the family moved on and I didn't take on another tenant. Before he met Madison, Conner and I had been talking about him trying his hand at farming. Who knows, maybe we'll give it a go together."

Irene shook her head and pursed her lips together in a frown. She didn't seem pleased with what he told her and I found that odd. Was it that she couldn't see her son as a farmer? Or was it that her uncle didn't need her and Seth helping him out?

"I'm going to go get a glass of lemonade from the kitchen. Does anyone want some?" I asked, standing up. Everyone declined so I took my time getting my drink as I thought about what Irene had said and her reaction to Duncan's response. I hoped I was making more out of it than it really was, but I had such an odd feeling about it.

"Would you like a snack?" Bea asked when I lingered in the kitchen drinking my beverage.

"I have fresh baked cookies, some sandwiches, and a cheese and fruit platter prepared to take in if they are going to be drinking. I know your aunts and they cannot drink without having a bite to eat. It isn't pretty."

I smiled at the maid. "What do they do?"

"They begin signing and neither one can carry a tune. Thankfully they have never had too much to drink with mixed company, but tonight might be different."

"I suggest a pot of coffee be brought in then."

Bea nodded.

I helped her carry in the refreshments and we set them up on a side table. I also brought in the pitcher of lemonade since I wasn't partial to liquor, even to settle my nerves.

The doorbell rang and a few moments later Bea showed Seth and Conner into the parlor. I hurried to

Conner and hugged him.

"I guess you have all heard?" Seth asked. Irene came over to him and kissed him on the cheek before hugging him.

"We are so sorry," Mossie said. "Please have a seat. Have a drink. Have some food."

"Moss, I think you've had enough sherry." Maude stood and took her glass from her.

"But I only had one."

Mom got up from the couch and walked over to Seth. "I know this hasn't been easy on you. Is there anything we can do to help during this time?"

"Thank you, Hope. Being able to spend time with family and friends tonight will be a great help to us. There is so much to deal with as far as father's estate, but I'm glad we won't have to get into that right away."

Conner dropped his arm from around me and stepped closer to this father. "There's nothing to settle or deal with. Grandfather was explicit about what he wanted to be done. I know you were not in the room when we discussed it earlier today, but he told me his lawyer had his will and that everything was taken care of if he shouldn't leave the hospital. The funny thing is I thought he was being paranoid because the doctor told me he was prepared to release him today. I left you alone with him to go get something to eat and when I came back he was dead."

"What are you insinuating?" Seth asked.

"Nothing about grandfather's death makes sense. How can he be doing better and then take such a drastic turn? Just like last week. He saw his doctor for his annual visit and was told he was in perfect health. Then you and mom show up. We come here for dinner and by the next morning he had a stroke. He told me he'd been talking with you after everyone went to bed that night. Coincidence?"

Seth paled. "He told you we were talking?"

"Yeah. He said he came down for a glass of water and you were in the kitchen. The two of you went outside to talk so you wouldn't wake anyone. That's when he showed you the envelope with my birth certificate in it and the letter from Richard Wyndam. He told you he was going to tell me the truth, that he'd given you years to do it yourself, and that he was tired of waiting. You argued." Conner shook his head. "I know you and your temper. And I also know you will stop at nothing to get what you want. "

"What's that supposed to mean?"

"I think you stormed off and he followed you back in the house trying to reason with you and that is when he had the stroke and fell."

"You honestly believe I would leave my father lying helpless on the kitchen floor and go upstairs to bed?"

"If it meant you got what you came home for."

"Conner, you don't know what you're saying." Irene reached for him, but he flinched away.

"Yes I do, thanks to Maude and Mossie."

I turned and looked at them wondering what they had done. Maude shrugged her shoulders and gave me an impish grin.

"What did they do?" I asked.

"Yes, please tell us what they did," mom echoed.

"They informed me what their private investigator found out about my father and why he and my lovely mother suddenly came for a visit. There never was a trip to the coast planned, was there, Dad? You came for the sole purpose of getting into grandfather's good graces again in hopes he'd put you back into his will. Somehow before you came, you also learned I was seeing Madison. How? Don't bother to answer. That is irrelevant. The main point is that my father is broke. He's been without a job for months and they've had to sell their home and the majority of their belongings."

Seth's jaw tensed and he glared at his son. "That is a far-fetched tale, Conner."

"I can't believe you'd think so poorly of us," Irene began to weep. "We came here only to visit you. We were going to the coast for vacation until Conrad became ill. How can you honestly believe what some stranger tells you about your own parents?"

"Conner, could you be wrong?" I asked unsure I believed Irene knew any of this, but then I recalled what she'd said earlier before they arrived. And decided that maybe she was a good actress with her tears.

"I wish I were wrong, Madison, but it's all true. The sale on the house was final the day they left to come here."

Irene looked up at Seth, shocked. She moved her head back and forth. "Tell him he's wrong. Tell me he's wrong that you wouldn't sale our home without my knowing."

Seth looked at her for a moment without saying anything and then stormed out of the room. The front door opened and slammed.

For a second I thought Irene was going to faint when her legs bent, but she quickly straightened her posture.

"No wonder he kept talking about us staying on and helping Uncle Duncan if something happened to Conrad." Irene staggered back to the sofa and sat down.

I didn't know what to say or do at this moment. I turned to my mother who looked as helpless and I felt. Conner had an expressionless look on his face so I couldn't read him, but he didn't seem affected by anything Irene had said. Duncan on the other hand got up and refilled his scotch glass. He also took Irene another sherry.

"Sorry, Irene girl, but I knew one day it would come to this. I just hate it has happened now."

Unsure of what to do, I hurried from the room and went outside in search of Seth. I hadn't heard the engine of his car start up so I was pretty certain he hadn't left. I found him out at his car with his hands resting on the back and his head down.

"Mr. Montgomery…Seth? Are you all right?" I asked as I approached so he knew he wasn't alone anymore.

"No. I've lost everything. How can I be all right? My son thinks I'm responsible for my own father's death."

"Were you?"

He turned around and stared at me blankly. "No."

"Then why didn't you tell him that?"

"It's obvious he already made up his mind thanks to those meddling aunts of yours. Did they really hire a private investigator?"

"Maude and Mossie mean no harm, even if they do cause it. It's their way…just like my great-grandfather." I couldn't believe I was defending them. When had my opinion changed? "They did hire a man to look into Conner and then because of a few things they learned they had the man look into you. I didn't ask them to, and once I found out I even told them not to do it, but it did help them see that Conner was suitable. I'm sorry if it uncovered things you didn't want anyone knowing."

"Losing my job and trying to keep it from my wife hasn't been easy. Selling our house fully furnished without her knowing it was even harder, but I had hoped coming here we could start over. But it hasn't been as easy as I hoped. Conner hasn't exactly been happy I'm here."

"Do you blame him? I understand why you objected to him going to war, but it appears you have objected to him all of his life."

Seth shook his head. "No. I don't blame him. I haven't made it easy for him all these years."

"And why is that exactly? Is it because you adopted your own child and you resented him because of it? Or was it because you couldn't have children with Irene, the women you loved, and had to raise the child you fathered with Ellen, whom you didn't love?"

"Boy, as a Wyndam you don't fall from the patriarchal tree. You sound just like your great-grandfather. You know what he told me all those years ago? He said, 'boy, you'll pay one way or another for what you've done. So go on and deny you're responsible for that girl's condition, but just remember we both know you're the one'. I was foolish enough to think he was wrong, but then Irene couldn't carry a child and I thought your great-grandfather had cursed us. So I allowed her to see the baby when he contacted my father and we did adopt Conner."

"Did you ever love me?" Conner asked, coming from around the side of the house. Neither one of us had heard him approaching. Nor did we know how long he'd been hearing our conversation.

"Yes, son, I did. The first moment I held you and looked into your eyes. You had such a grip. You held onto my finger tight and you cried when I had to give you back to the nurse on our first visit."

"Then why did you push me away?"

"I'm a foolish man. All I could see when I looked at you was Ellen in your eyes when I wanted to see Irene. Can you ever forgive me?"

"I don't know. It may take some time, but I will try," Conner said. "Mom said you lie to her. I think you need to start being honest with her instead. She's hurt and finding out you've betrayed her with my adoption and selling the house without her knowing is not going to be easy to get over. You've got your work cut out for you."

"I know."

"You also need to apologize to Ellen. It's time you start being the man you should have been, Dad. The father. The husband. You're a Montgomery and that means something around here. If you're going to live on River Road you need to man up."

"All right, son."

Conner stuck his hand out and Seth hesitated a moment before taking it. They shook on it and Seth pulled him toward him.

"I love you, Conner."

"I love you too, Dad."

Chapter Twenty

Getting through Conrad's funeral was rough. Tension was evident between Seth and Irene and even though Conner tried to help them work through it, Irene was clearly not ready to accept Seth's apology. In a way I didn't blame her, but another I found it hard that she could have lived with him all these years and not have noticed something was going on. I mean, if he wasn't working, how did they pay the bills? Where did he go every day? But then I'd never been a wife so what did I know about marriage?

Marriage. Watching them struggle through this made me wonder if I was really ready to dive into matrimony with Conner or not. Did we know enough about one another? Was feeling love for him enough to see us through the next sixty or seventy years together? Or would I find myself widowed and alone like my mother and grandmother had?

All these thoughts sent me down to the garden with my sketch pad and box of colored pencils early one morning. It had been so long since I had allowed myself the freedom of doing this that I immediately became lost in drawing and before I knew it my mother came looking for me, worried, because we had to go into town to pick up my dress for the mayor's party.

"Here you are. I should have known. We have to go get your dress and Maude and Mossie are insisting they come with us today. I thought we'd also go by and see Ellen. The aunts want to pay a visit to Sady and see how she's getting along."

I sighed, closing my sketch book. "I'm sorry. I forgot. It's been so peaceful down here. Free of all the drama and emotions we've been dealing with lately. I really hate to leave and go into town."

"I know, but we must do what we must. Conner is still taking you to the party isn't he?"

"He said he would, though I told him if he didn't feel up to it I would understand. I think everyone would under the circumstances if we didn't go. I even offered to send a letter of regret to the Peterson's, but he wouldn't hear of it."

Mom smiled. "That's so unlike him."

"Well, as heir to his grandfather's estate he has responsibilities he didn't before. Much is expected of him and he said he must set a good example for his father on that account. Seth has much to learn now that he has returned to River Road."

Mom laughed. "You know, Madison, what they say about you 'can't teach old dogs' new tricks' is true, especially with men Seth's age."

"Then please don't tell Conner that because it would burst his bubble. He has such hopes for his father."

Within the hour, we were on our way into Charleston to pick up my dress for the party and then we went over to Ellen Tidsdale's for a visit. She was in happier spirits today mainly because her mom was doing much better.

"Whatever it was has passed. I'm so thankful." Ellen beamed watching Sady with the aunts. "Just look at her. She's herself today."

"That's wonderful," mom said.

Ellen nodded. "How's Conner doing? I hated to hear of Conrad's passing. It was hard for me not to call him. And even harder to not come to the wake, but I didn't know what to say to Harold about it."

"He's doing well. In fact, he's doing better than Seth is right now," I said.

"Oh?" Ellen looked at my mom.

"There's been much family drama going on since

Conrad's death, but I'm sure it will all work itself out," mom explained. "Madison has just picked up her dress for the mayor's ball. Would you like to see it?"

"Yes."

"Really?" I asked.

"Of course. I am dying to see what you are wearing."

I sighed. "I'll go get it."

I went out to the car to get the dress box and my shoes from the car. And when I returned, Mom and Ellen took me upstairs to change in Ellen's bedroom. She'd strayed from the way my grandmother had decorated her room, but I was glad. I think it would have been a little creepy otherwise. It was nice to see Ellen's personal touch on my grandmother's bedroom.

"How are you going to wear your hair?" Ellen asked as mom helped me change behind the dressing screen.

"Her hair is so short there is not that many options, but we thought she could wear a beaded and sequined fascinator. The seamstress made it for her before we left the store today."

I slipped on my shoes and mom put the accessory in my hair before I stepped from behind the screen for Ellen to see.

"You look lovely, Madison. I love that color on you. It is so feminine and elegant." Ellen walked over to her dresser and opened up a box sitting on top of it. When she turned around she held a necklace of different shades of pink glass beads. "Will you do me the honor of wearing this on your special night with my son?"

I nodded. "Yes, thank you. I'll take extra special care with it."

"I know you will and when you come to return it I want to hear every detail about your evening. Maybe you can even bring Conner with you?"

"Absolutely." I felt my eyes begin to water and my heart swelled with joy that she'd called Conner her son and that she wanted to see him. He'd been concerned that she wouldn't and I knew he'd be pleased to learn she did.

Ellen put the necklace on me. "Now, I have one more request. Will you indulge me a little longer?"

"Yes, anything."

"Come downstairs so my mother can see you in your dress. It's more for me really than her, you see, because I'll be showing off my future daughter-in-law in her new dress."

Ellen's eyes were watering this time and I blinked several times to keep from shedding the tears in mine.

"For heaven's sake, Ellen, you're killing me here," mom said, wiping tears from her own eyes and I was thankful she'd said it because I felt the same. "Tomorrow afternoon the reporter and photographer from the newspaper will come by the house to interview them about their engagement. You must come by for lunch, bring your mom and that way you'll be there for it."

"Really, Hope? You'd allow me to be there?"

"Of course," mom said. "And if you were there for lunch and hadn't left yet then Irene can't object to your being there."

Ellen hugged my mom. "Thank you. A hundred times thank you. Mom and I would love to come for lunch and she always takes a long nap in the afternoon, another reason we couldn't leave."

I giggled and sniffed, wiping away the moisture from my cheeks.

We went back downstairs and I modeled the dress for Maude, Mossie and Sady and listened to all three of them make comments about my appearance. How they approved. Then Sady pointed a crooked finger at me and narrowed her beady eyes.

"She's stole your necklace, Ellen. Stop her."

"No, she hasn't. I gave it to her to wear. She'll return it after the party."

"It looks so pretty on Madison," Maude said. "Don't you think it will be okay for her to wear it with her new dress?"

"No! Make her take it off," Sady insisted, banging the palm of her hand on the arm of the chair where she sat.

Not wanting to upset the woman further I took the necklace off and handed it back to Ellen who looked apologetic to me for her mother's outburst. "It's no problem. I'll go change back into my clothes."

I hurried up the stairs feeling confused and sad for Ellen. It couldn't be easy taking care of her mom. Had Maude and Mossie went through similar days with great-grandfather? And they did it for years. Thinking about this as I changed I developed a new appreciation for their dedication to their father.

When I came back down with my dress box and shoes, Ellen was waiting for me at the bottom of the stairs.

"Please forgive my mom." She reached for my hand and put the necklace in it. "I do want you to wear this and I hope you still will."

"Yes. Thank you."

"Good. Now set your things down and come back into the parlor. We're going to have lemonade and cookies."

I did as she asked, opening up the dress box and laying the necklace on top of the dress. Then I followed her back to the parlor.

We had not been home long when Conner showed up at the door. Bea let him inside and sent him upstairs to my room where I was hanging my dress up. The door was open, but he knocked.

"I hope I am not interrupting?"

"No. I was just putting away my dress for the

party. What brings you by? Not that I'm not glad to see you, but is anything wrong?"

"Everything is as fine as they can be. Have you decided where you want that picture hung?"

"No, I haven't. So much has been going on I haven't really thought about it. Maybe over here?" I walked to where a collage of smaller pictures hung. "I could remove these and put it up here?"

He nodded. "I think that would be a good spot. The sunlight will not hit it directly as it would on that other wall. You don't want the light fading the colors."

"True. If you want to start removing those pictures I'll run down and see if Bea knows where the hammer is."

"Sure."

He sounded so solemn I feared something was wrong even if he claimed there wasn't. I hurried down the stairs to the kitchen and Bea instructed me to go out to the garage to get the hammer. When I returned, Mom was sitting on the settee in my room chatting with Conner.

"Madison, I was just telling him about our visit to Ellen's today and how she'll be joining us tomorrow for the interview."

"Isn't that wonderful, Conner, that she wants to be here for it?" I asked.

He nodded and sighed. "The attorney is coming by the house tomorrow morning to do the reading of grandfather's will. I'd like you both to be there. I know it's a private family affair, and I want Madison with me, but I don't know how father will react and it might be easier if your mom is there as well."

I looked at mom and she nodded. "Yes. We'll be there. What time?"

"Ten."

"We'll be there a little before then," mom assured him.

"Thank you." He took the hammer from me and removed the nails that were in the wall where the other pictures had hung. He picked up the painting and held it against the wall so we could decide which height to hang it.

Once the painting was on the wall, the three of us stood back and made sure it was hanging straight and that it was positioned centered between the two windows.

"Would you like to stay for dinner?" mom asked before she left the room.

"Thanks, Mrs. Franklin, but I really should be getting back home. I don't like leaving the three of them for long. Mom still isn't talking to dad so that puts Duncan on edge. It's not the ideal situation. So you see why I wanted you both there for the reading of the will?"

"Yes."

We walked him down the stairs, and I went outside with him to where his roadster was parked.

"You drove? Why not walk?" I asked.

He grinned at me sheepishly. “I had to go pick up my new suit for the dance and decided to drop by on my way home to ask about tomorrow morning.”

“Oh. So seeing me was an afterthought, huh?”

“Never.” He leaned down and brushed his lips against mine. “I always want to see you.”

I wrapped my arms around his neck and kissed him. “I miss our walks, our spending lazy days in the garden together. Why have things gotten so complicated lately?”

“That's life, Madison. I start my new job next week so we won't be seeing one another as much during the week and depending on how things go with the reading of the will tomorrow that could affect how much time I have to spend with you too.”

He turned to open the car door and get in. “I'll see you tomorrow.”

“Tomorrow.” I stepped back so he could turn his car around to head down the drive. I waved until I couldn't see the car anymore before I went back into the house.

It was raining the next morning, not hard, but a light drizzle that made it feel hot and muggy once it stopped. The sun was peeking through the clouds when mom and I went to the car. We took hers since Bea and Godfrey had already left for the market.

"I really hope everything goes well and there are no surprises in the will," I told mom when she pulled the car into the Montgomery's drive.

"So do I. I don't think Seth and Irene can take much more stress on their marriage right now. I feel for both of them, but Seth the most because he brought this on himself."

"But don't you feel as if Irene should have been more aware of what was going on? I find it hard to believe he was out of work for six months and she had no idea what was going on."

"I know I would have if it had been your father, but then, he never kept any secrets from me."

"That you know of."

"No. We did not keep secrets, Madison. He was my best friend. We talked about everything and I advise you and Conner to build your own marriage on that principle."

I nodded as she put the car in park, recalling how Conrad had advised us to cherish one another. Both had given us sage advice.

It began to sprinkle again and we ran from the car to the house. I knocked on the door and Conner opened it a moment later.

"Good morning," he said. "It looks like we are going to have sporadic rain showers today. There is nothing like a Charleston summer. Come on into the parlor. We have coffee and a coffee cake if you'd like a little refreshment. I've been thinking about putting on a record and turning it down low to help soothe emotions. Do you think that is a good idea?"

"It couldn't hurt," I said. "Do you have any Mozart. Mossie loves his music and I have come to appreciate the lighter pieces."

"I don't think we do. Most of the records we have are ones I've picked up and they are more on the jazzy side."

"Then you might not want to do the music," Mom suggested, pouring herself a cup of coffee.

"You're probably right." Conner opened the curtains wider then closed them back a little. "Is that enough light in here?"

"It's fine, honey. You're nervous aren't you?" I said coming over to stand beside him.

He nodded. "I know I shouldn't be. I mean it doesn't matter what is in the will. I'd rather have my grandfather here."

"I'm sure he knew that. You had several years together and you have your memories."

"There should have been more years," Duncan said coming into the parlor. "Hello, Hope, Madison. I was glad when Conner told me you were joining us today. How's Maude and Mossie?"

"They're the same. Maude said you should come over anytime you get to feeling lonely here," Mom told him.

"Well, how can I refuse an invitation like that? It's

hard to feel too lonely right now, but in a few weeks once Conner begins his new job and Seth finds something, I may be dropping by some."

Duncan had just settled in an armchair when Irene came in. She looked as if she'd not been sleeping well and she sat down on the couch with my mom.

"Thank you both for coming," she said softly.

A knock came at the door and Conner went to answer it. I sat on the loveseat and waited for him to return. A moment later, he escorted the attorney into the room and I was shocked that he was also Maude and Mossie's attorney whom they'd met with weeks ago before holding the dinner party. The man nodded at me and took the other arm chair. Conner had just sat down beside me when Seth came in, but instead of sitting beside Irene on the couch he stood near the refreshments table.

"Is this everyone?" the attorney asked.

"Yes," Conner said.

"Very well. We are here today for the reading of the last will and testament of Conrad Samuel Montgomery. I will tell you that he was of sound mind and body when this will was created in my office many years ago and even though there was a lawsuit trying to nullify it, the ruling of the court has determined it sound and abiding, and therefore this document stands as is. I ask that everyone please stay silent for the reading."

"To my son Seth and his wife Irene, I leave the

sum of one thousand dollars and his mother's cameo brooch." The attorney looked up at Seth before glancing back down at the document. "To my closest friend, Duncan Claiborne, I grant him a place to live in my home for as long as he lives or so wishes it. I also bequeath my cuff links, pocket watch, and my fishing pole for his abundant collection."

Duncan grinned. "He always knew I wanted that pole."

"And last, but not least, I leave my entire estate, savings and the sum of my stocks and bonds to my grandson, Conner with the stipulation that he must marry Madison Franklin within thirty days of the reading of this will if they are not already married or he forfeits his inheritance and she hers."

"What?" My mom and I gasped.

Seth roared with laughter. "Even from the grave those two are still conniving."

The attorney looked up. "I know. That last stipulation seemed off, but it was something Conrad and Richard Wyndam came to me about personally. I am just glad that it has all worked out and Conner and Madison have come together on their own accord."

I turned to Conner. "Did you know about this?"

He shook his head. "No. Grandfather never said anything. I didn't even know he had a will until you brought it up."

From the corner of my eye I saw Irene get up off the couch. I turned to see her walk up to Seth just in time to see her slap him hard across the face. I gasped and grabbed Conner's hand.

"This is your fault for trying to nullify your father's will. We have nothing. No marriage. No life. Even our son isn't ours. How could you have let me adopt your bastard and raise him as my own? You knew all about it didn't you. Admit it, Seth. For once in your life admit you never loved me."

In one swift motion Seth pulled her into his arms and kissed her, long and hard. She tried to twist free of his hold, but he didn't let go. In fact, it looked like he increased his hold and crushed her against his body. She soon wrapped her arms around him and held on tight.

Conner squeeze my hand as he watched his parents. I looked at the attorney but if he was embarrassed by the scene on the other side of the room he didn't show it.

"We had planned to be married before Christmas. Do we really have to get married within thirty days?"

"I'm afraid so. Maude and Mossie said they had told you about your inheritance. Didn't they tell you about the time limit?"

"What time limit?" Mom asked.

My mind raced back to my first night at Wyndam House and how Maude had urged Mossie because of time. They'd known all this time. I should be angry with them for not telling me, but I wasn't. They had been right to keep it from me because I had so much to learn about being a Wydam before I could truly appreciate what my great-grandfather had left for me.

"Your great-grandfather set a one year time frame for you to marry in order to receive your inheritance. That window of time closes next week. I stressed to Maude and Mossie to tell you as soon as you arrived, but they couldn't bring themselves to do it."

"And if we don't marry by the time stipulated in these wills?" I asked.

"Both inheritances will go to a charitable organization that each man designated."

I began to laugh. "This is grand."

"Then let's do it." Conner stood up. "There is no reason to wait until December. You have a dress. I have a new suit. We don't have to have a huge wedding. Couples elope all the time, even from prominent families."

"Absolutely." I surprised myself for agreeing so quickly, but would anything really change if we waited until the eighteenth of December? "Let's do it. We can have a small affair of our families down in the garden at the gazebo. Surely the Reverend Holster will agree to coming out and performing the ceremony."

"What will you wear? Mother's dress is too formal and much too hot for a garden wedding," mom said.

"I will wear my new pink dress. It will be perfect." I looked over at Duncan who hadn't been paying attention to us, but Seth and Irene who had stopped kissing but were talking softly with one another.

"What do you say, Duncan? Are you up for a wedding?"

He turned and smiled. "Always."

Chapter Twenty-One

The next twenty-four hours and thirty-eight minutes were a blur. Everything seemed to fast forward as we planned for a July first wedding. Conner and I met with the newspaper reporter and cameraman as scheduled, but the lunch with Ellen and Sady was focused on the upcoming ceremony. Conner called the reverend and explained the change in our plans and he agreed to perform the ceremony the next afternoon. Then we drove into Charleston to city hall and got our marriage license. Bea prepared a three-layer wedding cake for us and Ellen picked up a lovely bouquet of flowers for me to carry.

Everything appeared to be worked out between Seth and Irene and both were very helpful during the preparations. But the morning of the wedding, Seth and Duncan disappeared which had Conner panicking.

I didn't see him of course, but mom explained what was going on to me.

"That doesn't make any sense. Where would those two go off to today of all days," I said trying to not get upset. "Do you think they went fishing? You know how Duncan loves to fish. And only yesterday he found out Conrad left him his fishing pole."

"No. Conner said that was the first thing he thought of when Irene realized they were missing. He checked all of Duncan's favorite fishing spots. Poor Irene. She's beside herself right now. And I don't blame her. It's just like Seth to do something so…so irresponsible only hours before his son's wedding." Mom was pacing my room now and I could tell she was on edge. "This is supposed to be a happy day. We've worked nonstop to pull it together because my grandfather and Conrad decided to put stipulations on your inheritances. I can see my grandfather doing it, but not Conrad."

"Calm down. I'm the bride. I'm the one who should be antsy. I'm sure they'll show up." At least I hoped they would.

A knock came at my door and Mossie and Maude came inside. They had already got dressed for the ceremony and they both wore pretty new dresses they'd bought on our outing to town before the dinner party.

"We wanted to bring Madison this handkerchief that belonged to our mother for her something old and borrowed," Maude said.

"It also works for her something blue because of the embroidery of blue flowers on it," Mossie pointed out.

"Your dress and shoes are new and your necklace is borrowed so you have everything covered," Maude added.

"Yes I think I do. You both look wonderful."

"Thank you, dear," Mossie beamed. "Madison, Maude and I are so glad you're not angry with us for not telling you about the time-limit that father set on your inheritance. We were enjoying having you here so much it slipped our minds that the deadline was fast approaching."

"Actually, Madison, we didn't know at first how you'd react and now we see how our inability to follow through has caused you to rush into marriage without having the wedding you wanted. We're truly sorry." Maude handed me the handkerchief.

"And if we had known that Father and Conrad had stipulated they you marry Conner, well, we never would have objected to you seeing him," Mossie said. "Funny how it has all worked out."

I hugged her and then Maude. "Thank you both for bringing me here. You have changed my life for the better."

"All of our lives," Mom said coming over to wrap her arms around us and Maude. "Three generations of Wyndam women under one roof is a sight to behold."

"If only Father were here," Mossie said.

"Indeed!" I laughed.

At one thirty Ellen arrived and she came upstairs to join me and my mom before the ceremony. I slipped into my dress and they helped me with my hair. A few moments later Irene came in.

"We found them."

"Found who?" Ellen asked.

"Duncan and Seth. They went off somewhere early this morning without telling anyone," Mom explained.

"Where were they?" I asked.

"I wish I could tell you, but it's a surprise for you and Conner. They swore me to secrecy."

I frowned. "Another secret?"

"I know. I know. You and Conner are over secrets, but this one is really just a little wedding surprise, okay," Irene said coming over to give me a hug. "You are beautiful, Madison. Just like a bride should be on her very special day. I'll see you down in the garden. I told Conner I'd let you know all is well and then return to him. He's a little frazzled right now."

"Maybe I could go down with you and have a word with him?" Ellen asked.

Irene looked at her for a moment and then slowly nodded. "Maybe you could. Heaven knows I've tried everything I could think of already."

I walked over to my mom. "It looks like things might work out for the best all around."

She nodded. "Yes it does. Like grandfather always said, where there is a will there is always a way."

Mom and I walked down the stairs and picked up my bouquet of flowers tied together with a pretty pink ribbon lying on the marbletop table in the foyer. Then we went out the front door and around the house to the stone steps leading into the garden. We took our time and arrived at the gazebo at precisely two.

Conner smiled like a Cheshire cat from the moment he saw me until I came to stand beside him. I handed my bouquet to my mom and joined hands with him as the reverend instructed and before I knew it we had exchanged vows, slipped rings on each other's fingers and were pronounced husband and wife.

Conner kissed me and everyone clapped. When we broke apart he scooped me up in his arms and turned around with me until I began to laugh and I insisted he put me down.

The sound of soft music drifted through the garden. Inside the gazebo a table was set up with the cake and champagne punch. So Conner and I did the honors of cutting the cake and feeding the other a bite. Then Bea served everyone. Hugs and kisses were exchanged by all before Duncan and Seth pulled us to the side.

"I guess you both are wondering where we went

off to this morning," Seth said.

"You had everyone worried," Conner said.

"We didn't mean to, but we wanted to give you both somewhere special to spend your honeymoon. Since you both have a house of your own where others live, there really isn't any privacy at either." Duncan looked down at the ground and then back up at us. "Except for my farmhouse. So we were there cleaning the place for you. We stocked the cabinets with food and it's all yours to use for as long as you want."

"You did that for us?" I asked.

"Really?" Conner said.

"Really," Seth said.

"Thank you both." Conner pulled me to his side and kissed me.

"It's the least we could do," Seth said.

Duncan tossed Conner the keys.

The orange hues of the sun setting in the sky colored everything perfect as we hurried to Conner's waiting car to leave Wyndam House as man and wife a few hours later. Someone, though I suspected it was Godfrey, had tied an old tattered boot and a tin can to the bumper and had put a sign that said 'just married' on the back of the roadster at the rumble seat. Mom, Maude, Mossie, Ellen, Seth, Irene and Duncan tossed rice at us as we drove away.

"Well, what do you think about being married?" Conner asked, slowing the car down before turning onto River Road.

"Give me a day or two and I'll let you know. Right now, though, it feels perfect."

"It is perfect, Mrs. Montgomery."

I laughed and scooted closer to him on the seat. "And to think it never would have happened if I hadn't come to Wyndam House."

About the Author

Leanne Tyler is the author of sweet to sensual romance with a touch of paranormal thrown in. She loves writing about beautiful historic Charleston and you'll find it the setting of several of her stories.

Leanne loves to hear from her readers through reviews on Amazon or dropping her a note on her website leannetyler.com. She can be found on facebook at /leannetylerauthor or twitter @leannetyler.